Holiday

ᴬ Tiger Lily's Café® Mystery

By Kathleen Thompson

Holiday

Volume 4

ᴀ Tiger Lily's Café® Mystery

By Kathleen Thompson

ISBN-13: 978-0-9984023-3-8

ISBN-10: 0-9984023-3-8

© Registration # TX 8-309-116

Library of Congress Control Number: 2017904562

Kathleen Thompson

A List of Tiger Lily's Café® Mystery Series Books:

This cozy mystery series has everything you seek: an eclectic cast of characters, a mystery or two, and diligent detectives on duty. The detectives just happen to be feline.

Tiger Lily's Café is set in a Midwestern town nestled into the coast of a Great Lake. The setting itself acts as a character, bringing the reader into the sights, sounds and smells of the small resort community of Chelsea.

Read the series in order, or read any book alone. While characters grown and change, each volume stands alone with a clear beginning and a clear end.

- Turtle Soup (2014)
- Boo! (2015)
- Phishing (2015)
- Holiday (2016)
- A Rock And A Hard Place (2016)
- Splash (2016)
- Chasing A Butterfly (2017)
- Pumpkin Squash (2017)
- Snowblind (2017)
- Hearts On Fire (2018)
- Morel Of The Story (2018)
- Dragon Fire (2019)
- Beach Bunnies (2020)
- Shipwreck (2020)

Kathleen Thompson

Kathleen Thompson

Cast of Characters

Annie Mack, with the help of her "kids" and a talented staff, owns and manages a bed and breakfast, a cafe and other businesses on the south side of The Avenue. She has lived in Chelsea for only a few years, but her ancestral roots to the town date to the Civil War era.

Annie's SASHET Rainbow: (sa SHAY) a model that assigns color to each core feeling. **S**adness is blue; **A**nger red; **S**care green; **H**appiness yellow; **E**xcitement orange; and **T**enderness purple.

For more information, visit Liberation Psychotherapy: www.libpsych.com/articles/sashet/sashet.html.

Ben and JoJo are college students. They work part-time all over town, including most of Annie's businesses.

Boone is the person to call if you need anything: mowing, snow removal, landscaping, maintenance, preventative maintenance, and just about anything else. He is married to **Harriet (Hilly),** who provides business cleaning services. His sons **Daryl** and **Donny** work for him. Their roots are in rural Appalachia, and they are so much more than people think.

Candice is the head waitress at Mo's Tap. A native of Chelsea, her long, thick, dark hair is the envy of most women who meet her.

Carlos is the manager and baker at Mr. Bean's Confectionary. He is a citizen of the US but was originally from Mexico. He supports his mother and younger sisters, who still live there.

Cheryl inherited The Marina from her parents. It's a small deep water marina with basic amenities. Cheryl is married to Ray. She has known Annie since they were children.

Chris is Annie's special friend, although neither of them are ready to commit to a permanent relationship. He is the Officer in Charge of the Coast Guard Station. His stress relieving hobby is art. His sketches – in charcoal, pencil and pastel – are sold for charity.

Clara owns the flower and gift shop, Bloomin' Crazy. She is a citizen of the US, originally from Haiti, and has an ebullient personality. She keeps The Avenue decorated with fresh and silk flowers year-round.

Cookie probably has another name, but this is what he goes by. He cooks at Mo's Tap and learns what he can from Felicity at every opportunity. He's reticent at best, and he yearns to have his own restaurant.

Diana is the chief instructor at L'Socks' Virasana (Veer AHS ana). She is Mem's daughter. Diana left home right after high school and did not speak to her mother until her return ten years later. Their relationship, while tenuous, continues to grow stronger.

Felicity is the chef at Tiger Lily's Café. She is young, perky and extremely talented in the kitchen. She manages the Café, the upstairs catering facility and outside catering operations.

Frank recently moved to Chelsea to open an antique shop, Antiques On Main. He and Mem are in a relationship.

George is the bartender and manager of Mo's Tap. He is a top-notch bartender and can be counted on to keep confidences. He is a volunteer with the local Coast Guard.

Geraldine was the leader of the "it" crowd in high school, and somehow, life didn't turn out quite as she expected. Everything Annie isn't – perfectly dressed, perfectly coiffed, and perfectly awful – Geraldine is more than a thorn in Annie's side. **Everett** is her on-again-off-again husband.

Ginger is the daughter of Pete, the Chief of Police, and Janet. She works part-time at L'Socks' Virasana. Because she moved to town as a teen (when her father retired from the Marine Corps), and because she is one of the few African American teens in town, she sometimes feels like an outsider.

Greg is a progressive realtor in Chelsea. His goal is to get the right property to the right owner, always moving Chelsea forward.

Gwen is Annie's accountant. A motherly figure, her financial acumen is hidden from all but those lucky enough to have her in their corner.

Hank is a member of the Town Council. He opposes Annie in every way.

Harry is the regular driver for the rental company used almost exclusively by folks on The Avenue.

Henrie manages the KaliKo Inn in an elegant manner. He does not invite confidences and speaks little about himself. Always formal in tone, people have difficulty pegging his accent. Is it French? Cameroon? Rwandan?

Holly and Jolly, twins, own DoubleGood, an electronics and hardware store. Holly lives in a wheelchair. Natives of Chelsea, they used to hate the names given them by their parents. Now, they enjoy the novelty of it.

Janet is Pete's wife. She spent twenty years as a Marine officer's wife. She traveled the world and is now living in Chelsea. She is an outsider, not having grown up here like Pete. She is the ultimate community volunteer.

Jennifer and Marie, sisters and nurse practitioners, own The Drug Store and The Clinic. Folks call the sisters before calling nine-one-one. Chelsea natives, they know everyone. And their secrets.

Jerry learned how to make candy in a minimum security federal prison. He was not an employee. Jerry works hard to overcome his shyness, particularly around women.

Jesus manages Sassy P's Wine & Cheese and also selects the wines. His family, famous vintners in the Napa Valley, owned, farmed and made wine for generations before California became a part of the United States.

Joan is a member of the Town Council. She opposes Hank in every way. Clara's pet name for her is "Joan of Chelsea."

Laila owns Babar Foods. A traditional Pakistani, she is raising her children without the assistance of a husband. Her children are **James**, **Ava** and **Carl**, who lives with Autism.

Marco is a police officer in Chelsea. He is "second in command" because he was the only officer that didn't go off-kilter during a hostage situation. Marco prides himself on being one-hundred-percent-eye-talian-American.

Mem owns the health food store and cyber café, CyberHealth. Her wisdom is reassuring to everyone, including her daughter, Diana. She teaches the safe use of social media to all ages and has equipment and technology that is helpful to the small-town police department.

Minnie chooses perfect cheeses to accompany the rotating wine selections at Sassy P's Wine & Cheese. She comes from several generations of cheese makers in Wisconsin.

Nancy and Sam are Annie's mother and step-father. They have been married since Annie was a child. They come for extended visits in Chelsea and have learned to call this town their second home.

Pete is a native of Chelsea. He retired from the Marine Corps and is now the Chief of Police. Like Annie, his ancestors arrived in the Civil War era. His, however, came up via the Underground Railroad. He and his wife Janet have three children, the eldest of whom is Ginger.

Ray owns and operates The Escape, a yacht fashioned into a cruiser for fishing, diving and pleasure. He is married to Cheryl; Chris is his best friend.

Teresa is a newcomer to the area. She came to this community to serve. She pastors a small church, Soul's Harbor, and pastors the community through her outreach.

Trudie is the barista at Tiger Lily's Café. She is from Jamaica and ended up in Chelsea when a former boyfriend dumped her at the campground. Felicity saved her, and they have been the best of friends ever since.

Annie's Cats

Annie has seven cats. Most people would call them "rescue kitties." From Annie's perspective, each of them rescued her.

Tiger Lily is a beautiful tabby cat with soft green eyes. She is the titular manager of Tiger Lily's Café, the main gathering place for Chelsea. She is generally calm and logical.

Little Socks is a bright-eyed black cat with white socks. She has a commanding personality and is small and sneaky enough to serve as a cat burglar. She spends time at the yoga studio, L'Socks' Virasana (Veer AHS ana).

Kali, Ko and Mo are litter mates. They shared a secret language as kittens; Kali and Ko now speak "cat," but Mo still speaks "secret." Kali and Ko can be found at the KaliKo Inn, a lakeside bed and breakfast. Mo spends time at Mo's Tap, an upscale blues bar.

Sassy Pants is aptly named; it's difficult to keep this little girl's attention. She is overly sensitive and will react out of emotion instead of reason. She entertains at Sassy P's Wine & Cheese.

Mr. Bean is the baby of the family and is mostly gray with traces of tiger. He has two speeds: fast and love me.

Other Companions

Claire is a blue point Himalayan cat whose human is Frank. She's beautiful and loves people. She is stand-offish with other cats.

Cyril is an English setter whose human is Pete, the Chief of Police. Cyril is friendly and calm. He is an excellent hunter.

Fat Cat and **Scaredy Cat** are strays. They were lost (translation for humans: dumped) at the campground in a cold Great Lakes winter.

Honey Bear is a large, golden, long-haired mutt of a cat who believes it is his perfect right to be anywhere. Other cats hate him.

Jock is a Portuguese water dog whose human is Ray, the captain of The Escape. Jock is spirited and affectionate; he loves children.

Guests at the Inn

Alistair and Cressida Bartram, with their Jack Russell Terrier **Tillie**, are visiting from a rural community in England. They are not the seasoned world travelers they want everyone to believe.

Daniela is visiting from Mexico. She is a mother to Carlos and is traveling as chaperone to Isabel.

Isabel is a special friend of Carlos, visiting from Mexico.

Jeff Bennett is a Special Agent with the FBI. Now part of Chelsea's landscape, this week he takes time off to help with some investigations.

Nathanial and Lorine Kerschner are a young power couple in Chelsea for a romantic weekend.

Terrence and Jerald Timmer-Schmidt are a middle-aged professional couple in Chelsea for a romantic weekend.

Others In Town

Guy McNally is a marine carpenter, a preferred contractor with Ray's insurance company.

Tim and Susie Phillips open a restaurant, the Green Door, on the north part of town. It's a seedy section.

Cindy Stiles is an insurance adjuster for Ray's recent claim for The Escape.

Students

Billy, leader of the local bullies.

Dallas, a local bully, brother of Pam.

Ginger, daughter of Pete and Janet, a senior.

James, son of Laila, a senior.

Justin, a local bully.

Lia, a senior, caught up in a sexting scam by Billy.

Marc, a local bully.

Pam, sister of Dallas, bullied by him and his friends.

Penny, a freshman, bullied by her brother, Porter, and his friends.

Porter, brother of Penny, and a local bully.

Shellie, a senior, a friend of Lia.

1

Annie sat at her small kitchen table. She looked out the balcony doors that faced the lake, a chill, gray fog keeping the horizon at bay. She felt a kindred spirit with the lake: choppy, colorless, and hemmed in by the atmosphere. A storm was brewing.

A cup of coffee in her hands, she sipped slowly, wondering if she should get up and start her day.

Tiger Lily sat in the middle of the table. She looked at Annie intently, communicating silently but clearly, *"How could you do this to us?"*

At Annie's feet, Kali curled a tail around an ankle and cried. It was a plaintive, *"Do we have to go downstairs?"* cry that seemed to bore into Annie's heart.

Mr. Bean was behind the chair, reaching through the chair railings, stabbing at Annie's butt as if to say, *"It's all your fault!"*

Or maybe he was saying, *"Fix it!"*

Annie and her family of seven cats were in their spacious apartment on the third floor of a bed and breakfast in the town of Chelsea. It was early, but the town outside the Inn was bustling even before the full light of day.

Chelsea, a resort town, was nestled into a cocoon that kept it separate from the outside world. On two sides, the north and the south, were the wooded acres of a state park. On a third, the west, was a Great Lake. Positioned as it was, the town was noted for panoramic views of brilliant sunsets over the lake.

The KaliKo Inn enjoyed a prime position. It was separated from the lake by an expanse of white sand beach. Nothing hindered the view.

The Inn was one of several businesses owned by Annie. Her little patch of heaven took up the entirety of the south side of Sunset Avenue, known by locals simply as The Avenue, a broad expanse running from the town circle to the lakefront. The median was paved with brick and decorated with concrete urns holding flowers and greenery of the season. In between the urns were game tables and benches, used almost daily with the exception of some of the more stormy days of winter. Later today, the median would clear out as the storm brewing over the lake made landfall.

On the south side, a block-long 1880s era building was anchored at one end by the Inn and the other by the town circle. Through the decades the building had been well maintained, and for the most part the original brick fascia was intact. Windows ran the length of it, knee-height to a height of eight feet, letting walkers see within and allowing natural light into every space. The building held five unique businesses, each tailored to enhance the tourist atmosphere of the town.

Annie started most mornings with an actual walk up the block, stopping into each business. Today, she decided to take a virtual tour, pushing off the inevitability of the day for another few minutes.

Annie sighed again, took another sip of coffee, closed her eyes, envisioned the broad expanse of The Avenue outside, colored it with the gray hues of the day, and began her walk. Striving for realism, Annie mentally shrugged more deeply into her utilitarian coat and added boots, a scarf and gloves. She felt the bite of a winter breeze with a few sharp pieces of ice and snow in her face.

She looked to her right and saw the old mansion, the Inn, with a wrap-around porch reminiscent of southern mansions. The Inn was surrounded by gardens, now snow-covered. Outdoor furniture was in storage for the winter; the porch and gardens looked bare. The awning stood in stark contrast to the day, bright blue with pinstripes of green, red, yellow, orange and purple. The sign, with a picture of two large dilute calico cats standing side by side, proclaimed the names of both the Inn and the cats, the KaliKo Inn.

In contrast to the porch of the Inn, sturdy wrought iron café tables and chairs remained outside the block-long brick building year round. The arrangements were painted to mimic the awnings under which they sat. In one long virtual glance, Annie took in the expanse of outdoor seating that was used nearly every hour of every day. With this gray aura, however, Annie couldn't bring herself to picture either die-hard locals or tourists sitting at the tables, enjoying coffee or breakfast.

Stepping away from the Inn and toward the center of The Avenue, Annie reached the corner of the long two-story building, coming first to a sign with the picture of a small, spunky, multi-colored cat curling around the name of the business, Sassy P's Wine & Cheese. The sign sat atop a bright red awning accented with purple wine glasses. In her mind, Annie saw Minnie stocking the cheese display refrigerator while Jesus stocked wine racks.

She moved on. Mr. Bean's Confectionary was next. On this sign, a muscular gray kitten danced on hind legs, reaching for the top of a letter proclaiming the name of the business. His awning was bright green. White stars danced around the green canvas. Even on this gray morning, Annie had no trouble envisioning several people crowded into the small space, lined up for fresh baked goods. She could even smell it, and she saw Carlos, smiling, laughing, and enjoying personal conversations with everyone he served.

Mo, handsome long-haired gray Mo, sat with a sexy, sultry stare on a sign that proclaimed Mo's Tap, an upscale blues bar that for now, this morning and every other morning at this time, sat empty. Mo's awning was bright yellow, the silhouette of a black bar tap to one side, indicative of the artisan brews that George, the manager and bartender, kept on tap.

Lil' Socks' Virasana, a yoga studio, had a bright orange awning with the white silhouette of a yoga practitioner in the Virasana (veer AHS ana), or Hero, pose. The sign, in contrast, showed Little Socks in her signature pose.

Annie had received all of the building signs, made of sturdy resin, as a Christmas gift just a couple of months before. Her staff, the managers and assistant managers, collaborated to design each sign to go with the colors and tempo of their respective storefronts.

Diana, the head instructor and manager of the yoga studio, had taken great pride in this particular sign. It showed the lady herself, Little Socks, engaged not in the Virasana pose, but in the Lessiver Mon Derriere (LESS-e-vay mon DAIR-i-air). Translated to "wash my behind," this was a pose few human yoga students could emulate. Privately, Little Socks wondered how humans managed to keep their hind areas clean.

Finally, Annie came to the corner establishment, a large café with windows and awnings on both the north and east sides. Bright purple awnings with mint green pinstripes covered the windows on both sides, and of course Tiger Lily herself graced the new sign. She sat serenely, surveying her world. While Annie couldn't bring herself to see people at the outside tables, inside the windows of the Café she saw a bustling crowd.

Tiger Lily's Café served as the gateway to Sunset Avenue and the lake. It was the main gathering place for the town of Chelsea, locals and tourists alike. Annie allowed herself to step inside the virtual door, to smell the unique breakfasts that only chef and manager Felicity could produce and the coffees and teas that Trudie sent out from the coffee bar in the corner. Annie took a virtual turn and saw Tiger Lily at the hostess stand, ready to greet the next guest.

Except that she wasn't. There. At the hostess stand.

Tiger Lily was here. On her kitchen table.

Annie opened her eyes.

Yes. Tiger Lily was still here. Sitting on the table. Staring at Annie as only Tiger Lily could stare.

Annie's semi-solitude finally ended when a shrill *"Yap!"* came through the cat door. A guest of the Inn, a British Jack Russell Terrier, followed it in. She was British because she actually was from Great Britain.

Her name was Tillie, and she hailed from "outside Uppingham, a smallish town in Rutland County in the East Midlands. We're country people. Rutland is one of the smallest and most sparsely populated counties in England, you see. We don't have a lot of water like most Brits do. The closest thing we have to a beach is Rutland Water, a nature reserve. It's quite famous."

Annie's head bobbled back and forth as she recited this little ditty in her mind. She had heard the paragraph at least twenty times a day for the past few days. Make that thirty.

Well, probably only once a day, multiplied by the force of the delivery.

Annie couldn't forget the sentence that closed out the explanation. "And even with our country background, we are ever so much more sophisticated than anyone we've met here in the colonies." Annie wondered if anyone else, who lived in this century, still referred to the United States in this fashion.

Tillie had given Annie her usual good morning salute, a quick reach to her knees and a few sharp yips, and she ran out of the kitchen in search of fun playmates.

Tiger Lily stayed where she was and looked on. Mr. Bean and Sassy Pants joined in as Tillie ran around the apartment, onto and off of furniture as fast as her little legs would allow. Kali, Ko and Mo were probably hiding somewhere. Little Socks materialized on top of the refrigerator.

Not for the first time, Annie considered locking the pet door to the apartment. She had, at her guests' request, locked the outside pet doors, making for a tense situation with her own brood. They liked having the opportunity to leave the Inn whenever they chose, and most of them would have left the Inn long ago for their own places. Cat doors into the businesses allowed them easy access any time of the day or night.

While these guests were on hand, the cats couldn't leave until Annie went downstairs to start her day. And hopefully open an outside door for them.

On most mornings, Kali and Ko would have been downstairs long ago, helping Henrie as he served breakfast to their guests. There was something about the week, though, that kept everyone close to Annie. One reason might be that instead of breakfast, Henrie was serving "brekkie" this week. To two monsters.

Finally, Annie rose, sighed, took the empty coffee cup to the kitchen sink, sighed, pocketed her cell phone, sighed, opened the door, sighed, and headed downstairs. The cats followed close behind.

Annie hoped this would not be a typical Monday, long on angst and short on joy. She could hear the guests from her third floor landing. The British accent didn't waft up the stairs as much as it landed with a thud.

"All I wanted was a holiday! I didn't want to come to this God-forsaken place where they don't know a knacker from a hurdler!"

Low tones came in reply.

By the second floor landing, she heard, "I am being gracious. I am open-minded." Emphasis had been placed on the word "am." Two times. "These people are off their trolleys. All of them. I want to go to a city. A real city. A city with decent, intelligent people."

Low tones came in reply.

As Annie hit the first floor, heading for the dining room, she heard an anguished, "What do you mean we can't afford it? Where did the money go?" The words "mean," "where" and "go" had a long, drawn-out, especially whiny quality.

Annie tried to turn around before she was noticed, but both guests looked up. Alistair and Cressida Bartram stared at her, forks halfway from plates to open mouths, held in the manner one would hold a shovel at a trough.

Annie tried to smile warmly while correcting her step.

"Good morning, Cressida, Alistair. Have you made plans for the day?"

Alistair put his fork down. "We thought we would take our rental car and motor up the lakefront."

Rental cars were not available in Chelsea. The Inn allowed guests to use a car from their fleet, a gray all-wheel drive Ford Fusion, for excursions. This couple, however, wanted the car all day, every day. After the second day, Henrie handed the telephone to Alistair with a list of rental agencies in Marsh Haven. He locked away the keys for the Fusion.

Cressida stared at Alistair. "We thought what?"

Alistair resumed eating.

Cressida put the forkful in her mouth but didn't bother to either put her fork down or swallow her bite before talking. "Well, 'we' will have to rethink this motoring trip. 'We' did that two days ago, and yesterday, 'we' went in the other direction." For this paragraph, Cressida placed special emphasis on the word "we." "Honestly, Alistair, you are as boring as the people who live in this dreadful town."

Alistair nodded his head slightly to Annie in apology.

Annie had thought long and hard over the last few days as to just what it was that made the people of the town of Chelsea so boring, so unenlightened, so…whatever it was that Cressida disliked. She thought she knew what it was. No one in Chelsea bowed from the waist at the sight of Cressida, and no one deigned to kiss that dreadful, pudgy hand.

Annie kept the smile on her face and turned to inspect the breakfast dishes. She had completely lost her appetite.

Henrie entered, noticed that most of the dishes could be replenished, and turned back to the kitchen to do just that. He was stopped by Cressida.

"You! Stop there! I wanted biscuits again this morning. Biscuits! When will you ever get it right?"

Henrie looked again at the buffet, concentrating on the breads. He noted that his biscuit offering was depleted. Not a crumb could be seen on the dining plates. Surreptitiously, he glanced into the waste can. Nothing there, either. Henrie politely did not look at the oversized bellies of his guests.

Henrie was ever gracious. Never without his wits. An enigma to Annie and the rest of the community, Henrie left a stellar career in the five-star hotel industry in New York to become the chief cook, bottle washer, toilet bowl cleaner and concierge of a bed and breakfast in this small resort community.

He did not invite confidences and spoke little about himself. Most people, townsfolk and tourists alike, came away thinking, "What is that accent? French? Cameroon? Rwandan?" They also went away with the eerie feeling that he could read their minds. Indeed, whatever was needed or desired, he offered before a request was made.

The Bartrams had been guests of the Inn for several days. Cressida had immediately requested biscuits for their first "brekkie." Henrie erred. He mistakenly assumed – this would be the last time he would make any such assumption – that travelers to this country would want to sample foods of native origin.

Their first meal included flakey buttermilk biscuits with sausage gravy on the side. The Bartrams ate every smidgeon, then Cressida asked Henrie if he had forgotten the biscuits she had requested. She was peeved. Actually, "peeved" is a mild word, hardly descriptive of her ranting.

On the second day, Henrie offered biscuits supplied by Mem, the owner of a local tea shop. She had recently stocked vanilla flavored ginger snaps from Sweden. They were very thin, crisp, almost like a shortbread. The sweet flavor of ginger was heavenly as the cookie nearly melted in Henrie's mouth. Cressida had not been impressed, but she ate every one.

On day three, Carlos, from the Confectionary, made fresh biscuits after conducting research of British recipes. They were shortbread cookies filled with raspberry jam and were called Jammie Dodgers. Carlos learned this variety had been popular in Britain for over fifty years.

They were not popular with Cressida. Again, she ate every one.

Today, Henrie offered another biscuit from Carlos. Called rich tea biscuits, they were plain-flavored and especially good for dunking in hot tea.

After every one had been devoured, Cressida again declared Henrie had erred. Apparently in an egregious manner. Even though, according to Carlos, this type of biscuit had been a British standard since the seventeenth century.

Henrie, as close to wits' end as he ever came, looked calmly but with appropriately downcast face and eyes at Cressida. "I am very sorry to have disappointed. May I ask where you purchase your biscuits, or, perhaps, you make them yourself?"

Cressida barked, "We purchase only the finest biscuits from the East End Bakery in Uppingham. They," heavy emphasis on the word, 'they', "know how to make biscuits!"

Henrie made mental note of the name of the bakery as he turned to go to the kitchen. On his way he made eye contact with Tiger Lily and winked.

Tiger Lily gave Henrie a slow blink in return.

She sat by a six-person dining table that often was not needed. Typically it sat against the wall next to the kitchen door. Recently, Henrie changed the table covering to one that reached to the floor. A slit was cut into the cloth and stitched with a simple hem to make an opening. Henrie placed soft cat beds, pillows and blankets under the table.

A small resin sign hung from the table. Purchased at the same time staff made signs for the storefronts, Henrie fashioned this one with a detective cap, magnifying glass and the engraving, "Seven Cats Detective Agency."

Henrie explained the sign to the cats in a solemn ceremony. Proclaiming their importance to Annie, to her staff and friends, to her businesses, and to the town in general, he extolled their fine detective skills.

Henrie and Annie watched as the cats, first timidly, then with joyous abandon, claimed this "agency" as their favorite place to sit when gracing the dining room with their presence.

When, of course, they were not sitting in the window napping in the sunshine. Or on the buffet table sneaking bites. Or on the table bothering guests. Or under the table sniffing shoes.

While Tiger Lily stood guard at the door to the detective agency, Mo, Sassy Pants and Mr. Bean huddled inside it, together on one pillow, hoping to escape the evil eye of Cressida Bartram. Even Tillie hid from them. At the moment, she was inside the agency, hidden underneath one of the blankets.

Fearless Little Socks sat on the buffet table. She aimed a fierce green-eyed stare at the Bartrams. Kali and Ko hid under the television table in the library.

Annie could feel the angst of her kids and wished again that the guests would find a reason to leave Chelsea and the Inn. Sooner rather than later.

Once again she looked out the window and suddenly she realized she was not being a proper host. "You really should reconsider making a trip up the coast today. The weather is supposed to turn bad."

Alistair gave Annie a condescending look. "Do you believe we do not know how to drive in a little snow?"

"I'm sure you know how to drive in snow, but along the lakeshore, the snow and ice can turn wicked, especially if the wind kicks up. By the way, does your rental have either front-wheel or all-wheel drive?"

Alistair tried to maintain his condescending look. He said, "I'm sure our vehicle is adequate to the challenge."

Cressida joined in. "We are more than capable of handling a little winter weather, and it is so dreadfully boring in this town. Perhaps we will be able to find something worth our while if we drive north."

Annie's cell phone rang. Grateful for the intrusion, she picked up, only to hear the warm voice of Chris, her very special friend. And then, bad news.

"I hate to break our date tonight, but I have to stay on station."

"Is it the weather?"

"Yes. The shipping doesn't slow down, not even for Mother Nature, and tonight could bring some problems."

"Will you have to go out if there's trouble?"

"Probably not. I've called in the staff, and volunteers are ready. But I have to stay here. How are your guests?"

"Don't ask." Annie had wandered into the most distant corner of the library as she talked. She continued in a low voice, "Henrie struck out on the biscuits for the fourth day in a row."

"And that means that Carlos has also struck out. I think I'll hit the confectionary before Henrie has time to let him know. I'd rather see him in a good mood."

"I don't think anything can hurt Carlos these days. Last I heard, he was shopping for diamond rings."

"That can be therapeutic."

Annie smiled and gazed at her left hand, at the brilliant ring Chris had given her for Christmas. Well, for New Year. Actually, after the New Year. But it was a late Christmas present.

It wasn't a diamond. It was a deep purple oval-cut amethyst surrounded by white topaz and garnets of various colors. The smaller stones swirled around, encasing the amethyst in pinwheels of color.

It wasn't exactly an engagement ring. It wasn't exactly a pre-engagement ring. It wasn't exactly an anything ring, except a physical token of a promise to be faithful, honest and loving. Annie was still trying to think of something she could give Chris that would say and mean the same thing. Something a Coast Guard Captain would want to wear or keep near at all times.

She finally replied, "Yes, it can be. It's time for me to make the rounds, before the weather turns bad."

They hung up, and Annie, on her way to the dining room, swung by the television table to give tail tugs to the two cats who thought they were hidden. "I'll be leaving, girls. You have my permission to go back to the apartment. Henrie can get along without you today."

Two big cats turned around, faces rather than tails poking out. They looked at Annie with question marks in their eyes.

"I mean it. Go."

They squeezed out from under the table and ran for the door, taking care to look around first, just in case those horrid people were visible. In a second, Annie heard eight feet pounding up the stairs.

Annie checked with Henrie before leaving. Their guests had gone to freshen up before their trip north, and he was cleaning the detritus of the morning's breakfast.

"From the empty serving plates, it seems brekkie was a smash again today."

"You would never know it to hear them talk. I wonder if they put food into containers when I am not looking. I do not know how they can hold it all."

"Maybe they only eat one meal a day."

"Maybe pigs fly."

"Henrie!"

"So sorry. I will do an internet search and locate that bakery that makes the only edible biscuits on the planet. Perhaps they can send a recipe, or, even better, ship biscuits to us."

"Perhaps they can shed some light on the Bartrams in general, give you a clue how to break through that veneer of snobbery."

"Perhaps."

"I'm leaving. I know the kids want to get away from the house for a while, but I'll make sure they get home before the weather gets bad."

Annie bundled up for the weather and called Tiger Lily to bring everyone else. As they ran out the door, breathing in the fresh air – absent Bartrams – the cats felt the tingle of a brand new and exciting day. Well, okay, perhaps it was the tingle of an ice-and-snow storm on the horizon.

Annie had two styles of dress. Spring, summer and fall brought casual capris, flowing, colorful tops and almost flat sandals. Winter brought denims, longer sleeves, and either flat-ish mules – with crazy socks – or boots.

Today, she wore functional boots that were not too warm. She would be inside most of the time and did not want to carry shoes into which to change. She wore a rainbow-colored scarf and matching gloves with a thigh-length black coat, more functional than stylish.

Annie's straight, dark hair was graying gracefully and the lack of wrinkles belied her age, to which she carelessly gave little heed. What was in a number, anyway? High cheekbones gave just a hint of some hidden Native American blood in her background.

At Sassy P's Wine & Cheese, Annie chatted with Jesus and Minnie and grabbed a bite of sharp cheddar. The cats said a polite hello to the couple before heading to the back dining room to play.

Jesus was the manager and wine steward of Sassy P's. He was raised in the Napa Valley in the home of a famous vintner. While most thought of Jesus as a recent resident of the country, perhaps one generation at most, he claimed California as the family home for centuries. He loved everything about wines except the making of them; he found a perfect position with Sassy P's. He chose wines from an excellent selection of local and regional wineries and from around the world.

Minnie was the Wisconsin cheese equivalent of Jesus's California wine. She grew up in cheese country but preferred to choose them rather than make them. She traveled the United States and Europe to perfect her palate and, still a young adult, found Chelsea and Jesus. Her new home and her mate for life.

Annie admonished Sassy Pants to behave herself and went to the next storefront, Mr. Bean's Confectionary, four cats in tow.

She laughed with Carlos at the failure of his latest biscuit offering and took a truffle from Jerry. The cats accepted cat treats, one of the newer offerings of the Confectionary.

Carlos was a recent arrival to the United States. Before gangs took over his small town in Mexico, his parents owned a bakery. At his mother's side, Carlos learned the magic that made him a premier baker, no matter what country. Annie's father sponsored him and he was now an American citizen. He had begged his mother to come, or to at least send his sisters, now young women, but they did not want to leave. He went home as often as possible and sent most of his earnings to Mexico to support them.

Jerry learned his candy-making skills at a minimum security prison. He never talked about it and never talked about what he had done to get there. Recently Annie learned, as did the rest of the community, that he had helped his mother commit suicide. She had struggled long and hard with a terminal illness, and while the legal community empathized, what he did was a crime. Following his release, and having no other family, Jerry closed his eyes, put his finger on the map and chose Chelsea for his new life.

Annie hugged a muscular, prancing Mr. Bean and left for the next storefront, three cats still in tow.

At Mo's Tap, Annie watched Mo enter through the cat door, ready to take a nap on top of the bar until George and Candice arrived. Mo particularly liked the area where the clean glasses were stacked. He liked to press his face into the cool glass, wrap a paw around one side, and fluff his tail over the pile. George must love to clean the glasses. He did it every morning.

George, the manager and bartender, and Candice, the head server, were on-again in their up-and-down relationship. They both grew up in Chelsea, going through high school just a couple of years apart. George was a star athlete and heart throb who left town long enough to get a college degree.

Candice, whose long thick hair was the envy of most of Chelsea's women, had a quietly assertive way of managing both her love life and the bar floor. Mo's Tap would never be in need of a bouncer. Candice was the only manager or supervisory level employee that did not live in an apartment on The Avenue. In her on-again situation with George, however, she stayed in the apartment above the Tap most evenings.

Annie was down to two cats in tow. Little Socks seemed happy to get to L'Socks' Virasana, hopping to a windowsill to grab the meager gray daylight that passed for sunshine. Diana was busy with a class, so Annie waved and went on. Tiger Lily followed.

Diana grew up in Chelsea as well. She was rebellious as a teenager and was angry with her mother for divorcing her father when she was eight years old. Diana applied for and was admitted to the local community college, but before the start of the school year she took off without a word to her mother. She sent a Christmas card every year, with a different postmark on each card. They were all signed simply, "Your Daughter."

Ten years later, Diana came home. She apologized to her mother for the rebellious years and for the years of silence and begged her to ask no questions. Her mother welcomed her home and did as she asked. They obviously cared for one another, but a wall of secrets separated them. Her mother was Mem, owner of CyberHealth on the other side of The Avenue. Mem and Diana shared a large apartment above that business.

Annie and Tiger Lily finally entered Tiger Lily's Café, warm and fragrant, bustling with activity. Tiger Lily hopped to her place at the hostess stand. Annie waved at several friends having breakfast. Before going into the dining room, she made her way to the coffee bar.

Trudie was in the weeds. Annie's attention was caught by Felicity, as she sailed out of the kitchen and into the dining room. She held two trays high, filled with plates and bowls.

"Do you need help? Why are you serving?"

"Cindy and Shirley are in the back room. The Rotary Club is in there. I thought they were going to the new place, but they're here, and I didn't have enough people scheduled."

Annie put her coat on the rack behind the coffee bar, washed her hands and caught Felicity when she sailed out of the kitchen again. She took the tray.

"This one goes to table six."

Table six looked like all of the tables at the Café, except that none of them looked alike.

The Café had a casual chic ambiance. Because it was on the corner of Sunset Avenue and Main Street, two walls were mostly knee-height-to-ceiling windows with minimal coverings. Excess lighting was deflected by the awnings outside.

Most of the walls were mint green, but an accent wall behind the coffee counter and server station was bright purple. Lighting was an eclectic mixture of track, recessed and pendant lights. Each pendant light was colorful and unique in shape and design.

Chairs were matched in sets of four, but the sets were dispersed throughout the dining room, not arranged at any one table. The chairs were wooden and painted in every color of the rainbow. Each had a comfortable cushion to match the color of the chair.

The tables had brightly painted ceramic tops. There were cats painted on one, dogs on another, a lakeside sunset on another. When the tables were commissioned, the furniture artist was told to let her imagination be her guide. The tables had platforms on every side, designed specifically for Tiger Lily. The platforms allowed her to jump down from the hostess stand and up to each customer in the Café. Tiger Lily, especially with new customers, believed it her duty to point out menu choices by placing a paw on her suggestion. And sometimes, she just wanted to say hello.

At table six, Annie served a spinach, feta and mushroom omelet to Pete, the chief of police, a short stack of buckwheat pancakes with eggs and bacon to Ray, and steel cut oats flavored like carrot cake to Cheryl, Ray's wife.

Pete was a tall man, over six feet, with a physique honed by twenty years in the Marine Corps. He had a military haircut, mostly black on top but graying at the temples. Pete's family had been in Chelsea as long as Annie's. The difference was that Annie's great-great grandfather arrived from the east and settled into the lumber industry as a business magnate. Pete's great-great-great grandfather arrived by railroad from the south. The Underground Railroad. Pete returned to Chelsea after retirement, bringing a wife and children along for the ride.

Ray was retired from armed services as well, the Navy. He moved to Chelsea to marry Cheryl, a native, and a good friend to Annie since her childhood. When Annie visited her father during the summer, she and Cheryl spent every moment they could on the lake. Cheryl's parents owned the small deep water marina nestled into the harbor near the state and town parks. Cheryl owned it now, and Ray owned a yacht fashioned into a cruising and fishing boat, The Escape.

Annie looked at the oats. She was hungry. She had forgotten to eat breakfast, given the unwelcome atmosphere of the Inn's dining room. "This looks great. It must be a special of the day."

"Yep. Carrots, raisins, pineapple, pecans, maple syrup, cinnamon. Oh, and steel cut oats."

"Where are the boys?" asked Annie.

Pete motioned with his fork to the hostess stand. "The dining room got busy. They're behind the hostess stand."

The boys were Cyril, an English setter who claimed Pete as his human, and Jock, a Portuguese water dog who claimed Ray. Annie took a detour past the hostess stand to give the boys a love tap and returned to the servers' station to pick up another tray.

This trip took her to a table with two of her least favorite people. Geraldine and Hank. Two peas in a pod. Geraldine, married on-and-off again to the same man, and Hank, probably too mean for any woman. Geraldine and Hank, who hated Annie with a passion. Geraldine and Hank, who had both strayed into criminal activity but who seemed to have skins of Teflon. Nothing stuck. They remained free to deliver their vicious attacks on Annie and anyone else that got in their way.

Annie planted her most gracious smile as she served two breakfast specials, a two-egg feta cheese omelet with two lemon pancakes topped with powdered sugar and blueberry sauce.

"Good morning, Geraldine, Hank. I haven't seen you for a few weeks. It's good to have you back."

Hank grunted. Hank's head nearly met his shoulders. His short, stout neck was matched by his short, stout body, which, as ever, wore a rumpled polyester suit.

Geraldine was perfectly turned out. Perfect hair, perfect make-up, a perfect tailored red suit with a perfect pink silk blouse. Annie couldn't see, but she imagined perfect red three-inch stilettos on her feet. The shoes would be replaced with perfect stiletto-heeled boots by this afternoon. Red.

Annie thought about her sensible almost-flat boots. Oh, well. At least she was comfortable, and her ankles were not in danger of breaking.

Geraldine simpered, "We've been going to this absolutely divine new restaurant these days. You should try it. It's on the north side of town and is, I'm sure, the first of many places that will gentrify the area."

"I've heard of it, but I haven't had a chance to go yet. I haven't met the owners. Are they from here?"

"Yes. Well, no. They live here now, of course, but they're from…somewhere else."

"Oh. Okay. Well, it's nice to see you here today. How'd we draw the lucky penny?"

Geraldine and Hank looked at one another. Geraldine answered. "They had to close today for something. Some kind of carpentry work, or plumbing, or something. I'm sure by tomorrow you'll be missing us again."

"That will be our loss. Pardon me, but I'm needed…"

As Annie turned to go, Geraldine exclaimed, "Oh, my! Such an exquisite ring!"

Annie turned, not knowing if the statement was made for her benefit. It was. Geraldine's hand was out, beckoning Annie to come closer and allow a good look. Annie obliged, placing her left hand into Geraldine's right.

"An amethyst. And are these diamonds?"

"White topaz."

"And what are these other pretty stones?"

"Garnets."

"The red ones, yes, but the others?"

"All garnets. Orange, yellow, green, even the blue."

"So. Every stone is semi-precious. A pretty ring, but so little value, after all."

"That depends on your perspective." Annie smiled. "Have a wonderful day, Geraldine. Hank."

Annie could hear Geraldine and Hank laugh out loud as she walked away. To Annie, this ring was more precious than life itself. She continued to smile, looking at the ring as she returned to the kitchen to pick up another tray.

By the time the breakfast rush was over, Annie had served two more tables and bussed most of the dining room, taking carafes of coffee to the back room in between.

As the Rotary meeting broke up, Greg, the club president and a local realtor, beckoned for a private word. "I'm sorry we descended upon you like this today."

"Not a problem, Greg. Did we cross wires somehow?"

"No. I didn't have a chance to explain it to Felicity, but I'll call her later today. We got to that new place, and it was closed."

"Closed for the day, right? Carpentry or plumbing or something?"

"I'm afraid it may be closed for good. I tried to work with the couple when they were first looking for a place, but they went with Jones & Tribbett instead, and they got a bad deal. That property was overpriced and a lot of renovation was needed."

"Jones and Tribbet. Isn't that Hank's..."

"You got it. Hank's brother is one of the owners. Hank loves to broker deals. Tim called me one day – Tim Phillips, he and his wife Susie are the owners – and said they'd met a nice man from the Town Council, and…well…you can figure out the rest of the story."

"I'm afraid I didn't make it to the restaurant. I've been too busy to slip in for either breakfast or lunch, kept thinking I could do it 'tomorrow.' But you went? Even though they used another realtor?"

"Sure. Well, I moved the Rotary meetings over there just to give them some regular business, you know, until they got their feet on the ground, but they didn't have a feel for the food industry. The food was second rate. Heck, it was third rate. And the coffee was awful."

"At just a few weeks they didn't have time to work out all the kinks. But I can't imagine a Rotary meeting with awful coffee. It's a wonder you didn't lose members!"

"We had some complaints, but this is a civic-minded group. They understood the concept and were willing to put up with it. But we're back here now, again and probably forever."

"Please, Greg. Don't say that as if it's a life sentence. I'm sure Felicity will take great care of you. And we appreciate the business. By the way, what was the name of the other place? The Red Door?"

"The Green Door."

"I never met the owners – you said Phillips? – and as far as I know, they've never been to this part of town. It's odd, that someone would move in, open a restaurant, and not even look at the other places in town. Or maybe they did, and I just didn't know…."

"I think you're right. When I first met them, I tried to arrange a business lunch here. They said they didn't want to be unduly influenced by Chelsea's old fashioned eateries. They wanted a bright new idea. It was odd, but then, I'm an old goat. Maybe I'm no longer on the cutting edge of…whatever it is I'm not on the cutting edge of."

Ginger was bored. Pete's eldest daughter and a senior in high school, she was faced with a school snow day. The weather wasn't bad yet, but school buses wouldn't be able to get through the country roads by early afternoon. School would probably be called off tomorrow as well. The day before, correctly calling the weather issue, she had completed both days of e-learning.

She worked part-time at Lil' Socks' Virasana, but Diana had assured her class attendance would be light, limited to those who lived close enough to walk in. And who wanted to walk in during a storm?

Ginger checked her mad money and determined she could afford to spend $40 at the mall in Marsh Haven. She wouldn't be able to get there tomorrow, but, if her mom and dad approved, she could go this morning, as long as she returned home before the roads got bad.

She called her father. Pete said, "No way. Stay home today." She hung up, deciding to ask her mother without telling her she had talked to her father. Janet moved slowly down the deli counter at Babar Foods. She wanted emergency food supplies and had time to stop at her favorite grocery store, one of the shops on The Avenue. She picked up her cell phone as it rang.

"Mom, I've finished all of my school work. I need a new t-shirt for yoga. I've got enough money saved, and I was hoping you would let me go to the mall? I'll be home by 2:00. I promise."

Janet looked out the window. The snow was still light, most of it blowing, not much landing on the road. "I don't want you out that late, but if you leave soon, you can have a couple of hours at the mall and still be home by noon."

"Noon?!"

"Noon."

"Alright. I'm leaving right now."

"Wait until I get home. Just in case, I want you to use the Fusion. I'll be there in a few minutes."

Janet smiled as she hung up the phone. Ginger was a responsible teen. She worried about her driving in this weather, but this is where they lived. She had to learn to drive in it.

Ginger put on her fashionable boots. Warm winter boots were for old people. She added her best jacket and a hat, scarf and glove set that she thought made her look more mature. She took a glance at the second family car, an old rear-wheel drive sedan, and was glad her mother would let her take the new one.

Janet left the car running as she got out with her groceries. She gave Ginger a peck on the cheek and couldn't resist. "Drive the speed limit. Or below."

At the mall, Ginger got her shopping out of the way in minutes. She found an inexpensive T-shirt on the spring racks. She didn't really need it. The purchase was merely cover for an excuse to come to the mall. She put the bag in her purse and walked quickly to the food court. If anyone else was hanging out, she would find them there.

She saw about a dozen girls and boys in the center of the court. It was not unusual to see teenagers gathered together, noses buried in their cell phones. It was unusual for them to be looking at their individual phones but apparently laughing at the same thing.

She approached the group. "Hi! How's it going?"

The group, almost as one, looked up with smiles. Then, again, almost as one, the smiles faded and phones went into pockets and backpacks.

"Hey, Ginger," said a girl named Shellie. "Shopping, or just hanging out?"

"A little of both." Ginger didn't drop her friendly demeanor. As the daughter of the chief of police, she was used to this type of response, although not in quite so large a group.

"We, um, well, we're getting ready to go over to Forever 21 and look around."

"Sounds good. I'm in."

A few of the girls peeled off, looking back at the rest of the group. Ginger joined them.

As they walked along, Ginger asked, "What were you all looking at?"

Shellie replied, "Oh, nothing. We were just hanging."

Another girl, Lia, gave some more detail, as if it would help cover up the truth. "I was checking the weather. Mom told me I had to be home by suppertime, but I'm thinking I'll leave sooner."

"Good idea," said Ginger. "I have to be home by noon."

"Your folks are so strict."

Ginger didn't agree with them, but she said, "They are. I can't catch a break."

As they got to the store, they heard some ugly words behind them.

"Shake that thing!"

"Make it work!"

"Come with us for a good time!"

They turned. Five big, dull-looking boys. The school bullies. Certainly they wouldn't try anything here. Certainly.

One of the boys moved forward. Ginger, unused to being approached by the bullies, froze. For a few seconds. Then she walked forward, putting herself in front of the group of girls.

She looked at the leader, a big, rather dirty boy named Billy. "I don't think going with you would be such a good time."

Billy stared. He hadn't recognized the daughter of the chief pig from behind.

Another one of the boys, Porter, spoke up. "Hey, Marc, maybe this one would do for you. Billy wants you to ante up."

"Shut up," said Billy, still looking at Ginger but aiming the remark to Porter.

Porter, safely behind Billy, raised a middle finger in salute. He looked around to the other boys for a laugh. The other boys shuffled their feet.

Billy continued to stare at Ginger, turning the stare into a menacing leer, looking from her toes to her face and back down again, lingering on her breast and pelvic areas both times. Ginger didn't move. She continued to look at him as if he were a boil on the hind side of a rat.

Billy looked around at the rest of the group, eyes coming to rest on Lia. "You didn't tell me you hung out with such grand friends."

Lia blushed and looked away.

Shellie said, "Go away. We didn't come here to hang out with you."

"Pretty brave, now that you've got little Miss Piggy here with you."

Ginger was too busy staring Billy down to see Lia. Lia had buried her face into Shellie's back.

Billy finally blinked. "Well, you don't look like you'd be such a good time after all. Come on guys. Better pickin's back at the food court."

When they were a few yards away, Ginger gave a sigh and turned around. She saw Lia move away from Shellie, keeping her back to the rest of the girls. She swiped at her eyes.

Shellie spoke quickly. "They bother us a lot. They've never gone away so easily before."

"Why are they still allowed to come in here? Doesn't mall management care?"

"Who's going to kick them out? All the stores get business from us because of them. We have to hide in the stores until they go away, and usually someone buys something."

"What did Porter mean, about me being one that would do, that Marc still had to ante up?"

Shellie, Lia and the other girls looked at one another. Lia tossed her head and said in a fake nonchalance, "Who knows? They're just idiots."

Ginger looked around Forever 21 for a while, then decided she had better things to do with her time. As she walked toward the car, she pressed the keyless door system. She heard the beeps, but when she got to the car, it wouldn't open. She tried the key in the door. It didn't turn.

Ginger looked up at the sky. This wasn't good. The weather was turning from bad to worse, and…as she brought her eyes down, she saw another gray Ford Fusion a few spaces away. She looked more closely at the car she was trying to open and realized there were things - fast food wrappers, soda cans, trash – in the back seat.

She pressed the keyless system again. The other car's front lights blinked and she heard the beeps again. She walked to her car and drove home.

2

Tiger Lily continued to greet guests as they entered and left. Most people were leaving, because Tiger Lily arrived after the breakfast rush was in full swing. She hated to be late and always gave extra friendly good-byes when that happened.

Sometimes, guests left tips for her. A crystal bowl sat on the lower ledge of the hostess stand, beside the crystal vase with fresh flowers. In front was a sign for the current charity, the American Cancer Society. The tip bowl was almost full. As coins and dollar bills dropped in, the big girl purred and preened.

When she had time, she lay on her stomach facing the back, draping her paws over the edge and looking down at the large, napping dogs.

"Don't you ever get tired of sleeping?"

One dark brown eye opened. Jock gave her a scornful look. It closed again. Jock sighed and went back to sleep.

Outside, the wind picked up. Swirls and puffs of snow darted through the air. Whenever the door to the Café opened, a brisk bite of air ruffled her fur. Tiger Lily didn't mind. She loved snow and winter in general. Being out in the cold made being inside a warm place all the more enjoyable.

For a period of time, no one entered or left. The dogs slept peacefully until time to go. Pete, Ray and Cheryl gave Tiger Lily some love, then quiet descended upon the hostess stand.

Tiger Lily turned to look outside at the wind and weather. She thought she saw movement at the side of the

church. Soul's Harbor was across The Avenue. The State
Park was behind the church, so it wasn't unusual for wild
animals to come close, but the movement she saw was on
the side facing the town hall. Rarely did she see activity on
the part of wild animals on that sidewalk.

Tiger Lily peered intently until three guests walked to
the door on their way out. Back in "working mode," she
preened, purred, offered her head for pets, and graciously
accepted yet another donation for charity. When she
looked back and saw nothing, she assumed it had been an
opossum that lost its way. Or two.

An icy snow mix pelted the window now. Annie
appeared, bundled up again with a large thermal bag over
her shoulder.

"Let's go, big girl. It's time to go home."

Tiger Lily stomped her feet. She wanted to stay for the
lunch crowd. It was her job, after all.

"Don't argue with me. The weather is going to be
awful, and I want all of you to come home with me."

Tiger Lily turned her back and prepared to jump to the
floor behind the hostess stand. Annie was ready for her.
She put two hands around Tiger Lily's soft middle, turned
her and pulled her close, head and front paws nestled
under Annie's chin. "Come on, big girl. We'll come back
tomorrow."

They walked out, Tiger Lily allowing herself to be
carried.

When they reached the yoga studio, Annie rapped on
the window to get the attention of Little Socks. The lithe
black body stood, stretched, stretched some more, rolled

her head around a few times, washed her nose with a paw, then slowly hopped down to follow Annie home.

At the Tap, Annie opened the cat door with her foot and called out, "Mo, let's go!" Mo, typically a lover boy who couldn't be bothered with Annie when other women were around, was bored. George had arrived, but there were no guests yet. So Mo, unusually pliant, sauntered through the cat door to go home. He looked at Annie's shoulder, the shoulder where he, Mo, was typically enthroned, and huffed. Tiger Lily wasn't exactly on the shoulder, but Annie never carried two at a time. Oh, well. He could walk. Just this once. As they walked toward the Inn, Tiger Lily stuck her tongue out, goading Mo into a hissing fit.

Mr. Bean danced in the window as Annie neared the Confectionary. He looked over his shoulder at Carlos, who waved, and ran out to join Annie and his siblings. At the Winery, Sassy Pants seemed to expect them. She waited on the sidewalk, dancing in the now-driving ice and snow.

Back at the Inn, Annie paid no attention to the hissing fit as she placed Tiger Lily on the floor. She shrugged out of her coat and took the thermal bag to the kitchen.

"Henrie?" she called. "I have lunch. Practice meals for Valentine weekend."

Henrie had been in the basement doing laundry. He came up to look into the bag.

"What has Felicity conjured for lovers?"

"Herbed roasted chicken with lemon potatoes, honey-soy glazed salmon with mushrooms and peppers, pancetta and Brussels sprouts linguine, and a pork tenderloin stuffed with dried fruits and herbs."

"We will have to suffer through and try them all."

"My feelings exactly."

As Henrie set the kitchen table and arranged dishes, Annie checked through the mail from the hall table and made two cups of coffee at the guests' Keurig corner.

"Nothing but bills," complained Annie as she sat down with the coffee.

"Did you expect something else?"

"No. I must have the February blues. Light gray days. Dark gray nights. Guests from H-E-double-hockey-sticks."

"I placed a call to the bakery that apparently makes the only decent biscuit in the world. They were busy at the moment and promised to return the call."

"Did you tell them why you were calling?"

"I was able to say, 'Alistair and Cressida' before they finished the sentence with, 'Bartram.' They will be pleased to help me in any way they can."

"This pork is outstanding."

"Have you tried the salmon?"

"Not yet. I'm going for the linguine next."

"Which part of the chicken would you prefer?"

"Take yours first. I'll eat anything."

After a few minutes of quiet eating, Henrie sat back with a satisfied smile. "I will call Felicity. Each dish is remarkable."

The phone rang. Henrie picked up the kitchen extension and immediately hit the speaker button. The call was from England.

A friendly, booming English voice came from the other end of the line. "So you have the pleasure of the company of the Bartrams. How is that working out for you?"

Henrie, always the professional, was brief in his reply. "We are learning much of English customs."

The voice boomed with laughter. "How can I help you with the biscuits?"

"Apparently we cannot seem to find the right kind of biscuit, or something about our recipes are wrong. We have not hit upon the, shall I say, correct biscuit to please the Bartrams."

"And you never will. How is it, may I ask, that you've come to call us about it?"

"They say your bakery is the only place, apparently on this earth, that can make a proper biscuit."

Another burst of laughter. "I'll tell you my secret."

"Please do."

"I lay in a supply of El Loco's Coyotas, a sugar cookie made in Mexico. When the Bartram's come in, I go back to the kitchen, open a fresh box, put them in one of my bakery boxes, and sell them as something that just came out of the oven that morning."

"You are joking."

"Honest truth! I could ship you some, but you can probably get them easier if you just do a Google search yourself. That's El Loco's Coyotas, C-O-Y-O-T-A-S."

"Thank you so much. You have no idea."

"Oh, yes, I do have an idea. It took me months to get it right. I kept them just for the Bartrams. No one else in this area of the world will ever taste a Coyota."

"I shall make haste."

"Oh, Henrie?"

"Yes?"

"Be prepared for them to say you still can't get it right!"

"Understood. By the way, what can you tell me about them?"

"I think we've seen the last of them. Neither one of them worked. They made do with some inheritance from both sets of parents until that was gone. I heard they left Uppingham with many a bill unpaid, sort of in the dead of night, if you get my drift. You might want to ask for payment of your bill upfront."

On the other side of The Avenue, two stray cats stopped running long enough to catch their breaths.

"I think that cat saw us."

"We were too quick. She didn't get a good enough look. And it's snowing. It would have been hard for her to see."

"Yes, it's snowing. And we're going to be out in it if we can't find a place to sleep tonight."

"I think that doctor's office is a good place. No one will be in there this evening. We can sleep on that cot. It will be soft. We'll wake up before anyone gets in. We'll hear them walking around upstairs."

"Why don't we just stay in that church?"

"They have meetings and stuff almost every night. Scouts and people who drink and stuff. They'd see us."

"I wish we had an apartment to live in. Or a house. Even a barn."

"*We'll be okay. We just have to get through the winter. It's too bad that restaurant closed. We're going to have to get better about catching mice.*"

In the other room, seven cats and a visiting dog gathered inside the detective agency. Tiger Lily, beginning to doubt herself on the issue of the opossum, asked, "*Has anyone seen or heard of stray cats in the area?*"

She was answered by a chorus of no's and a trill.

"*Keep an eye out. I think we may have strays in the neighborhood. I might have seen an opossum, but that snow was making for some tricky viewing. I think I saw the tip of a tail, maybe two.*"

Sassy Pants had a worried look on her face. "*It's awful cold out dere. Where duz dey stay?*"

Little Socks, knowing she was smarter by far than Sassy Pants, had a quick answer. "*Cats were made for the outdoors, but we've gotten soft. We're used to soft beds and heated rooms. Other cats can handle it.*"

"*But dey shouldn't has to.*"

"*We should go look for them.*"

"*Maybe they followed you home. Let's look outside.*"

This last comment was from Kali, who got up as she spoke. She trotted out of the dining room to the library and up to the window, She peered through the snow, still swirling, but more thickly now. She was followed by Ko and Mr. Bean.

Mr. Bean's sharp little eyes caught sight of a long tail twitching as it went through a cat door on the other side of The Avenue.

"There! Something just went into The Clinic. It's closed now. No humans are inside."

All eyes peered at the cat door of The Clinic. Nothing happened. Tiger Lily jumped to the windowsill herself. *"One or two of us should go over there."*

"What for?" asked Ko. *"It's cold and wet out there."*

"It's not our problem."

"They could be hungry. There wouldn't be any food over there at The Clinic."

"What if they're mean?"

"What if they're sick?"

"What if they don't like other cats?"

Tiger Lily huffed. *"What if, what if, what if. What if Mommy didn't save us? What then?"*

Chastened, some of the cats hung their heads, others continued to stare at The Clinic.

Finally, Sassy Pants said, *"I'll go."*

"Wait," said Little Socks. *"You can't."*

"Why not? I can do portant stuff!"

"Mommy locked the outside doors so Tillie can't get out."

Tillie, on the floor looking up at the windowsill, whined in embarrassment.

Tiger Lily, exasperated at herself for forgetting this detail, jumped down as she said, *"They're inside now. They're warm. They can take care of themselves."*

The other cats jumped down, one by one. Sassy Pants, lingering for a moment, said, almost to herself, *"I hopes dey's okay."*

Back on the pillows in the agency, Tillie asked, *"So is this what you do? Is this how you do your detective stuff? Can I be a detective? What do I have to do? Is this like an active case? The Case Of The Cats In The Clinic? Will we go over there later and put hot lights on them? Will we have to take them into custody? Do you have a jail?"*

Tiger Lily bopped her on the nose and went to sleep.

For the first twenty miles, Cressida complained that they could not use the Inn's car for their daily journeys. Then she complained about the price of everything along The Avenue, chief among them the price of their room. Then she complained that brekkie had not been at all satisfying and when would he, Alistair, stop for some decent food.

Alistair treated this conversation as he had all others throughout their marriage. Most of the words went in one ear and out the other. Besides, he had to concentrate on his driving. Perhaps they should have listened to Annie about the weather. This was only a thought. He knew better than to say it.

Finally, he could bear no more. "Cressida, stop rambling on."

"What?"

"Shut up. It's time we had a serious discussion about our finances."

"Yes. What did you mean about our money being gone?"

"It's gone. Both of our inheritances. Gone. Somehow we have managed to spend it all."

"Well, we still have our home, and certainly there are other assets."

"Gone."

"Gone?"

"The house is gone. Foreclosed. We have no other assets."

"Foreclosed? Our house?"

"By now they've emptied it of our possessions, sold them off, and the house is owned by the bank."

"All our possessions? Alistair! Did you know that would happen? All of our things? My jewelry? The china?"

"You didn't notice that I sold the china before we left. Your jewelry is in my big suitcase. I just didn't have the heart to tell you."

"What are we to do?"

"I've given this some thought. There are several places along the lake in this area that look like our kind of place, where we can find our kind of people. They'll be our ticket up."

"Up where?"

"Up anywhere. We can find the proper lot, the lot that can be, let's say, made to believe we have more than we do, and they'll be the ones to get us back on our feet."

In a town about eighty miles from Chelsea, they pulled into a parking place outside a seedy-looking bar. They went in, sat at a rail near a billiards table and ordered burgers and fries with whatever beer was on tap.

The beer, a pale light beer, popular, for whatever reason, throughout the country, was served in room temperature glasses that had not been completely wiped clean. Cressida wiped lipstick off the edge of hers with a napkin. Without complaint.

The burgers arrived. Thin, greasy meat-like patties on cold dry buns, floppy dill pickle spears, and fries, crinkle cut, dripping in oil and under-cooked. They had learned not to ask for vinegar, and instead slopped mayonnaise – actually, a cheap substitute – on top of the fries, mustard on the burgers and ate heartily. They did not complain about the quality of the food.

They struck up a conversation with the bar owner and a few regulars and asked about places they could rent on the cheap while they got their new business going. When asked, Alistair said it would be a property management firm with upscale apartments.

They had a few more beers, bought rounds for the house and received several leads for rental places that could be had for a song. A few maps were drawn on bar napkins, most of them requiring specific directions, because they were in the country.

Alistair paid and tipped lavishly using travelers checks. Eventually they left the comfort of the bar, driving further north in search of the places on the cheap. They left with the telephone numbers of a few of the regulars, helpful men that looked forward to having big spenders such as themselves in their community.

Alistair worried again about the weather, but they did not have time to waste. They left the highway, following a napkin map, and found the country road to be covered with heavy, wet snow. Instead of turning around, they did the unthinkable. They plowed ahead until they plowed right into a fence.

Henrie logged onto his reservation accounts. Time to see what those people are up to, he thought. He looked at the charges adding up on the Bartram's account, daily, it appeared, from at least one, sometimes two or three, of Annie's businesses.

He noticed a charge from Mr. Bean's. Two dozen Jammie Dodgers. Egads.

No need to bother Annie about this.

He got to work.

3

Annie sat in the kitchen as Henrie handled a reservation. She looked out the window, snow swirling faster. She thought how lucky she was. Most businesses were going to close early today, and even more would be closed tomorrow due to weather.

Most of her key personnel lived right here on The Avenue. It was the same with the businesses across the street, as the owners, to save costs, had modern, attractive apartments on the second floor.

The second floor of the Café was a catering and party venue, but the rest of the businesses in the long brick building had upstairs apartments.

Her managers and supervisors didn't have to drive through snow to open, so Annie's places – and everything on The Avenue – would be open regular hours. Unless absolutely no one walked in. Then they would close early. Tomorrow would be a light, easy day for them.

Boone and his boys would make sure the sidewalks were clean and that paths were cleared on the median to allow access from one side of the street to the other.

Henrie put the phone down. "Our next set of guests, due to arrive tomorrow afternoon, have put their travel plans back for a day. They will arrive Wednesday."

"Wise decision. Who are they?"

"Married professionals from the south. One is a psychiatrist and the other a heart surgeon. They are the Timmer-Schmidts. Middle-aged, I believe. Terrence and Jerald. They look forward to a short vacation ending in a romantic weekend."

"Have you heard from the Bartrams?"

"No. That lot is unwise. The snow is blowing far too much for them to be driving."

"Should I put out an alert?"

"Whom would you notify?"

"I don't know, but if something happened to them, no one would know to call us."

"That is true. I will call Pete. He can notify the State Police."

"They probably didn't put anything out for Tillie. I'll get some dog food for her."

"I hope, for your sake, that Tillie is not as particular as her parents."

The storm was a typical February coastal storm. Heavy, wet system snow came over the lake and up the lake coast, augmented by lake effect snow, reacting to the warmer temperature of the lake. Wind blasted from the northeast and met the lake winds from the west, resulting in a swirling effect. Gusts of up to fifty miles per hour sent the snow in circles and made a treacherous cover on the earlier freezing rain, now ice, on the roads and sidewalks.

Waves on the lake were dangerously high, at twenty to thirty feet. When Annie looked toward The Marina, she saw waves crashing into the wharf and the one large boat still anchored in the harbor. It was The Escape, Ray's yacht-for-hire. Annie hoped it would weather the storm.

Annie worried about Chris and thought again that perhaps she should invest in a radio to stay informed of Coast Guard activity. Chris had encouraged her away from that notion, but on days like today, she wondered....

"I'm going to call Laila to come over for dinner this evening, Henrie, to keep my mind occupied. Would you like to join us?"

"No, thank you. I have been holding on to a movie for just such an evening. I will make popcorn and have my own theater experience."

Annie made plans with Laila and found enough frozen and prepared food in her kitchen to make a feast fit for mad kings. She had a bottle each of dry red and dry white wine, two packages of frozen meals from the Café, cheese curls, her go-to junk food, frozen pastries from Mr. Bean's, and a frozen pizza and hot dogs for Laila's kids.

Plans for the evening made, she curled up on a sofa in the library, one eye reading a book and the other watching the storm. The phone rang. Annie picked up.

"Ms. Mack? This is State Trooper Jones. I have information here that asks me to call you if a certain couple was found to be in trouble?"

"Yes. The Bartrams. Are they okay?"

"They're fine, ma'am, at least they are at the moment."

"At the moment?"

"If they say one more word about our troopers driving them through this weather down to Chelsea this evening, my men will lose it and shoot one of them."

"Dare I ask which one?"

"Ma'am, I believe that would be the female."

Annie laughed. "Where are you?"

"We're about a hundred twenty miles up the coast from you."

"And beyond the personality deficit, they're really okay?"

"They got lucky. They were stopped on the side of a country road and weren't found for a couple of hours after they ran out of gas. They're cold and hungry, but otherwise fine."

"Where will they stay the night?"

"We'll get them to a hotel and have their car towed to a gas station nearby. They should be on the road home to you as soon as the weather lets up tomorrow."

"I can't thank you enough."

"That voice sounded pretty dry and sarcastic, ma'am."

Annie chuckled.

"Oh, I should tell you," he continued, "this nice couple said they are going to have the hotel bill you, for some convoluted reasoning that includes their reservation at your Inn."

"Well, we'll see how that works out for them."

"My thoughts exactly. Have a great evening, ma'am."

"You, too. Stay safe out there." Annie hung up the phone and told Henrie the news.

The storm was in full force now, but Ginger, unable to concentrate on anything at home, asked her mother if she could run over to The Avenue.

Janet, looking outside, realized the town streets were still in pretty good condition, and that the houses were, for the moment, keeping drifting at bay.

"I don't like you going out, but is there something specific you need?"

"Yeah," lied Ginger. "I forgot to get, you know, my monthly supplies."

Janet, chagrined that she had forgotten to check the supplies herself, said, "Alright. But be back in an hour. I don't want you driving in this weather, even in town."

"Okay, Mom."

Ginger had an ulterior motive. One of her best friends lived on The Avenue. She could run into The Drug Store, get some supplies she didn't really need, then go to Babar Foods.

Once inside the grocery, she said hello to Laila and asked if she could see James.

"Sure. He's out in the back yard with Ava and Carl."

Ginger slipped through the back storeroom and went to the yard area behind the building. The "yard" extended from one end of the building to the other, and since Laila was the only person with children, everyone else who lived and worked here assumed it belonged to this family. The back of the yard was bordered by trees of the state park, fenced off so they really couldn't make use of the trees in their play.

They didn't need the trees. James was huddled behind a snow fort on Ginger's left. His sister and brother were behind a fort on her right. They kept James pinned down with heavy fire. Ginger slipped into the fort beside James, scooping up snow to make a dozen medium-sized bombers. James had at least two dozen ready to go.

They looked at one another. James said, "Are you ready?"

Ginger nodded.

They rose as one and began to fire back at the other fort, forcing Ava and Carl to duck for cover. Gathering speed, they packed supplies into their left arms and ran toward the other fort, right arms high and armed with snowballs ready to throw.

As they reached the other fort, Carl, in a high-pitched scream, cried, "Give! Give! We give up!"

"Speak for yourself!" cried Ava.

She jumped up and pelted James and Ginger with snowballs, receiving in return more than she could give, until she, too, was forced to cry, "I give up!"

Laila called from the door, "Get in here, all of you, and dry out before you catch your death!"

In the back room of the store, coats hanging here and there and hands cupped around steaming cups of cocoa, Ginger quietly told James about her encounter at the mall. She told him first about the bullies, then about the strange comment made by Porter, then about the curious behavior of the group of teens.

James listened intently. Then he asked Ginger to wait, went upstairs and came back, cellphone in hand.

"This is what they're talking about," he said.

James showed her a picture of a waif of a girl. Naked. Obviously in the shower and trying to cover herself, but showing both buttocks and a breast.

Ginger put facts together in her mind. This was a girl named Penny. She was a freshman and lived in the hard section of town. She was Porter's sister. Porter had taken this picture, and he had goaded Marc to take a picture of Ginger to share with the world.

"Did you show this to your mom?"

"Are you kidding?"

"How long have you had it?"

"Just got it this morning. I was going to delete it, but, I don't know, I think something more should happen. I think, you know, this isn't right."

"Is this the only one?"

"What? Whoever it is just sent one picture of Penny."

"But are there pictures of others?"

"I think so, but I haven't seen them. Last week at school I heard about maybe two others."

"Who?"

"Um, maybe Pam, she would be the sister of one of that group, Dallas. Dallas is a junior; Pam is in junior high, in Ava's class."

"You're joking! A kid like that?"

"I know. When I heard that, the first thing I thought about was Ava, and what I would do if anyone did that to her."

"And there might be more?"

"I heard about a really bad one, someone in our class, but no one would tell me who. They know you and I are friends. I'm surprised I got the one of Penny. Someone forgot to delete me from a distribution list."

"We have to tell Dad."

"We won't be able to walk back into that school if we do."

"Yes we will. Why wouldn't we?"

"Maybe you could, but I couldn't. Look at me! I'm brown! And I just moved here a few years ago. Some of the meaner ones send me notes to 'go back home, towelhead.' And some just outright call me that to my face."

"You've never said anything."

"What would I say? That I'm a teenager and I'm being called names? Get a grip, Ginger. I'm an outsider here, and you know it."

"I guess I didn't pay attention…"

"You don't pay attention. You say you're my friend, but all we ever talk about are fun things. We never talk about real stuff. Face it, you don't have to deal with real stuff. You're the daughter of the chief of police."

"I'm the black daughter of the black chief of police and I didn't grow up here, either. You don't think that gives me status as an outsider? In this lily white resort town?"

"In this town, black has a higher status than brown."

Ginger stood, picked up her coat, and looked down at James, who stared into his cup of cocoa.

"Delete the photo. Just having it on your phone is a crime."

She walked out. She was a teenager with feelings of anger, sadness and fear boiling around, each competing for top status.

4

Laila and the children leaned into the wind to make their way across The Avenue. Laila felt the parental effects of the snow day and knew it would be worse tomorrow. It didn't take long for the cats and Tillie to feel the same effects. The children, normally quiet and reserved, ran through the Inn, chasing the cats and the pup through the apartment, down the stairs, through the library, upstairs to the apartment, and...Annie put her foot down. She ushered the children into the living room, put an Avenger movie in the DVD player and pointed sternly at the television.

"Stay here. Pizza and hot dogs are on the way."

When Carl started to get up she met his face with a look that brooked no argument. He sat back down and transferred his energy to the movie.

Laila was a single parent. She owned the grocery store across The Avenue from the KaliKo Inn. Her oldest child, James, was in high school; Ava attended junior high; Carl, the youngest, was in grade school and lived with autism. Annie's best friend, Laila was an eclectic combination of contemporary conservatism. Always dressed in traditional Pakistani style and faithful – to a degree – to religious rules, Laila embraced everything about today's acceptance of lifestyle choice and technological chic. Her grocery store was filled with organic foods and regionally-grown produce and meats. Her deli selections were unique to the area and featured many Indian and Pakistani dishes.

In the kitchen, as Annie and Laila put the meal together, they watched waves crash over the beach. The moon wasn't full, but it was bright enough behind the clouds to give a gray sheen to the sky. Annie again worried about Chris, but Laila refused to allow her mind to linger.

"So, who's the pup?"

"Tillie. She's a Jack Russell terrier, from England, no less."

"She belongs to those horrible people?"

"Yes. They've been to your store?"

"They've been in every day for the last three or four days. They're awful! They walk through and complain about everything. The selection, the prices."

"Do they ever buy anything?"

"They 'buy' things by stuffing them into their coats. The first time they were in, they took a large bag of dog food. He picked it up and walked out the door; she saw me looking and told me she was shopping and she'd pay for that when she finished. Of course, when I looked up again, she was gone."

"Oh, no. Make a list of everything you think they took. We'll take care of it."

"Don't worry about it. But listen, they should have plenty of food for Tillie in their room. Is that what you're feeding her now?"

"Henrie always has dog food on hand, and I think she and the cats have helped themselves to some people food here and there."

Once the children were fed, Laila and Annie settled down with food and a movie of their own. They paid more attention to the storm than to the movie. The television sat near bay windows overlooking the state park, with a view to the sky over the lake. They watched as the storm continued to roll through. Heavy snow piled up, blowing as it fell, but too heavy to drift.

"I love a good winter storm. Always have."

"I'm getting used to them. The kids had a good time in it this afternoon. The snow was perfect for making a snowman and a couple of snow forts."

"I thought you were having an e-learning day."

"We got in some physical education time."

Annie laughed. "You had snow forts. Were snowballs involved?"

"You know it. Ava and Carl had one fort; James had the other. I think, by the time Ginger got there to help James, a clear winner was determined."

"It will be even better tomorrow. We'll have a little less wind, and the snow will still be heavy and easy to pack."

"That will give them the incentive they need to get their e-learning out of the way early."

"Use any tool at your disposal."

Laila glanced occasionally at Annie's ring. Of course she had seen it before, but she often wondered why Annie didn't talk about the meaning behind it. It wasn't an engagement ring, so what did it mean? Was it just a gift? Tonight was not the time to ask, with the Coast Guard on alert.

Annie moved the conversation in another direction. "How do you think Ray and Cheryl are doing at The Marina? The Escape is still in the harbor."

"I thought about calling them before we came over tonight. Do you want to see if they're home?"

Annie got a cell phone and made the call to their house. No answer. No answer at The Marina. No answer on Cheryl's cell. "Well, let's hope that means they are busy enjoying the storm, not having to do damage control."

Annie and Laila settled in, conversation moving from one topic to another, as they watched the storm and the movie progress. When the movie ended, they walked in between cats and a dog to wake the children. Laila bundled Carl into winter gear; Ava and James grumbled as they got into their own.

Annie watched from the window as they made their way back across The Avenue.

At The Clinic, two stray cats looked out the window.

"Thank goodness we found a place to stay tonight."

"Let's hope we find a place for the day tomorrow."

"And tomorrow night."

"And forever."

5

Annie woke from a fitful night of sleep. She wasn't alone in bed. Not only were seven cats sleeping in various locations, under or on top of the covers, but Tillie was there as well. She was snuggled into Annie's shoulder.

When Laila left with the children the night before, Annie let Tillie out. The pup took care of business quickly, not liking the snow and the wind. This morning, not used to the needs of puppies, Annie almost missed the code. When Tillie awoke and started to yip, Annie covered her head and tried to go back to sleep. It was only on the prodding of Tiger Lily, a paw on Annie's nose, over and over, that she realized she needed to take care of the situation.

Annie threw an old, ratty robe over her baggy sweats, put her bare feet into floppy gardening boots, and took Tillie out the back way. As they came in through the all-season porch, Henrie met her with a cup of coffee.

"I have prepared a small breakfast. Come back downstairs when you are ready."

"I'm ready now."

Henrie looked her over carefully, head to toe. Disheveled hair, face unwashed with mascara drooping negligently underneath her left eye, sweats that sagged in unflattering ways, a robe that should have been thrown out years ago. And those boots.

"I believe some repair is in order."

"Since when do I have to dress for you, Henrie?"

Henrie gave a slight harrumph. "I took the liberty of calling the Coast Guard station. One boat went out last night; everyone is back safely. Chris stayed on station and is ready for a break. He will join us shortly."

Annie gave Henrie a grateful hug and danced up the stairs to shower and dress.

Outside, the snow had stopped. The wind was a mere breeze at twenty miles per hour. Things were looking up. Tuesdays were always better than Mondays. After dressing and feeding all of the four-legged creatures, Annie picked Tillie up to hold her tight and opened the front door to let the cats out.

She saw Boone, Daryl and Donny at work blowing and shoveling snow from both sides of The Avenue and the median. They had to shovel and blow the same direction the wind was blowing, but they were making headway. Annie went inside to grab her coat and shrugged into her boots. She picked Tillie up again and went out to say hello.

Boone and his wife Harriet, known to all as Hilly, were responsible for keeping Annie's businesses in good shape. They removed snow in the winter, landscaped the rest of the year, provided preventive maintenance and building repair, and cleaned the interior of each business, even, starting recently, the Inn. Daryl and Donny, both part-time college students, worked with them.

Annie loved this family. They were unassuming, taking on the air of common hill folk. They were from the Appalachian region, which allowed them to keep up the façade. In fact, they were hard working, well-educated and financially comfortable, possibly wealthy. With Annie's complete acceptance of them, they were slowly letting more of their true nature become visible to others in town.

Boone turned off the snow blower as she approached. "I think we've seen all of the snow from this system. Probably won't have any more until later in the week."

"Aren't you glad you moved to an area that has lake effect snow?"

"Well, it does keep a body busy."

A four wheel drive vehicle came down the newly cleaned streets and turned into the Inn's parking lot. Chris emerged, looking a little bedraggled. Annie wondered why he didn't keep a shaving kit at the station, but to her, he looked good no matter how long he had gone without attention.

Boone gave a knowing grin and slipped into his practiced drawl. "I'll jes be gettin' back to work now, ma'am."

Chris met Annie halfway with a long, deep hug, not caring that a little dog shared the space. He finally pulled away.

"New pet?"

"This is Tillie. You haven't been here for a few days, so you've not had the pleasure. Her mommy and daddy were caught up north in the snowstorm. They should be here later."

Chris was a little under six feet tall and had the slim and erect bearing of a Navy officer. His hair, prematurely white, had some length to it. He also sported neatly trimmed facial hair, both mustache and beard. At least it was generally neatly trimmed. Today, he could use a little help.

He was the child of a privileged, old-money family and had arrived several years ago on assignment from the Coast Guard. This was his fourth assignment, after two in coastal waters and one at another Great Lakes station. His family did not immediately warm to his choice of a career in the Coast Guard. Or his life in Chelsea. They were still cool-ish on both.

Inside, Annie put Tillie on the floor. The little dog headed at a fast clip to the dining room and treats. Finding nothing, she went on to the kitchen, followed at a more sedate pace by Annie and Chris.

The small table was set for breakfast. Henrie arranged orange pancakes with pomegranate sauce, eggs scrambled with bacon, mushrooms and onions, a variety of scones from the Confectionary, juice and coffee.

Chris told them of the one call-out of the night, a tanker that had engine trouble in the high waves. The crew had to be off-loaded before the tanker possibly rolled. It was a small crew and, given the weather, an easier rescue than could have been hoped. Boats were on their way now, in calmer water, to attempt to save the tanker itself.

Annie gave silent thanks for the safety of everyone involved and an extra special thanks that Chris had remained on land.

Chris said, "By the way, Ray stopped over this morning needing some help with The Escape. It took quite a bit of damage last night."

"I wondered about that. The waves were crashing into the harbor something fierce. I tried to call them; didn't get an answer."

"They were at The Marina all night, watching the storm slam into their pier and The Escape. They probably didn't want to talk to anyone."

"How bad it is?"

"He doesn't know yet. His biggest concern is turning in another insurance claim so close on the heels of the last one."

"This will be the third claim in about a year, won't it?"

"Yeah. All for very different circumstances. But insurance companies aren't in business to give it all away. Anyway, I helped him secure it, and he was going to call the insurance company. If they don't cover it, he'll have to pay for the repairs himself."

Henrie said, "If they need physical labor to make repairs, I would be happy to be involved. I am a skilled carpenter."

Chris and Annie looked at him in wonder. Was there anything the man could not do?

It was the kind of day that had the resort community moving slowly. Businesses on The Avenue were open on time, but people who didn't have to get out stayed indoors with that extra cup of coffee. Henrie, Annie and Chris were slipping into the same slow "snow day" mode.

They sat, drank more coffee, talked a lot about not much of anything, spoiled Tillie, Kali and Ko, drank more coffee, talked about possibly getting going, had more scones, laughed at some funny Coast Guard rescue stories, and finally had to admit that they really, really did need to get moving.

The front door banged open, and loud, angry footsteps could be heard in the entryway. Kali, Ko and Tillie skippered into the dining room and under the cover of the detective agency.

Then those voices. Cressida and Alistair were back. Annie took a look at the time. 11:00. She looked at Henrie and said, "You stay here. It's my turn."

Annie headed to the entryway, but didn't get any further than the dining room when she was confronted with two faces, one angry, one apologetic. Cressida, of course, took control.

"I have never been so insulted in my life!" Special emphasis had been placed on 'never,' 'insulted,' and 'life.' As if Annie could not comprehend the meaning without proper emphasis.

"What happened?"

"You know very well what happened! That hotel said that you would not be covering the expenses of our overnight stay, our dinner and our brekkie. The nerve!"

"The hotel didn't call us, but had they done so, you're right, we would not have chosen to cover those expenses for you."

"Why on earth not? We are your guests!" Emphasis on the words 'not' and 'guests.'

Annie tried to diffuse the situation. "First, why don't you take your coats off, freshen up, and then come in for some coffee or tea, and we'll talk."

"We'll have our brekkie now."

"Excuse me?"

"I'm sure you have charged us for use of the room last night, so we will have our brekkie. Now."

Henrie came through the door to rescue Annie. "We did not know the time of your return. "Brekkie" is not prepared at the moment. Please take the time to freshen up, and I will prepare a meal within the hour."

Somewhat mollified, Cressida huffed, "In view of the time, make it a proper English luncheon."

She stomped off and Alistair, like a meek puppy, cast an apologetic smile in their direction before he followed her up the stairs.

Annie looked to Henrie. "Proper English luncheon?"

"I do not have a clue. I shall Google the issue."

They went to the kitchen to find Chris, arms covering his head on the table, body shaking with laughter. When he finally came up for air, he said, "The best part of that? To hear you, Henrie, use the word 'Google' as a verb in a sentence."

Henrie did 'Google the issue' and determined a proper English luncheon that could be prepared without notice. He and Annie made calls to Felicity, Carlos, Minnie, Mem, and, as an afterthought, George.

Deliveries were made promptly. By noon, Henrie laid the dining table with a proper lunch. Thick slices of crusty bread, sliced roast beef, a large wedge of stilton cheese, a bowl containing sandwich slices of both sweet and dill pickles, onion chutney, a sliced apple, lettuce, and frosty mugs of ale.

As Henrie laid the plates and sliver, Cressida stormed into the dining room, prepared to roar. She stopped short, looked around, sniffed, turned to Alistair who had meekly appeared, and said, "It's possible they have finally gotten something right."

Henrie retreated to the kitchen, where Annie and Chris still lingered, listening to the exchange. Not wanting to ruin the moment for the Bartrams, they remained silent. Cressida and Alistair did not realize Annie and Chris were in the kitchen, and they continued to treat Henrie as the common, and, when necessary, deaf, "help." They paid no heed to him as they discussed their problems.

Money problems.

Big money problems.

"So, we're broke. I don't know why you couldn't just tell me that before we left Uppingham."

"I did not want to bore you with the details."

"The details! I would have taken more from the house before we left! I didn't know the collectors were coming. We'll never get anything out of it now."

"I told you I got the jewelry, and I sold the best stuff."

"We'll never be able to show our faces there again."

"I thought we decided we did not want to show our faces there again."

"You're right. We'll find a cheap place here somewhere. But where? We have to go somewhere we can live on the dole."

"Oh the dole? Us?"

"Yes, us, unless you have another source of income you have neglected to mention."

"No. No income, and very little money left."

"How much do we have in traveler's checks?"

"About $500."

"And cash?"

"Less than $100."

"We wasted hundreds on that trip yesterday. And there is the rental car to pay."

"We can cash in our return tickets to England."

"That will get us a few hundred. Remember, we got them on the cheap. What else do we have?"

"We have the one credit card, the only one with a balance. Of course, the Inn expects to be paid from it."

"Blast the Inn. Let's use up the credit card before we check out Sunday."

"Why are we going to leave? We have to live somewhere."

"Much as I hate to say it, Alistair, we cannot afford to stay here. And we didn't even get to see those places yesterday, the places we could get on the cheap. They could have been hovels. We don't know what 'cheap' means to these idiots."

"What else can we do?"

"I know. I'll go over to that tea house and chat up the woman who owns it, see if she could do some computer research on the issue of going on the dole. Maybe there are places where it's easier than others."

"You must go today," came Alistair's plaintive voice.

"I'll get round this afternoon. At least that woman, Mem, I think her name is, prepares a pot of proper tea, and she is not as vulgar as everyone else."

In the manner of the upper class, assuming Henrie would hear what they were saying only as it applied to him, Cressida raised her voice just a bit and said, "You! You there!"

Henrie appeared at the door.

"More ale."

Henrie nodded, picked up her empty mug and returned with another frosty mug filled with ale. Cressida was talking again.

"Maybe we should take Tillie for a 'ride' while we're here. Certainly if we find a lightly populated country road, someone will find her and take care of her. That would be one less expense."

Kali and Ko gasped and without thinking moved to hide Tillie – already hidden under a blanket – with their big bodies.

Henrie held his facial expression and said nothing, except to ask, "Will there be anything else?"

Cressida merely glared and said, "You can leave now."

Henrie, back in the kitchen, whispered, "We must do something."

Annie and Chris were wide-eyed and open mouthed. Finally taking a deep breath, Annie answered in a whisper of her own, "What if I ask them if we can keep her?"

"What would you do with a dog to add to your herd of cats?" asked Chris, as softly as he had ever spoken.

"That's not important. Certainly the first thing is to rescue her from those...those...those people!"

"What reason would you give?"

"Well…um….the cats have grown so fond of her?"

"I could say I want her."

"Don't be silly. It wouldn't make any sense for you, someone who has barely met the pup, to come out and ask perfect strangers to just hand her over."

"I can offer to buy her. Tell them I've always wanted to have a…what kind of a dog is it, again?"

Annie looked at Chris, then at Henrie. "It has to be me. But I can hardly say anything right now," she whispered. "They'll know we heard everything they said."

Henrie leaned closer. "Go along through the kitchen door to the back. Certainly Boone has cleared all the sidewalks by now; he is very thorough. Come into the dining room as if you have just come downstairs and let them know how much you enjoyed having Tillie last night. Ask them if they would consider allowing you to purchase her."

Annie nodded and slipped silently out the kitchen door. When she entered the dining room, she came from the stairwell as if she had just been upstairs.

"How was lunch?"

"Bearable," answered Cressida with a sulk. "At least he made an attempt at a proper repast."

"Well, I'm glad to hear it. Listen, I want to ask a huge favor of you."

"What?"

"It's about Tillie. You see, the cats have grown quite fond of her. I was wondering, since she is such a sweet thing, would you be willing to let me buy her?"

Annie smiled and looked back and forth, from Cressida to Alistair. Alistair started to nod in answer, but Cressida stopped him with a hand on his arm.

"He is a part of the family, you know."

"She, dear. Tillie is a she."

"Yes, of course, I meant 'she.' She is part of the family."

"Oh, I'm sure. I'm certain she is very valuable to you."

"He…she…is, at that. We would have to discuss this and let you know the proper price."

"I would be willing to pay anything fair," said Annie, knowing she would probably end up paying an outrageous sum.

Cressida's eyes narrowed. "Those cats. They are valuable to you?"

"Oh, yes. Very valuable."

Her look turned shrewd. "What kind of price would you set for them?"

Annie's eyes narrowed to match Cressida's gaze. She caught herself and put an innocent look back on her face. She breathed in, looked thoughtful, and said, finally, "Well, of course I would only sell them to a person who would truly love them, and, well, I can't imagine an appropriate price."

"Then you see our dilemma. We'll let you know in a day or two."

"But you will consider it?"

"Of course. We will consider it."

Kali, Ko and Tillie trembled together in the detective agency, hardly daring to hope that Annie would really purchase Tillie and get her away from those awful people.

Susie Phillips put another bag of clothing into the trunk of their car. She opened the back door and sighed. And held her nose. Oh, well. Why bother to clean it? It will just get dirty again. She returned to the car, trudging over snow they had not bothered to shovel.

Tim was in the kitchen. A few boxes of kitchen utensils and what few groceries they had left were on a pile on the kitchen floor. He stood on the counter top with a hammer in one hand, a black plastic trash bag in another, and nails in his mouth. Through the nails, he said, "Lass woom."

Susie took one more trip through the house. When she passed the bathroom, she closed her ears – and her nose – to the plaintive meows and yips. They had food and water. And a blanket to pee on. They should be fine. For now.

She looked around at the furniture they were leaving. Easy come, easy go. Most of it was from Goodwill, anyway. No great loss. But still….

Back in the kitchen, she looked up at Tim as he put the last of the nails through. A corner at the bottom of the trash bag, just over the counter, flapped open. "Missed one."

"Didn't miss it. Ran out of nails. No big deal."

"Well. This is it. Want to stay here one more night?"

"May as well. The utilities won't turn off until sometime tomorrow."

"Did you call those idiots up north?"

"I did. They're keeping their eyes and ears open. Something will come up. It always does."

6

Cressida and Alistair put on coats and were once again away from the Inn. Annie was on her hands and knees. She knocked on the top of the detective agency table and pulled at the opening. Sticking her head inside, she peered at Kali, Ko and Tillie, huddled together and trembling.

"Don't worry, girls. I'll take care of everything. Tillie, how would you like to stay here? At least for a while? I'm sure the kids will take good care of you until we figure out what to do next."

Tillie seemed to understand what she said. Her tail wagged just a little bit. She snuffled and reached up to lick Annie on the nose.

Annie got up and went once again to the kitchen. Chris had his coat on to leave. "This is all you need. Are you going to try to rescue every dog or cat you meet?"

"Not every dog or cat. Only some."

"Oh. Only some. Okay. No problem then. We won't have to add a kennel out back."

"We?"

"Well, let me just say that I love your cats. Love them. All…seven of them. And the little dog seems really…cute. But, Annie, there is only so much room in that bed…."

Chris seemed to realize Henrie was still in the room. Henrie realized it as well. He cleared his throat and said, "I must clean the dining room."

Annie stared at Chris. He turned and walked to the kitchen door. At the door, he turned around, started to say something, closed his mouth and left.

Annie fumed. She went into the dining room to help Henrie and remembered a nugget of conversation from last night. "Laila said they bought some dog food from her a few days ago." She stopped. "That's not really what she said. She said they 'picked up' dog food, and they walked right out of the store without paying. That's pretty awful, but where I started to go with this thought was to say that maybe you can find out what they picked up, so we can at least feed her what she likes."

Annie banged her fist on the table. "Can you believe that they haven't even asked about her? Haven't called for her? Haven't looked around the house for her? But she's 'family'! She's 'so important' to them!"

Henrie patted her shoulder. "Do not worry, Annie. We will take care of her."

"We should probably take care of the grocery bill, too."

"I have a plan."

Kali and Ko turned to one another. *"We have to tell Tiger Lily about this. We have to protect Tillie."*

"We'll have to wait until she gets home. We can't get outside."

"What if we tricked Henrie into opening the door?"

"How are we going to do that?"

"I can help!" said Tillie. *"I'll bet I can undo that lock."*

"Never!"

"I can!"

"If it could be done, Tiger Lily and Little Socks would have figured it out before!"

"Let's take a look."

Two big cats and a little dog poked their heads out and looked around before scampering to the front door. Tillie looked closely at the lock. It was a simple privacy lock found in most hotels, a buckle swing arm. It was metal and sturdy. It looked hard to open, but Tillie put her paw firmly in place and pulled. It popped open.

"Well, I never!" exclaimed Kali.

"Let's go!" cried Ko.

They ran out the door, Tillie close behind them.

"You have to stay with us!" "Stay with us!"

They ran down the stairs and up the sidewalk, as fast as the big girls had ever gone, until they reached the Café. As soon as they got there, they realized a parade had followed them. Sassy Pants, Mr. Bean and Little Socks noticed them from the windows, and they scurried along as well.

Breathless, they entered the Café and looked around until they saw Tiger Lily. She was on one of her table ledges, pointing out a particularly interesting entrée to a new customer. She heard the commotion, turned and realized she might have a problem on her hands if she let that yappy dog run around the restaurant. She gave a quick nod to the customer, jumped down and gathered the cats and Tillie behind the hostess stand.

Hissing, she said, *"Why are you here? Why did you bring Tillie?"* Thinking about it, she said, *"How did you get out of the house?"*

Ko, puffing up in importance, answered in an uncharacteristically bold manner. *"Which question do you want an answer to first?"*

Sassy Pants, breathless, said, *"Da one about how you gots out of da house!"*

Little Socks bopped Sassy Pants on the nose, then turned back. *"Yeah. How did you do that?"*

"Tillie did it." "Tillie used her paw." "It just opened." "Mommy is going to be so mad."

That gave them all pause. For a second.

Tiger Lily pressed them. *"What was so important?"*

Quickly, Kali and Ko told the story in the way only they could. One would start; another would finish the sentence. So they went, back and forth, until the whole sad story was out, about the nasty Bartrams, how they planned to take Tillie to the country to dump her out, how Mommy had been in the kitchen and how she sneaked into the back door and came in to ask if she could buy Tillie.

Kali and Ko looked at one another before silently agreeing they had to hear it all, so they told how Mommy had discussed actually selling them, the cats. This got gasps and looks of alarm, but they quickly went on to say that it seemed like Mommy was only saying it because she wanted to make sure Tillie was safe.

"They didn't even ask for Tillie. Didn't look for her. Didn't ask if she needed food or anything."

Tillie stood with her head down, waiting the word from Tiger Lily. Would she say they could help? Would she kick Tillie out of the house? Of course, Tillie wasn't thinking rationally.

At that moment, Cyril's big body came around the corner of the hostess stand. Tillie looked up in alarm. Cyril merely came close, sniffed her head, moved her around with his big nose and sniffed her behind. He sat down and asked, *"Who's this?"*

Everyone talked at once.

Cyril put down a big paw, rather swiftly, and they all shut up. Cyril looked at Tiger Lily, who introduced Tillie and told Cyril the problem.

"I see. Well, pup, Tillie, is it? It seems you have a group of very good friends that are going to make sure you're safe."

Tillie looked around in wonder. Was it really true? Were they going to save her? The faces looking back at her said, *"Yes."*

Tiger Lily quickly took charge. *"There's nothing we can do now. Tillie, why don't you spend the afternoon going around to all of our places, so you know where to go if you have to run away."*

Looking around at each cat, she said, *"Take care of her. Don't let her wander off. Introduce her to your managers. I'll go first, then one at a time, go into each place. And so nothing looks out of place, all of you stay where you belong until time to go home today. Kali and Ko will make sure she gets back to the Inn."*

Everyone nodded. Tiger Lily looked at Tillie. *"Come on, then. Let me introduce you to Felicity and Trudie."*

Tillie followed obediently. Tiger Lily took her behind the coffee counter where Trudie kneeled down to give her some special pets. "Who is this, Tiger Lily? A friend of yours?"

Tiger Lily blinked slowly, nudged Tillie on the shoulder with her nose and took her back to the kitchen.

Felicity turned around and saw Tiger Lily with a little dog. In the kitchen. Tiger Lily knew better than to bring another animal into the kitchen. She knew better than to come into the kitchen without another animal.

Instead of ordering them out, she beckoned Tillie to come forward, leaned down to give her a pet and said, "Any friend of Tiger Lily is a friend of ours."

Tillie yipped in delight, and they left.

"Go on, now," said Tiger Lily. *"You all know what to do."*

Tillie made the rounds of all of the businesses, including Mo's Tap. She met the managers, some of the other employees, several guests, and realized she had found a new home.

The roads were clear and Ginger once again asked for permission to leave.

Janet, knowing the roads to be safer than they had been the afternoon before, still asked the parent questions. "Where are you going?"

"Um, I thought I would stop in at the yoga studio to see if Diana needed me."

"And after you find out she doesn't, where are you going then?"

"Maybe that box store on the east end of town."

"Are you meeting anyone?"

"Um, no, I might see some kids, but I'm not planning on it."

Janet sensed a bit of subterfuge but had no reason to say no. "Be back before supper."

"Yes, Mom."

Ginger left. She waited until she was in the car and on the street to hit the call button on her phone. She had looked up the home telephone number for Penny, and she hoped the girl would answer the phone. She did.

Ginger didn't know why the girl, a virtual stranger, agreed, but in a few minutes, she pulled in front of a house in need of much repair. The waif of a girl jumped into the front passenger seat.

Chris sat in his living room, a large room with a wall of windows looking over the lake. The upscale condominium community was north of the historic lighthouse museum and just south of the Coast Guard Station. It wasn't possible to walk to the Inn via the beach. Past the museum was an area that abutted the state park, and a rocky cliff and lagoon took over the beach. Of course, he could go up and over...or he could swim...or...having that barrier was probably a good thing.

Where had that argument come from? Why was he talking about "we" to Annie – in front of Henrie, no less – when he and Annie had never discussed "we"? And what had upset him – really – about the rescue of a pup?

Chris worked on a watercolor. Art was a stress-relieving hobby. He enjoyed working in watercolors, pen and ink and charcoals, and he was passably good. His work was sold at charity events, and many people, seeing his work, commissioned additional pieces.

He appreciated his Coast Guard salary and benefits, but he didn't need them. He was from an old money family. Trust funds established by his grandparents were available to him with few strings attached. If he were to add it up, he would probably be the richest man in Chelsea, but he didn't think about it. Most of the funds were hard to get to, taking some time and work on the part of the family's attorney to untangle.

He could live higher than he did, but he didn't have the need to do so. And he had never told Annie about his financial circumstances. She was aware his parents were, in a word, "filthy," but she had no idea he was "filthy" in his own right.

Thoughts of this nature floated in and out of his mind while he finished the watercolor, a sunset as seen from Annie's third-floor balcony.

He put the paints away and got a pad and set of pencils. The thoughts of his situation, his un-we-ness with Annie and everything else, went away as he concentrated on a likeness of Annie. The detail was precise. The feeling on her face was of contentment. As the picture came together, he placed her on a rocking chair of the front porch of the Inn. One cat went into the picture. Tiger Lily, on the table beside her, one paw on her arm. Annie looked past Tiger Lily toward the north side of The Avenue. He added some movement of her hair, to indicate a light breeze.

He added one piece of color. On her finger he placed a ring with a riot of colorful jewels. He took one last look at the picture, signed and dated it. And put it in a closet of private collection pieces, pieces that Annie would see only when he was sure she was ready. As he put this one away, he realized how large the collection had grown over the last year.

7

Cressida and Alistair split up.

Alistair went to Mo's Tap, where he ordered several more frosty mugs of ale. He spent most of the time on his cell phone at a corner table. His self-appointed assignment was to make contact with one or more of the stellar friends made during their jaunt north. He had a special request.

Mo's Tap was not a typical bar. It was upscale, with a classy, clean, light look. Most of the walls were a buttery yellow, and light taupe served as an accent color. Most of the tables were burnished oak with comfortable oak chairs. There were booths, also oak with dark taupe cushions, and several areas with overstuffed chairs and accent tables in private arrangements. A few tables looked like oaken barrels.

Each seating area had unique pendant lights that looked as if they could be turned up or down as the mood struck. And candles. The candles were lit only after Mo was gone for the day. Those who had seen Mo's little butt alight from a careless dance around the flames knew why. To add to the ambiance, blues music played through the sound system quietly, just enough to be heard.

While Alistair did his telephone research, Cressida went across The Avenue to CyberHealth, the combination health food store, internet café and tea shop, a shop as eclectic – some would say eccentric – as its owner.

Mem puttered around her displays, straightening some items and rearranging others. When she saw Cressida, she smiled and said, "Mrs. Bartram. How nice to see you again."

"So nice to see you as well, Mem. Please, call me Cressida."

"Cressida it is. How can I help you today?

"I was hoping for a proper cup of tea."

Mem brewed tea the old fashioned way, and she served it in whimsical tea pots, covered in even more whimsical cosies, poured into mismatched china cups with saucers. For Cressida, Mem selected English Breakfast tea. She boiled the water, placed tea – loose tea in a tea ball – in the pot, filled the pot and allowed it to steep for a minute before bringing the tray to the table. In the meantime, she filled a small china creamer with milk and placed a plate of scones on the tray.

Bringing the tray to Cressida's table, she asked, "May I join you?"

Cressida, delighted she didn't have to beg for Mem's time, answered in the affirmative.

Cressida told Mem about their travels north, omitting the parts about running out of gas and having to be rescued by the state police, intimating they had planned to stay overnight in another town to get a feel for the communities in the area. In what she believed to be a skillful manner, she asked Mem what she knew about "the dole."

"I have a friend that feels the need to move to this country. I can't imagine why. But she will, you see, have to be on the dole, as she has never held a job. Would she be able to do that, do you think?"

Mem was not the blooming idiot Cressida apparently thought. She answered in a polite manner. "Well, I'm not sure about all of the requirements. I know that every state, including this one, would have residency requirements of some type. I'm not sure what those requirements are, but they would involve either citizenship or some other residency status, for example, being here on a work visa. I'm not sure how it would work for someone to travel here on a passport or visa for, let's say, tourism, to qualify for public assistance."

"I see. Well, would it be possible to find these things out if one were to have a computer?"

"I'm sure it would." Mem knew she was being baited. She didn't take it.

Cressida cleared her throat. "My friend will be calling on me in the next day or so, and I'm sure she will ask my advice. I don't have a computer, you see, and I was wondering if, perhaps, you could check that out? Perhaps in this state, and perhaps in one or two other states?"

Mem smiled. "Certainly, Cressida, I would be happy to do that. I have a consultancy fee for such search requests, they do take some time, you know. Would your friend be willing to pay the fee?"

Cressida drew herself up to a haughty stance. "I see. Well. As I said, she does not have an income to speak of." Softening a bit, she asked, "Would you be willing to just help me out? Sitting here, perhaps? On one of those laptop computers you have?"

Mem looked around. She had two customers in the cyber café, neither of whom needed her assistance. "All right. I'll get one of the units."

Mem went to her cupboard and pulled out her personal laptop. She made room by moving the tea tray to another table, waiting for Cressida to help herself to another cup of tea, milk and two more scones.

Then she got busy. She checked this state, which had easy-to-find residency requirements. She checked the state to the south, whose requirements could be located but were more obscure. She checked the state to the east, the state across the lake to the west and the state through which they would have driven if going from one side of the lake to the other by car.

The answer was similar in every instance. Residency for some period of time was required and citizenship or some form of legal alternative to citizenship was also required.

"I'm sure your friend could make this happen, but she would have to move here with some legal reason and be able to support herself for a year or more, depending on the state, before an application would be accepted."

Cressida, being Cressida, argued with Mem, as if Mem herself had created the system rules that would keep her from public assistance. "That's rubbish! Rubbish, I tell you! This country should be more accepting of persons from their mother kingdom. They should jump at the chance to have people of culture and breeding come to live amongst the peasants, as it were!"

Mem had tired of the charade, but she knew this woman would only be here a few days more. She could suck it up for that period of time. "I know, I know. You just can't imagine the rules and regulations under which we labor. To hear people talk, we open our doors and our pocketbooks for everyone, but, alas, that is just not the case. We're ungrateful, that's what we are."

Cressida stuffed the last scone into her mouth and said, around the bite, "Well, I suppose I should be grateful to you for looking it up."

"No bother at all. I was happy to do it."

Cressida stood, conveniently forgetting to pay for her tea and scones, and left the building.

Mem, laptop still open, sent a quick email to Annie to let her know of her guest's boorish manner. While she sat at the computer, she watched as Kali, Ko and Sassy Pants went into Sassy P's with a dog. A terrier of some sort. She added that to the email. "Who's the little dog running around town with your cats?"

Annie's cell phone chirped at the arrival of an email. Sitting in the library, going over some financial reports, she opened it, saw it was from Mem, and, expecting a chatty message, started absent-mindedly to read. Soon she sat upright. She read the last sentence over. And read it again.

She got up to look in the two most likely places to find the big girls. They could be hiding under the television table here in the library or under the table in the dining room. Not there. She scanned windowsills in the library, entry and dining room. Not there. A quick look up told her they were not in the common area of the second floor.

Holding her breath, she looked at the cat door at the main entry. It stood open just a bit. How had that happened?

Annie threw a coat on, forgetting her boots, hat and gloves, and hit the door at a run. She took a deep breath and slowed down. She couldn't spook them, or Tillie might run. She walked slowly past Sassy P's, looking into the window. There they were. It looked like they were having a conversation with Minnie. She opened the door and closed it behind herself, reaching down to lock the cat door from the inside. Three cats and one dog stood in a semi-circle, bodies facing the bar and Minnie, faces turned back toward Annie.

Uh oh. Busted.

Minnie, not realizing there was a problem, said, "What a cute dog. Is she visiting, or have you added to the crew?"

Annie didn't quite know what to say. "Well, Minnie, I'm not sure. I can tell you there has been some mischief going on today. For now, let's just say she's visiting."

Sassy Pants faced Mommy to explain the situation. She said, clearly, *"I has to introduce Tillie to Minnie an Jesus, so dey knows to protect Tillie if she needs to run aways."* To Annie, it sounded like, "Meh, meh, ick, purr." Of course, the purr occurred as Sassy Pants hit the floor with her back, body twisting so she could look at Mommy and beg for a pet of her tummy.

Annie shook her head, leaned down to pet the proffered body part, picked up Tillie and said to Kali and Ko, "Come on, girls. You have work to do at the Inn."

Cressida crossed The Avenue to Mo's Tap. She joined Alistair at his corner table. Less than a minute after her arrival, Candice was at their table. "It's good to see you again, Mrs. Bartram. What can I get for you?"

"It's about time! Give me a menu and the same ale he is having. And make sure that mug is frosted."

When Candice set the mug in front of her, she handed over a menu. "We have a few small plate specials this month. Instead of featuring Valentine's Day, here at Mo's Tap we've decided to honor Mardi Gras and Fat Tuesday. Would you like to hear about them?"

"Well, it can't do any harm to hear about them."

We have buffalo cauliflower bites. That's cauliflower soaked in pepper sauce, fried and served with celery and bleu cheese dressing. And we have blackened shrimp and grits. The grits are made with chipotle cheese and garnished with bacon. That's served with a white wine Dijon cream sauce. If you don't want a spicy meal, we have a mini meatloaf topped with a mustard and porter sauce with onion straws on the side.

"Ghastly! Give us two of your horrid burgers again."

"Shall I charge this to your account?"

Cressida glared; Candice left to put the order in. She ordered what they had ordered twice before. Two half pound burgers, medium well, served on large grilled buns with melted cheddar, pulled pork, barbecue sauce and coleslaw. Black pepper fries on the side.

The casual onlooker wouldn't realize they had eaten a proper English luncheon only an hour before, and that Cressida had a few scones after that. For the next hour they pooled their information and made plans for the rest of their lives. They talked in low tones, stopping every time Candice drew near.

Late in the afternoon, Henrie informed Annie that yet another couple would spend several days at the Inn. "A young couple from the city, escaping their jobs in the finance industry for a long romantic weekend."

Susie picked an outfit and checked that it was clean and pressed. They were getting a late start, but what did they have to get up for? She heard the bathroom door open and listened as the cat and dog scampered out. They ran toward Susie, but when she turned to look at them, they stopped, turned and ran to another part of the house.

Facing the animals, she saw Tim holding his nose. "What?"

"It stinks in here. It's a wonder our clothes don't stink."

"They might, but I can't smell it anymore. Why did you let them out?"

"They can't stay in here. We have to do something with them."

"Well…we're running late. Get a move on or we'll be late for that meeting with Hank."

"Hank Hank Hank. I'm sick of hearing about Hank. He's not going to get us anything."

"He might. He's always got ideas."

"Nut case ideas."

"Your friends up north aren't going to do much better. When do you think we'll hear from them?"

Tim's cellphone rang. He looked at the display. "Right now." Tim answered and listened intently, said, "Yeah, we can do that."…. "We've got something in a bit, won't take long." …. "What's the number?" …. "Okay. Yeah. We'll take care of it."

Tim looked at Susie. "Things are looking up. We have a job to do, starting tomorrow."

8

That evening, Annie and Chris had dinner with Carlos and Jerry. It had not been planned. Chris wanted to pick up some truffles for Annie, just because, but he caught the two men in a chatty mood. He invited them to Sassy P's for a light supper.

The interior of Sassy P's Wine and Cheese was bright and modern with wooden touches. Display counters, shelving and the bar had a light walnut finish, and the bar had a delicate hand-carved trim. The wall behind the tasting bar was painted cranberry red; the other walls were lavender. At the end of the bar were a few café tables, but most customers sat at the bar in highly polished wooden stools with seats resembling hollowed out wine barrels.

Annie and Chris preferred the outside garden area for seating. To be honest, it was an outside area in warmer months. Now winter, temporary exterior walls allowed for a smaller seating area but still added expandable space for diners and parties.

Jesus brought a bottle of dry red that was featured for the month. It was a wine he had cajoled from a Chicago winery. They would not give him bottles with their own label, as it was a special, tenth anniversary blend. They did give him a good supply with a separate label. Labeled Exxcess, it was a mix of cabernet sauvignon, merlot, zinfandel, syrah, petit verdot, petite sirah and malbec. Minnie brought the suggested cheese pairings: cashel blue, an artisan cheese from Ireland, and manchego, a Spanish cheese made from sheep's milk. She returned to the other room.

Annie, rolling her eyes over Exxcess, said, "Please don't bring it, because I don't need it, but I haven't tried your dry white of the month."

Jesus smiled. "It's too late; here it is."

Minnie was already on her way in, an open bottle in a chiller and yet another small tray of cheeses. Jesus pulled a bottle of pinot bianco from the chiller. "This is one of the lesser known Italian white wines. If made by the proper vintner, it is exquisite."

Minnie's cheese pairings were camembert and an Italian cheese, taleggio. Chris, happy to have chosen the winery for the evening, ordered a plate of meats and crackers and called it supper.

As usual for this particular week, talk turned to the horrible Cressida and Alistair Bartram. Carlos laughed. "You know I've changed the special of the month to those Jammie Dodgers. They're flying off the shelves. And guess who came in to purchase two dozen?"

"No!"

"Yes. And of course she charged them to her room at the Inn. She's charged a lot of things to the Inn this week. I hope Henrie is keeping an eye on the account."

Annie laughed as she told the story of Mem's email and her discovery of the cats and dog here. As Carlos and Jerry told her the story from their perspective, she and Chris looked at one another in wonder.

Jerry noticed them first. Mr. Bean had been in the window, dancing as usual as people walked past, but suddenly, he was on the floor and out the door. Jerry, curious, had gone to the window to look. Kali, Ko, Sassy

Pants and a terrier of some sort were running toward the
Café. Mr. Bean followed. Jerry stuck his head out the door
and watched as Little Socks joined the parade.

They stayed in the Café for quite a while. They finally
emerged and, one by one, they went into each business.
They stayed a while, then came out to go to the next place.
By the time they reached the Confectionary, both Jerry
and Carlos waited in front of the counter. They greeted
the dog, as the cats seemed to expect, and, as Mr. Bean
took his place on the windowsill, the others left, headed
toward the winery.

Annie took out her phone to call Felicity. Felicity told
essentially the same story. Tiger Lily brought the dog into
the kitchen, as if by way of introduction, and she had
introduced the dog to Trudie as well. Annie called Diana.
Yes, she was teaching a class, but Little Socks felt the need
to interrupt her so she could meet this little dog. Then the
other cats and the dog left. Diana noted it was unusual to
see Kali and Ko out, especially on a cold day. Annie called
George. Yes, the cats had come in and they brought the
dog up to him and to Candice. Mo joined them for a bit,
but he had a little bit of a fling going on with a hot female
customer, so he didn't hang out for long. Then they left.

Annie sat looking at first one person, then the next, and
finally, she shook her head and laid it on the table. For just
a minute. She only needed a minute. What it the world
were they up to, and how, yes how, did they unlock that
door?

Carlos took the long view. "Annie, you have a very
independent family. They have always been well-behaved,

and you can count on them to do the right thing. Whatever that is."

"You're talking as if they are children, growing up to be adults."

"Well, they are your children, aren't they? I hope my children will be so well behaved. Especially when they become adults."

"Are you having children?"

"Not this minute. Oh, my goodness! I've been so caught up…I forgot to ask! Do you have a room for Isabel and either one of my sisters or my mother over the weekend?"

"Sure. We don't have too many guests for some reason. We're normally full over Valentine's Day. But what's had you so caught up?"

Carlos looked a little nervous, then he pulled a box from his jacket pocket to show to Chris and Annie. It contained a beautiful diamond ring. "I want to ask her to marry me this weekend, and you know she can't travel to visit me without an escort, so someone will need to be with her."

The conversation turned to ideas about the proposal, where it would happen, when, what would they be doing and with whom, and went all the way through the wedding. Annie was planning the reception when Chris finally said, "Hey, wait a minute. Do you think the bride might want to be involved in the planning?"

"Spoil sport."

"Yep. That's me. Hey, Jerry, how about bringing out that present I chose for Annie? Well, for all of us."

Jerry reached into his coat pocket and brought out a box large enough to hold four of his famous truffles. He opened the box with fanfare and said, "My newest creation. Champagne, with white chocolate."

Annie picked one, took a bite, and said, not for the first time, "Jerry, will you marry me?"

9

Wednesday dawned bright and sunny. Annie looked out the window from her apartment and could tell much of the snow would be gone before the day was over.

Once again, she awakened to Tillie curled into a shoulder. She went downstairs to take her out, being careful to wear better clothes, since the guests were back in residence. Tillie ran out, took care of business and came back in, following Annie up to the third floor.

"Do you think your mum and dad will ever say hello to you, now they're back from their trip up north?"

Tillie looked up at Annie. She either understood, or loved the sound of Annie's voice. She wagged her tail. Annie put some dog food into a bowl and watched as the pup ate her fill.

She showered, dressed and enjoyed a cup of coffee before going down to the certain bad humor of the dining room.

She was surprised when she got downstairs. The Bartrams had not yet made an appearance, but Ginger was there, with a waif of a girl.

Henrie sat with them and had placed cups of cocoa in front of them. Before Annie could speak, however, they heard the dulcet tones of the Bartrams arguing their way downstairs to the dining room.

Henrie said, "Girls, go into the kitchen. Let Annie and I get breakfast started for this couple, and we will be in to join you."

Ginger and the girl rose obediently, taking their cups with them.

Annie turned to say good morning, but the words stuck in her throat. Cressida was already scowling, looking around at Henrie's always outstanding buffet. She turned to him. "So, you aren't even going to try to get the biscuits right this morning?"

"On the contrary. I waited until your arrival. I did not want them to sit for long."

Annie looked at Henrie with a question, but he merely turned to go to the kitchen. Cressida and Alistair heaped three plates (each), a bowl, two glasses and a cup with everything else: a sausage egg soufflé, bacon, English muffins with apple butter and orange marmalade, cinnamon flavored French toast with maple syrup, oatmeal with fruits and nuts, Danish pastries, coffee, orange and cranberry juices.

While they filled their plates, several of the cats and Tillie entered the room carefully. They stayed close to the wall and headed straight for the detective agency and good cover. The Bartrams didn't notice their own precious, valuable pet and family member. Annie didn't think they had set eyes on her since their return.

As Cressida and Alistair sat down, surrounded by their bounty, Henrie returned with a crystal platter. On the platter was an offering of wafers, the like of which Annie had never seen.

Cressida's eyes widened, and even Alistair perked up a bit. Henrie set the platter on the table between them and backed away. Cressida picked a cookie up, tasted it, and said, "Now this is almost the proper biscuit. For someone serving us in the colonies, it will do."

Alistair nodded as he tasted one himself.

"I trust," Cressida continued, "you will be able to supply these for the rest of our stay."

"I shall make every endeavor."

"See that you do. You may go now."

Henrie gave a small bow from the waist and backed into the kitchen, every inch the dutiful household servant.

Annie marveled that he didn't do a step-n-fetchit routine. She followed him, not having said word one to her guests.

She placed a hand on Ginger's shoulder to acknowledge the girl, but her first words were to Henrie. She whispered, "Where did you get those?"

He whispered in return. "I Googled them. They were available on Amazon dot com. I paid extra – pardon me for the expense – to have them delivered overnight. Yesterday I took delivery of six boxes. We will see today how far a box will go, and if I need to order more to extend to the rest of their stay, I will make an order tomorrow."

"Worth every cent, no matter what you paid or why."

Henrie set a platter of the cookies in front of the girls. Annie got a cup of coffee for herself and sat at the table, taking a cookie as she did so.

"Ginger, so as not to disturb our, um, very pleasant guests, let's keep our voices down. Why don't you introduce me to your friend?"

Ginger made introductions. The shy girl, Penny, was a freshman at the high school. She lived on the north side of town. Ginger didn't have to say it, but Annie could tell she lived in the part of town that was known for having trouble with various petty crimes.

"And why aren't you girls in school today? You were out for two days in a row already this week."

"Penny, um, she and I saw one another at the store yesterday. We were just out, doing, you know, our thing, and I noticed that she was, um, upset a little, and I, you know, thought I would ask her what was up, and, um, I told her that maybe when she got off the bus today, maybe she and I could, um, come here and see if you could help us with something."

"Okay. Happy to do whatever I can. What's the issue?"

"Well, um, it's kind of hard to say…"

"Take your time. I'm just sitting here having a cup of coffee. And a cookie, or biscuit, as the Brits say. This is outstanding, Henrie." Annie kept her tone as light as she could, not showing the concern she was beginning to feel.

Tiger Lily materialized on the table. She sat in between Penny and Ginger. Annie knew that her presence would be a calming influence, and assumed Tiger Lily knew it as well. Ginger and Penny took turns stroking the big girl's back.

Ginger cleared her throat and tried again. "First of all, I wanted Penny to talk to my dad, but she wouldn't do that. Refused. Said she wouldn't say anything to anyone if she had to do that and if I said anything to him, she would deny it."

Penny looked at the cup in front of her and said nothing. Ginger gathered her courage.

"You see, Annie, it's like this. There are some boys at school that do bad things to a lot of people, mostly girls, and they did a bad thing to Penny last week. There wasn't anything she could do to stop them; it just happened. Her brother isn't a good person. He's one of them. The bad boys. He took a picture of Penny when she was in the shower and he showed it to these boys, and then they sent it around to a lot of other people, and then they sent it to a lot more people, and now, almost everyone in school has seen that picture of Penny in the shower. There wasn't a thing she could do to stop it."

Tiger Lily moved closer to Penny.

Annie and Henrie sat still as stone, saying nothing, barely breathing, not knowing the best way to proceed. Annie finally took a deep breath. "Penny, do your parents know about this?"

"No, ma'am. And if they did, they would be mad at me. They don't care what he does."

"Has anyone at the school, a teacher or an administrator, said anything to you?"

"No, ma'am. I don't think they've seen it. I would be really embarrassed if they did."

"Has anything like this happened at the school before?"

Ginger looked uncomfortable. "Yes. To a couple of girls."

"And what happens?"

"Nothing. The kids are real careful not to tell anyone – any adult – about it."

Annie concentrated. "You know, the school would probably expel anyone who did this and brought it onto school property, and I'm assuming this is on personal cell phones on school property. And it's against the law."

Penny started to get up. Ginger on one side and Annie on another put soft hands on her shoulders to keep her in place.

Tiger Lily moved even closer to Penny.

Annie continued in a soft voice. "Penny, what's the worst that could happen? Most of the students know about it or have seen the photo already, correct?"

Penny's voice trembled, and a tear rolled down her cheek. "Yes, ma'am."

"I have to assume that some adults have seen it also, probably adults that are, shall we say, not the right sort of adult."

"Yes, ma'am."

"You are afraid to let your parents know, is that right?"

Penny paused and wiped her eyes before she responded. "Yes, ma'am."

Henrie passed a box of tissues to Penny; she took one.

"You're afraid they will punish you for it and, even worse, involve your brother in the punishment somehow. Let him be a part of it."

Penny looked at Annie in surprise. "Yes, ma'am."

"It's pretty awful at home, isn't it?"

Penny held Annie's gaze. "Yes, ma'am."

"But even so, you don't want anyone to look down on your parents or punish your parents for anything they have done to you."

"I don't want nobody to get them in trouble."

"Do you understand that could be unavoidable?"

"What?"

"Do you understand that for me to help you, the right adults are going to have to be told, and your parents might be in trouble?"

"Can we do that without them knowing?"

"I think you already know the answer to that. And I think you know that since I know, I have to tell the right adults."

Another tear slid down Penny's cheek and Ginger hung her head down. Ginger said, "You have to call my dad?"

"Yes."

"Now?"

"Yes."

"He's going to be mad at me."

"What for?"

"Because I came to you and not him."

"He is going to honor your decision and he'll know you did the best you could possibly do in the circumstances. Who you told will not be an issue. The important thing is that you are doing the right thing to help a friend."

They sat for a moment in silence until Henrie, without Annie noticing the movement, handed her the telephone. She called Pete on his cell and asked that he come to the kitchen door with one of his female reserve officers as soon as he could.

For the next half hour, Henrie was in and out of the dining room seeing to the guests, and Annie sat with Penny and Ginger. She refilled the cookie plate, poured more cocoa, and threw away used tissues. No one spoke.

Finally, Pete came through the door with Jenny, a female reserve officer, behind him. Cyril bounded in and sat underneath the table. Pete nodded to Ginger but said nothing to her. They sat at the table, coffee cups already waiting for them, and Annie started to tell them the story. Ginger finished it.

Tiger Lily listened intently. She didn't know if there was a single thing the cats could do to help this poor waif, but she knew they would do what they could when necessary. She and Cyril made eye contact and made their silent pact.

Billy gathered his gang around Porter's locker. "Porter, where's that ugly sister of yours?"

"I dunno. Why do you care?"

"I wanted to show her what she could have if only she was worth it."

"Yeah, right. I already showed her mine. She didn't care." Porter got a hopeful look on his face. "But she might like it if you showed her yours, Billy."

"Serious, man. Where is she?"

"How should I know? We get on the bus, we get off the bus, we go our separate ways. What the hey?"

"I thought I saw her leave school this morning with that little Miss Piggy."

"Why would she do that?"

"That tramp has shown her ugly face twice now in a couple of days. Just, I don't know, got me to thinkin'."

Billy turned to Marc and Justin, the two boys who had yet to ante up a photo. "If you two was to get a photo of that Miss Piggy, it could count for the both of you."

Marc and Justin looked at one another, expressions unreadable.

"The picture would have to be good. Better than Lia."

Justin said, "I dunno, man. She's the daughter of Chief Pig. That's kind of scary."

"You think she'd tell her old man if she was naked in a picture?"

"I think she might."

"Well, then maybe we all need to help out, give her a taste of the good side of life. Give her an in-cen-tive to keep her mouth shut."

Justin looked shaken. "Hey, man, you know, we could really get in trouble. If my folks found out..."

Dallas cut in. "You ain't done nothin'. Now my folks, they might have a gripe if they found out about Pam."

"How are they gonna find out? Pam gonna tell 'em?"

"No, she won't tell. She's embarrassed to death. She's only twelve, man."

"So? You took the photo. What are you complaining about?"

"I dunno. Somehow it don't feel right."

Porter stuck out his chest. "I didn't have a prob takin' a pic of my sis. You a big sissy, Dallas? Huh? Billy asked us to do it, and, well, I done it for 'im."

Dallas threw a hard glance at Porter, then looked back at Billy.

Justin said, "I'm just sayin' we ought to be careful before doin' anything to Miss Piggy."

The boys left to go to their next class. Porter, who had put on a show of bravado, turned back to his locker as the others left. When he was sure they wouldn't turn around, he went the other way, turned at the main intersection of hallways, and walked out the front door.

Hank waited at the gas station on the far north side of town. He watched as cars pulled in and out. In and out. Where in the danged heck is she. He hit his fists on the dashboard a few times, until he heard a "crack." Dang it to heck. What broke this time?

Then she pulled in. She waved, pulled out, and he followed. They drove south, until she pulled into the lot of a fast food restaurant.

Hank parked next to her, got out of the car and slammed his door. "Why can't we at least get a decent cup of coffee?"

"I don't have time to drive all over, Hank, and we have to stop meeting in Chelsea. There isn't any place in that town that won't tell that...that...her!!! what we're up to. Remember, we have history in that regard."

Inside, they stood quietly at the counter and ordered a fast food breakfast with fast food coffee and asked for fast food cream to tone down the bitter taste. At a table in the corner, they were passably friendly again.

Geraldine asked, "How did the meeting go?"

"It went good. Good. They talked about something they've got going up north, something that should give them some cash that they need, but they're interested in the proposal."

"How soon can they get to it?"

"They can do it in the next day or so, or it will have to be sometime next month."

"Let's do it quick."

10

In the early afternoon, Tiger Lily enjoyed a bit of rest. No customers entered or left and the sun shone companionably on the hostess stand. She lay mostly on the stand, her head off to one side, her tail off to the other, lazily flipping up, then down. Up, then down. Up, then down.

Suddenly she was awake.

There they were. Two of them.

This time they were sneaking out of the cat door at the church. One of them was fat. That was a boy. He was mostly a dark tabby with a white chest and belly and white trailing down his legs. Tiger Lily couldn't feel sorry for him, because he looked as if he had never missed a meal.

The other was a girl. She followed close behind the fat one, looking left and right like a scared rabbit. She had similar coloring as Tiger Lily herself, but there was less brown, and her face was thinner, her chin more pointed.

Tiger Lily jumped down and headed out the door toward them. They stopped, sensing her presence, as they made the turn to go around the church and, Tiger Lily assumed, toward the state park. Tiger Lily stopped as well, and they stood there. Three statues. Looking one another over.

Tiger Lily came back to life first. She sent a loud cat message across The Avenue. *"This is my territory. If you want to be a part of it, you have to talk to me."*

The fat one hissed, and they turned to run around the corner and out of sight.

Tiger Lily heard another hiss and turned to find Little Socks at her side.

"You saw them, too. Did you see them come out of the church?"

"Yes. They must be hiding there during the day. It would be easy, at least through the week, because so few people go in and out."

"And they stay in The Clinic at night. I wonder if they have ever come into our places."

Little Socks, at once concerned for Tiger Lily's health, said, *"Is something wrong with your sniffer?"*

"No, why?"

"We would have smelled them."

"You're right. I wasn't thinking. They must stay on the other side of The Avenue because of us."

"I noticed you told them this was your territory."

"And?"

"What am I? Chopped liver?"

Tiger Lily sniffed. *"I didn't have time to think. I needed to send them a warning. And what kind of a warning would it be, anyway, to start listing the names of all the cats that call this side of The Avenue their own?"*

"Next time, I'm going after them."

"Next time, we'll be better prepared. We'll be together. And you are not going after them. We need to get to know them. They could become friends."

"We should try to corner them before they get into The Clinic tonight."

"Or we can watch for them, and when they get in, we can follow and, um, have a chat."

The two girls stood for a while, watching the corner of the church, just in case. Then the cold sidewalk got the better of them and they turned to go to the yoga studio and the Café, each with thoughts of her own.

The two strays stopped running.

"Maybe we should introduce ourselves."

"I don't know. She didn't want us in her space."

"She didn't say we couldn't be here. She just said we had to talk to her first."

"That little black one looked mean."

"We're going to have to trust someone sometime. We're not used to living like this."

Annie walked up the sidewalk toward the Café and watched as her two oldest girls parted company. What now?

As usual, her walk was lengthened as she took time to stop at each place, have a brief conversation with the staff and a quick piece of love from her cats. By the time she got to the yoga studio, Little Socks was once again asleep on a black pillow in the windowsill.

Annie sat close, but went through the routine. "I wonder where that pretty kitty is today?"

Soft purr.

"I'll just sit here for a minute and see if she shows up. Maybe she's in the dressing room."

Soft purr.

"Huh. This pillow looks softer than the others. I think I'll sit here." Annie rose, put a hand on the other side of the pillow in question and started to sit down.

The little girl stood up before Annie could sit down, stretched, and gave her a lazy stare.

"Oh, my gosh! I almost sat on you! Have you been here all this time?"

Head bump, soft cat forehead to Annie's arm.

Annie gave the girl a little love and then asked, almost as an afterthought, "So, what were you and Tiger Lily conferring about on the sidewalk?"

Little Socks stared deep into Annie's eyes with those hypnotic green eyes and then rolled into a ball to go back to sleep.

"Secrets, huh? Okay. I'll just pretend I didn't see it."

Flick of the tip of her tail.

Annie gave her a final pet and left for the Café.

Tiger Lily was asleep again in the sun. It was moving and had almost left the hostess stand completely. Tiger Lily was as far to the edge as she could getwithout falling to the floor. Annie, recognizing the last-gasp-of-ray stance, passed her by and went in to chat with Felicity and Trudie. They had taken a coffee break at the table by the front window.

"How was lunch? Sorry I missed it."

"We were fine. It was busy. People were happy to be out in the sunshine today."

Annie pointed to Tiger Lily and asked, "Has she been okay?"

"Yeah. Well, you know she was late today, but other than that… What's up?"

"I saw her on the sidewalk with Little Socks. They seemed to be stalking something on the other side of The Avenue."

"Oh, that. Tiger Lily has been watching that side for a while now. I think there are a couple of strays that hang out over there."

"Even in that awful snow storm?"

"Yeah, but you know, strays have a way of making out. I've seen them. Tabbies. They don't look like feral cats. Maybe they were dumped by someone at the campground."

Trudie added, "Like me. At least I was dumped during warm weather."

The women chatted for a while, as much good friends as owner, manager and employee. Felicity, the best chef for miles around, was perky, to the point of annoyance at times, and managed both the restaurant and a catering business. Trudie, her best friend, was the barista and a trusted second for the business. Trudie was Chelsea's only Jamaican. When she was stranded at the campground by a boyfriend, Felicity rescued her, gave her a job, and set her up in an apartment above the yoga studio.

Annie finally rose. "I'm going across the street to talk to Mem. Keep an eye on me. I don't want to be attacked by wild cats."

"Will do. We'll sic Tiger Lily on 'em if they come near."

Mem saw Annie come across the median and met her inside the door. "Have a seat. I have water on for tea."

Before sitting, Annie fixed a tray with two mismatched cups and saucers, a dish of dark chocolate covered coffee beans and two spoons. Mem carried a teapot with a cosie resembling a squirrel. Inside, orange ginger tea steeped.

As they sat together at a table in the sunshine, Mem asked, "So, do you have a dog now?"

Annie laughed. "That email got me outside pretty quickly. The dog is a guest, well, is the pet of a guest, the charming Bartrams."

"Oh, them."

"Enough said. Anyway, I promised to keep the exterior cat doors locked so she couldn't get outside, but...I don't know what happened. Maybe one of us kicked the lock open. Maybe Hilly, when she was cleaning, thought it should be open. Maybe that awful woman opened it herself, hoping Tillie would get out and get lost."

"Really? You think she would do that?"

"A small illustration. They went north on the day of the storm, against advice, of course, and they got stuck in a snowdrift. They had to stay overnight about a hundred twenty miles up the coast, and since their return, they haven't so much as looked at, asked for, cared for, fed or otherwise given a rat's patoot about that sweet thing. Except to discuss getting rid of her. Taking her for a ride on some country roads and dumping her."

"No! Why would they do that?"

"Money troubles. I didn't let them know they had been overheard but made an excuse to purchase Tillie from them. Told them the cats were fond of her. They are considering the price, since she is of such value to them."

"No wonder the dog – Tillie? – is spending so much time with the cats. She probably hopes they will adopt her. She made it home alright yesterday?"

"Yes. I went out as soon as I got your email. They were at Sassy P's. I picked her up and carried her home, just to be safe. They stopped in at every single place, from the Café to the Winery. It was as if the cats were making introductions."

Mem closed her eyes and chuckled softly. "Annie, you assign characteristics to your cats as if they're human. You know that, right? Do you really believe it to be true?"

Annie laughed and decided to stop there. She changed the subject. "So what properties does orange ginger tea possess?"

"You know ginger is my go-to tea for just about everything. It relieves stress and tension, improves your mood, improves your circulation. It can even increase your fertility, so be careful. Oh, it can aid erectile dysfunction. Another reason to be careful. The orange just adds flavor."

"So, the perfect Valentine's Day tea?"

Mem laughed. "Possibly. Although I might also suggest a dessert flavored tea for lovers. Perhaps a Ceylon tea flavored with chocolate and strawberry, or any creamed or vanilla flavored dark tea. But if it's action you seek, stick with ginger."

They laughed again. Annie enjoyed Mem. She was the matriarch of The Avenue. The wise one. The one to whom everyone could come with a problem. The one that accepted everyone on their own terms. She had a few issues with her daughter, Diana, the head instructor at the yoga studio, but who didn't have issues with family members?

"Tell me about your guests."

"Thank goodness by this afternoon the Bartrams won't be our only guests. What can I tell you about them that you don't already know? They are...um...let's go with dreadful. On a lighter note, two couples are coming in today, a young power couple from the city and a middle-aged couple from the south."

"Thank goodness. New blood. Your current guests really are dreadful. I told you she left without paying for her tea. That wasn't the first thing left unpaid and will probably not be the last. But that's the least of my concerns about them. I think she is trying to figure out how they can stay here, or at least somewhere in this country, and collect welfare."

"There is no reason they can't find gainful employment. Even at a fast food place. Except, apparently, they are better than everyone else in this country. Perhaps the elite of New York City might make the cut, but certainly no one in Chelsea."

"We can only hope they dislike us enough to move on. How long are they staying?"

"I think until the weekend. Perhaps they intend to have a romantic Valentine's Day." Annie's laugh turned into a snort at the thought.

"Is there anything else about them? Besides the fact they are extremely unlikeable? Do you think they've stolen from you?"

"I can't be positive about that, but my main concern is that Tillie stays with us when they leave. And if they try to take her out some day for a 'ride,' I want to think of a way to stop it."

"Are you and Chris doing anything special for Valentine's Day?"

Annie got quiet. She finally said, "We haven't discussed it." Annie gazed at her hand and her beautiful ring as she said it. She looked up again. "And you? Do you have plans with Frank?"

"That was a great way to deflect, Annie. What's up?"

"Oh, nothing. Not really"

Mem stayed silent.

"Well….do you remember, a couple of months ago, when you were worried about 'terminal politeness' with Frank?"

Mem sat back in her chair, crossed her arms and said, "Yes."

"How'd that turn out?"

"We got past it. He got through his open house, we got past the holidays, and then we had a rip-roaring fight."

"About?"

"Taking one another for granted."

"And you got through it?"

"Of course. We're still together, and every now and then we have a spicy conversation about one thing or another. It's good for the spirit. So…have you and Chris had a fight?"

"I'm not sure."

Mem stared for a moment, then she reached over to pat Annie's hand. "Take a deep breath, Annie. First of all, if you aren't even sure you've had a fight, then you need to clarify it. And then, if it's worthy of a fight, go for it. What's it about, anyway, if you don't mind my asking?"

"Cats. Dogs. Kennels." Annie didn't say it, but silently, she added the word "we" to her list.

11

Joe Palco, the superintendent of Chelsea Community Schools, looked at Pete, wishing he had stayed home another day. What a way to end a forced four-day weekend.

"So, tell me again what you want to do."

Pete took a deep breath. He knew time was of the essence, and this man was taking a precious hour just in the explanation.

"We need to go to the high school and take five boys into custody. Do I need to tell you their names again?"

Joe shook his head.

Pete continued. "We have a wagon coming from the county jail. The sheriff will take them in for questioning and will contact their parents. They will go through their telephones. We are pretty sure those five boys are the original source of several compromising photos of girls who attend your schools. And we're certain that a large percentage of your students have these photos on their phones. Some will have shared them, others will have just held onto them. Some may have deleted them. As I said before, time is of the essence. We need to do this, and at the same time, arrange for all of the junior and senior high school students to gather in your gyms so we can explain the situation, and we'll confiscate their phones."

"I just don't know…"

"Mr. Palco, time is of the essence. We need to do this before students leave for the day and conveniently 'lose' their telephones."

"The parents are not going to like this."

"The parents are going to learn that their children, many of them, are felons."

"That's pretty harsh, chief."

"Child pornography is a harsh business."

"I don't know."

"Do I need to show you the warrant again?"

Pete and Joe stared at one another. Marco and the two principals stared at the table.

Joe sighed and said, finally, "Go ahead. I'll stay here and make some calls. I'll start lining up some counseling and training on the proper use of social media. And get the attorney ready to field angry telephone calls."

Pete's heart lightened a little as both principals offered their personal services and the services of other administrative and teaching staff to assist in collecting cell phones. As they left the administration building, the county van pulled into the parking lot. Marco motioned to the Chelsea officers, who split up, some to follow Pete to the high school and some to follow Marco to the junior high school.

The high school principal made calls to three classrooms, asking that five boys be sent to his office. After the last call, he checked his computer and he looked at Pete.

"It appears Porter is no longer in school. He must have left after third period, because he was here for that class."

They waited. Pete, the principal, and two deputies.

Billy sauntered in first, looked around and saw the uniformed officers. His bravado left him for a few seconds, then he looked at the principal and said, "Yeah? Whatdaya want?"

The principal didn't answer him right away and waived him into the conference room.

He did the same as Dallas, Marco and Justin trailed in.

Once the boys were seated, Pete and the deputies standing at the door, the principal asked the group, "Where's your friend, Porter?"

Billy answered for the group. "How should we know?"

"He was here through third period. Did you see him after that?"

Billy looked at the other boys and continued to take the lead.

"Yeah. We saw him after that class. What of it?"

"Did he say anything about leaving school at that time?"

"No. I thought he went to the next class."

"Let's just move forward with the problem at hand. These officers are going to take you to the county jail to discuss an issue. They'll call your parents when you get there. Before you leave with the officers, you'll hand over your phones."

Four angry voices spoke at once.

"No way!" "You got no right!" "I'm not goin' nowhere!" "What if we don't wanna go?"

Pete stepped forward. "Don't make the mistake of thinking you have a choice in the matter."

Pete talked to every high school student in the gymnasium in a hastily-called convocation. Reserve officers, teachers and administrators sat at tables placed strategically at each door. At the middle school, Marco led a similar group with full time Chelsea police officers and school staff. Pete and Marco had a script, hastily written and agreed upon. They stuck to it.

"We have been made aware of a situation involving compromising photos. These photos have been passed around to many of you here in school. This is called sexting. Sexting can have serious consequences, especially when a picture is taken without the victim's knowledge or consent, is forwarded without the victim's knowledge or consent, or is used to bully and harass the victim. The embarrassment can do more than just disrupt the victim's life. It can damage his or her reputation, his or her self-esteem. It can lead to problems at home, problems at school. It can lead to suicide. There are crimes associated with sexting. Even if you are a minor, if you have taken this type of photograph or forwarded a photograph, even just possessed a photograph, you can be charged with child pornography."

Pete and Marco scripted the next part, as well. They moved. They now strode back and forth in front of the students, looking at as many as they could, straight in the eyes. "I'm going to give you one scenario as an example of crimes that may have been committed. Let's assume an underage girl has taken a picture of herself. A sexual, semi-nude picture. She sends that as a phone message to her boyfriend. She has just committed three felonies. She created, disseminated and possessed child pornography. Now assume her boyfriend asked her to send it. He has now committed two felonies. He solicited and voluntarily possessed child pornography. One indiscretion, five felonies, two teenagers branded as child sex offenders for the rest of their lives."

They stopped walking and faced their audiences. "First, let's talk about prison. Child molesters have a hard time in prison. Child pornographers don't fare much better. You can go to prison from one to fifteen years. Prison. Every bad thing you think you know about prison doesn't begin to describe it. Then you will come out of prison. Your first stop will be to your local police department. My office. There, you will register as a child sex offender. And then, you can spend the rest of your life with a label. That label, that legal description of you, will be available to anyone and everyone, online and in legal documents, for the rest of your life. For the rest of your life, you will never be trusted. For the rest of your life, you cannot be on school grounds or loiter or live within five hundred feet of a school building. Even if you are able to find someone to marry you and you have children, you will not be able to come to school to speak to their teachers, or to watch a ballgame. You can probably get a job in the fast food industry, unless, by the time you come out of prison, that avenue is no longer open to you. Say good-bye to your family, the college of your choice, the career you had in mind. You don't have to be the person who took the photo. You don't have to be the person that requested the photo. If you received and held onto a photo, or if you received and forwarded a photo, you are a child pornographer."

Again from the script, they started to pace again. "I see many of you trying to hide the fact that you are deleting things from your cellphones right now. That won't work.

We will be able to find anything that has been there. We will know when you received it and when you deleted it. And that's the next step. Each and every one of you will step over to one of the tables at the exit doors. You will turn over your cell phone. We will bag it and tag it, and for the next several days, we're going to call your parents to come in while we go through them, one at a time. This is not a joke. This will not go away. You will deal with it, each and every one of you."

The beginning of each convocation had been met with smirks and elbow jabs, knowing looks and winks. By the time Pete and Marco had finished, not a sound could be heard from the sober faces in the audiences.

Henrie welcomed two sets of guests, arriving at the same time via the regional airport's limousine. He was helped by Kali and Ko, who gave their ultimate welcome. They sniffed shoes, pants and luggage until they were satisfied the guests felt at home. Henrie did not shirk his duties when it came to welcoming guests. His tours started and ended the same way.

Nathanial and Lorine Kerschner had the look of a modern power couple. Both medium tall and slender, they had dressed for a small town vacation in J.Crew. From the information at Henrie's disposal, both worked in the financial industry, he as a financial manager and she as a budget analyst.

Terrence and Jerald Timmer-Schmidt had the rumpled look of middle agers comfortable with themselves. They dressed in jeans and shirts with cardigans and spoke with the slow drawl of the south. Henrie knew one to be a psychiatrist and the other to be a heart surgeon. They were old enough to be the parents of the Kerschners.

Henrie seated his guests in comfortable chairs that surrounded a low table. In the middle of the table and within easy reach of all sat a silver tray with freshly baked cookies, lemon, sugars and creamers. He offered drinks and served one hot tea in a china cup with saucer, one hot coffee in a ceramic mug, one iced tea in a tall glass with a silver tea spoon and one sparkling water in a crystal water glass.

When giving an introductory tour, Henrie always looked at the Inn from the perspective of a new guest. He knew they would find the furniture to be both elegant and comfortable, that they would note the slate blue and gray upholstering and the touches of light-hued walnut. He seated guests so they could see into each downstairs room. They would note the pastel-painted walls: blue, lavender and rose. He was particularly pleased when groups were welcomed as the sun shone through the minimally-covered windows. He did not have to point out the fresh bouquets. They burst into view. An over-large welcoming bouquet with blue blossoms in the foyer and a smaller, similar bouquet in the dining room.

When his guests today were ready to walk around, they paid polite attention as Henrie showed them additional amenities, including the coffee and snacks corner, books and movies in the library, and the computers, televisions and reading nooks in other common areas at their disposal. Henrie invited them to view the evening's sunset from the all-season porch.

Rolling the luggage cart to the elevator, Henrie invited the couples to take the stairs to the second floor. He met them as the elevator opened to the common area and showed them down the hallway. As Henrie escorted the middle-aged couple to the room facing the lake, he received a surprise. One of the older men asked the young couple, "Would you like to take the room facing the lake?"

If it were not for the professional veneer, Lorine would have gushed the reply. "Do you mean it? Thank you!"

The older couple watched as Henrie let the young couple into their room. Henrie pointed out the television and computer access point, the locked armoire, and the spacious seating area. Kali and Ko helped by jumping on the bed to demonstrate its comfort.

Even in the winter, he made a point to open the balcony doors. "You will not spend a good deal of time outside in this brisk weather, but should you desire, the furniture is all-weather and has been cleared for your use." Kali and Ko again helped by jumping onto the balcony when Henrie opened the door.

"And one last thing. Kali and Ko are great hostesses, but should you tire of their services, this latch can be used on the cat door." Kali rubbed against the legs of both Terrence and Jerald with a heavy purr, assuring them they would never need to lock the door. Ko kept her distance but looked at Lorine in an attempt to mind mold her of the same notion.

Henrie opened the door to the room facing the winery for the older couple, and he left the four with a reminder of the afternoon snack. Today's offerings would be chocolate covered strawberries and English tea sandwiches.

At that moment, at the end of another tour given to perfection, came the bang of the entry door as it slammed open and shut. Feet, loud, angry and stomping, went from entry to dining room and back again. And then, the dulcet tones of one loud English accent and one whiney respondent. "That dolt should have food ready for us! This is a foul establishment!!"

Murmurs of something in reply.

"And where is that dog? Have you even bothered to look for her? If we're lucky, she's run off."

Murmurs.

"Where is that man? You! You! We are ready for our tea!"

Henrie looked apologetically at the two couples. Terrence and Jerald were wide-eyed, mouths agape. The younger couple didn't look surprised. Henrie thought, perhaps, they traveled often and met all sorts of people.

"Excuse me while I tend to other guests. Please...make yourselves at home."

Kali and Ko were long gone.

Porter walked quickly home. His parents, drunk already, didn't seem surprised to see him.

His father sat in a corner chair, a beer can in one hand and several empties on the table beside him. An ash tray sat on the table, filled to overflowing with butts. As he lit another, he slurred a question to Porter. "Szchooloutaready?"

"No. We got problems.

"Probems?"

"Yeah. I think Penny snitched me out."

"Thaprincesz? Whadshedonow?"

"I think she told the cops about a picture I took."

"Whapitcher?

Porter opened his phone and handed it to his father.

A leer spread across his face.

"Shesgotsome…somesomethin. Sheputtinoutferyouboy?"

"I just took the picture."

His mother stumbled in from the kitchen and took the phone. Her eyes widened and narrowed as she tried to bring the picture into focus. "Whyyoudothis?"

"My friends wanted me to. They all did it, too."

"PitchersaPenny?"

"No, pictures of other girls. They wanted me to take a picture of Penny."

"Anyoudiditwhy?"

"If I'm going to get along at school, I have to do what they want me to."

"AnPennytoldacops?"

"I think so. They might be comin' for me. I need to get outa town. You got money?"

"Weaintgotnuttin."

Porter grumbled under his breath, "You got enough for booze and cigarettes."

"Whayousay?"

"If you don't have money, how can I get out of town?"

"I'llcallJoe."

"Joeain'tgotany."

"Wellwhoyoucall?"

"GonnagetPenny'smoney."

Porter's mother lurched into Penny's room and stumbled out with a cigar box. She opened it and showed Porter a small stack of bills. "Sheduzn'tknowIknow."

Porter took the bills, counting quickly to $56. Not enough to get very far. He put the bills in his pocket, then went to the kitchen. He found his mother's purse on the counter on top of a six pack of beer. Her billfold contained several ones and a five. He took those and a debit card that was probably dry.

Someone knocked on the door. Porter moved quickly from the kitchen to the living room. He whispered, "I'm not here!" and ducked into his bedroom, shutting the door behind him. He wished, not for the first time, that his window wasn't nailed shut.

He listened at the door while his mom yelled, "Whosit?"

"Police, ma'am. Can you open the door, please?"

"He'snothere."

"Ma'am, can you open the door, please?"

"Goway."

"Ma'am, I'm here with social services. We need to talk to you about your daughter, and we need to get her clothes and some personal things."

Porter cracked open the bedroom door. He and his parents stared at one another, shaking their heads. Fearing an arrest, this turn of events was confusing to their booze-filled – or teenaged – brains.

Porter's mother opened the door to the officer and a social worker. She held onto the door, but stood back while they entered. The social worker had just started to explain the situation with Penny when the officer took a radio call.

He stepped to the porch for a minute, walked back in and said, "Ma'am, is your son Porter at home?"

"He'snothere."

"Ma'am, I'm going to have to check the house."

"Youcan'tdothat."

"If I don't have your permission, we'll all just stand here while I call for back-up."

From the corner chair could be heard, "Thalilprincesz. I'llteacherathingortwo."

Annie arrived home with five cats in tow. She knew Henrie's snack would be ready, and having missed lunch, she was hungry. She headed for the snack corner, made a plate and walked toward the voices in the all-season porch.

Four people, a young couple and a middle-aged couple, ate in a companionable manner.

"Hi. I'm Annie. You must be Lorine and Nathanial. And Terrence and Jerald? Which one is who?"

"I'm Terrence. Very pleased to meet you."

"Has Henrie told you of our sunsets? The sunset tonight will be beautiful."

"He has, and we are trying to plan our dinners around it."

"It's February; since you're having a snack now, you can probably eat dinner after the sun has set. There are two places within walking distance that will be open, and of course you could use the Inn's car to find a place in town or up the coast."

Terrence said, "Jerald and I have decided to try Mo's Tap tonight, so we'll be walking."

Mo heard his name and trotted in.

"This is Mo himself. He won't be at the Tap tonight, but I'm sure he wants to say hello."

Mo found the woman. He was already on her lap. He preened and curled his tail around her face. He was in love. So was she.

More cats came in, Sassy Pants and Mr. Bean clamoring for introduction. Tiger Lily and Little Socks held back. They wanted to make sure these were the proper sort of guest.

Kali and Ko, who had been hiding under the television table in the library, trailed in, Tillie at their tails.

Jerald held out his hands to the pup. "I didn't see anything on the website about a dog. What a beautiful Jack Russell Terrier."

"This is Tillie. We hope she will be able to stay with us for a while, but she came in with our other guests, Mr. and Mrs. Bartram."

A chorus of "Oh." "Poor thing." "I hope she can stay with you." And "Dear me."

"I take it you've met?"

"Not face to face. Just mouth to ear."

"I'm so sorry. They do not spend a good deal of time at the Inn, but of course, they do have breakfast here. This may be a good time to tell you that breakfast is served in the dining room, but we have trays beside the buffet, and many people find dining on the all-season porch to be delightful."

She received some smiles and a chuckle.

Annie turned to Joline and Nathanial. "Have you decided on a place for dinner?"

Joline answered. "We thought we would stay in tonight." She sent a suggestive look toward Nathanial. To Annie, she said, "Do you have a list of places that deliver pizza?"

Tiger Lily gathered her crew, now including Tillie, in the corner of the all-season porch for a chat. She and Little Socks took turns telling them about Fat Cat and Scaredy Cat, adding as much information as they could.

Sassy Pants, always up for an adventure, said, *"Let's setted a guard up to watch Da Clinic. We needs to find out if dey goes in dere."*

Mr. Bean chimed in. *"We can take turns watching."*

Kali and Ko reminded them, *"Tillie can let us out when they go in. She can open the lock."*

Tiger Lily took charge. *"Sassy Pants and Mr. Bean, you have the first watch. They'll probably go in soon. The Clinic has already closed for the evening."*

The two young cats set off for the library and its comfortable windowsill. Tillie went with them. While Kali and Ko were her protectors during the day, she preferred the company of the younger, more active cats.

When they left, Tiger Lily told the remaining cats about Penny, and the problems she had with the bad boys. *"Pete and Cyril were here. Maybe we'll have a chance to talk to Cyril later tonight or tomorrow."*

12

Alistair made a telephone call. On the other end of the line, he heard, "Everthin's set. They's in town now. They'll call you. Don't act no differnt to nobody. You ain't gonna know who it is. I'm only gonna tell ya it's a couple. A married couple. They'll git the job done fer ya."

Chris came to the apartment for supper. He and Annie shared two appetizers from Sassy P's, Mexican drunken shrimp wrapped in bacon with tequila lime butter sauce, and chicken pot stickers with a ginger soy sauce. The meal was paired with a merlot made in the region. They opened a second bottle and now sat on the overstuffed sofa surrounded by seven cats and a yappy dog. Actually, the dog wasn't that yappy at the moment. Tillie had curled into Chris's lap where she slept peacefully. Chris's hand lay softly on her back.

Mr. Bean had to make do with Annie's lap. He loved to sit on Chris's lap. On occasion he reached out a paw to slap at Tillie's tail.

The humans watched, saying nothing, but catching one another's eyes to share a smile. Annie took a deep breath and started, "Chris, when we…"

She was talking on top of, "Annie, about my…"

This time they laughed. Annie said, "Please. You first."

"I'm sorry. That's what I should have started with. I'm sorry. I jumped into a fantasy where you and I lived here together, and…"

"And that fantasy is so far-fetched?"

"No, that's not what I meant. What I meant was, I shouldn't have questioned your intention…"

There, a silence reigned, until Annie broke it. "My intention to save cats and dogs?"

"Well, to add to your family. Before you consider adding another human."

They didn't realize the activity in their laps came to a halt. They didn't see six other cats creep around to find hiding places nearby.

Annie considered her response carefully. "Chris, my life is complete, just the way it is. With seven wonderful cats, everything Dad left to me, the people in this town, and you."

"I was in last place there."

"You were the last to enter my life. That doesn't mean you're in last place."

"But…"

"But there will be times that others come and go. Let's talk about Tillie. We couldn't possibly let those horrid people take her away from here."

"You're right."

Tillie couldn't help it. She was trying to be still as a church mouse, but her tail gave a few involuntary wiggles. Enough to draw Chris's attention to her. She looked into his eyes with rapt puppy dog love.

Chris continued. "But now what? This is the first of what I'm sure will be countless rescues for the rest of your life."

"Now, we wait for those horrid people to leave, and we find a home for Tillie. Preferably one close by, because the cats love her so."

They sat in silence, until Annie said, "So…what do you think?"

"About Tillie?"

"No, about me. My tendency to rescue strays and abused pets. Is this something you can accept? Or live with?"

On that last sentence, a slow smile broke across his face. He was leaning toward Annie for a kiss when they heard the whine of the elevator.

"Henrie?" asked Chris.

"He would call first. Well, frankly, anyone would call first."

The third floor was locked to guests of the Inn, but a few of Annie's good friends had keys and could come up on their own.

Chris shook Tillie off his lap and rose to go to the door. He got there just as a knock sounded. He opened it to find Pete and Cyril.

"Sorry I didn't call. I should have. I'm just, well, just not thinking too clearly this evening."

"Sit, Pete. Let me get a glass for you, or would you prefer a beer?"

"Beer. Please."

The humans sat at the kitchen table while the companions went silently to their favorite corner of the living room. Cyril would tell them everything.

Pete took his time, finished about half his beer and picked half-heartedly at the drunken shrimp and pot stickers Annie placed in front of him.

"This is bad business," he said.

"Did Ginger's information turn out to be helpful?"

"It sure did. We started with the five names she gave us. Apparently, this group of boys made a pact. Each was supposed to come up with a naked photo of a sister, or cousin, or girlfriend, so they could pass them around. Penny was number three."

"What about the five boys? What happened with them?"

"One of them wasn't at school. Penny's brother. The rest were transported to the county jail, and their parents had to meet them there."

"So, Porter is still out there? That can't be good for Penny."

"No, we got him. Porter isn't too bright; it appears he takes after his parents. He went home, and they actually tried to hide him. Because they obstructed the officer trying to take him in, they were all arrested. But back to all five, the county's tech gal did an initial search of the phones and found that three of them had taken photos to send out to others. All five of them kept the photos on their phones, but the district attorney put initial charges only on three: Billy, Dallas and Porter. By now, the other two are back in town and will be free to go to school tomorrow, until the school decides what punishment, if any, they will face. Porter's parents are back, too. The DA declined to file charges."

Pete paused for a drink and a bite. "While county deputies took custody of the boys, we called the rest of the students together. Put them all in the gym for a chat. We wanted to get to them before cell phones were somehow lost or destroyed. I took the high school, Marco took the junior high. We bagged and tagged every cell phone from every student in school today. The superintendent sent a notice home to parents, and now we get to talk to them. All of them."

"I'll bet that was fun."

"Not so much. Actually, we're taking care of the parents that call us first, then we'll eventually get to all of them. Some of the parents are angry about what they call the overreach of the law. Others are happy to help. One of the first parents to call was Laila. She signed permission to open the phones of both James and Ava."

"Have you looked yet? Was anything on their phones?"

"I took the time to look at hers, so she didn't have to wait for days. When did every kid from the age of ten have to have a smart phone?"

Chris and Annie kept quiet, rather than send Pete off on another tangent.

He got back on track. "There was nothing on Ava's phone; James received one photo. He got it Monday morning, and he deleted it Monday afternoon. He didn't request the photo and he didn't pass it on. He didn't say anything to a responsible adult, but he didn't keep it. It's not going to be so easy for some of the other parents. For those that received and deleted the photos, like James, there will be only a minor consequence. For others, those that kept them, or those that passed them on...I don't even want to think what they'll go through. But the DA let those two boys go."

"What happened with Penny? Certainly she can't go home."

"Child Protective Services placed her in a foster home out of town. She will finish this school year in another school, and by then, her case will have come through the court system, and someone else will decide if she stays in foster care or goes home."

"You said hers was the third photo. How bad were the other two?"

"There was another sister, a girl in junior high. Her parents were more understanding, and they're considering their options about bringing the brother home. And there was a girlfriend. That photo was pretty raw. It looks like she was a willing participant. Her parents are, well, ready to sue just about everyone. The boy, the boy's parents, teachers, principals, administrators, police department – apparently for not mind-reading the situation – you name it."

"And Ginger? How is she doing?"

"She's going to have a hard time at school for a while, but she's prepared for that. We may take her out and home school her for a while. Or not. This is life, and she has to learn how to face it. She's smart, and she's strong. We'll take it as it comes."

Pete paused again. "Annie, I want to thank you for being there, for being calm, for being the person that Ginger and Penny could approach. We need more people like you in the community."

"There are lots of us in the community. It was just my turn."

Annie had a feeling the community of youth would not rally around Ginger and Penny. At least not right away.

In the living room, Cyril gave the companions essentially the same information Pete had relayed to the humans. Moving to another subject, Tiger Lily started to tell Cyril about Fat Cat and Scaredy Cat.

Cyril surprised them. *"You mean those two cats that are living on the other side of The Avenue?"*

"Yes. Do you know them?"

"I haven't had the pleasure of meeting them face-to-face. I've tried to tell Pete there are new scents at the cat doors over there, but he doesn't understand me."

"We've seen them at the church and The Clinic, but better than that, we met them!"

"What?"

"Tillie saw them go into the clinic this afternoon."

Mr. Bean and Sassy Pants looked at the floor. They had been arguing with one another about who was the most important when Tillie had cried, *"There they are!"*

Tiger Lily continued. *"Tillie was able to unlock a door again. This time we had her unlock the door going outside from the basement. It won't get locked again, because Mommy won't think to look there. Anyway, we went out and ran over to The Clinic."*

Mr. Bean, wanting to tell the story, picked it up. *"We ran in there and we were ready to kick 'em, scratch 'em, knock 'em silly!"*

Little Socks hissed and Tiger Lily picked it back up. *"Not really. We just needed to meet them. They aren't bad cats at all; they're just lost."*

"Lost?"

"They think their mom and dad thought they were in the camper, and they left to go back home, pretty far away. They were here ice fishing."

"How have they lived?"

"Their folks are outside kind of people, so they always hunted on their own. They had real food and could come inside when it was cold, too, but they know how to make do."

"Are they going to be okay on the street?"

"I think they'll be better when we can find them a home. We'll have to think about that."

Kali had remained silent, but her eyes took on a dreamy glow. Cyril noticed. *"So, Kali, are you in love?"*

"Fat Cat is so handsome," she purred.

Sassy Pants spat, *"Ooo! Ick! Gross!"*

Mr. Bean made a face and Ko laughed. Mo trilled.

Mo still spoke the secret language that he and his litter mates, Kali and Ko, spoke as kittens. Kali and Ko now spoke cat, but Mo had not progressed. Kali and Ko generally had to translate for him. In recent months, however, Sassy Pants had shown an ability to read minds. She saw pictures rather than words, but she was still able to translate for Mo. Tiger Lily and the other cats had to remember she could read their minds as well.

She was still grossed out over the thought of gushy stuff, so Ko translated Mo's trill, *"He said he has a girlfriend, so it's okay for Kali to have a boyfriend."*

"What girlfriend?"

"That sissy cat, Claire."

Claire was a blue point Himalayan whose human was Frank. She lived at the antique store and was not allowed outside. Sometimes, though, Mo could go to the store with Mommy, and sometimes Frank brought her to community events.

"I thought she didn't like other cats, except for your awful Uncle Honey Bear."

"She doesn't, uness that other cat is a long-haired philanderer like Mo," sniffed Little Socks.

Kali and Ko said together, *"You'd better watch out."* *"Don't flirt with her when Honey Bear is here."*

"Hey! Let's tell Cyril 'bout Mommy an Chris!" Sassy Pants turned to tell the story herself. *"Dey fighted over Tillie an now dey's not fightin' any more."*

"Over Tillie?"

"Yeah. Cuz Mommy rescues strays and such. Like us."

"But…"

Tiger Lily got them back on track. *"Enough, Sassy Pants. It was just a little spat. Mommy and Chris agree about Tillie."*

Tillie didn't know whether to wag her tail or look sad. She did a strange combination of both.

"Let's concentrate on Fat Cat and Scaredy Cat."

Cyril asked, *"Those are really their names? They don't have real ones?"*

"They seemed happy with the names we gave them. Apparently, both were called 'Here, Kitty Kitty' by their humans."

From here on, everyone, including Tillie, contributed to the conversation.

"What do we need to do about them?"

"Keep an eye on them. Make sure they have a warm, dry place to sleep and enough food and water."

"How are we going to do that?"

"At night we could sneak them upstairs and let them eat our food."

"How does we do dat wiffout Mommy finding out?

"Trill!"

"He means we makes sure Mommy is asleeping."

"She won't put out enough food."

"After a day or so, she'll see we're more hungry and she'll leave more."

"In the meantime, we'll all starve!"

"I know where there is some dry dog food. No one will miss it because it's supposed to be for me, but it's in my bedroom. Well, the bedroom I should be staying in."

"Can we get to it?"

"It's probalby in the same place, on the floor by the door."

"We'll try to drag it out."

"It's too big for the cat door."

"*When Hilly is here, she'll have the human doors open. We'll sneak in and get it out.*"

"*How?*"

"*Someone will have to spill something downstairs and make noise doing it, so she will hear it.*"

Kali and Ko, together said, "*I know just the thing!*" "*That big flower vase!*"

"*You'd do that to Clara's flowers?*"

"*Do you have a better idea?*"

"*No. If you think of something else, though, do it. We don't want Clara to stop bringing flowers.*"

Clara owned the flower shop on the other side of The Avenue. She kept the Inn – and all of Annie's businesses – decorated with fresh flowers. The vase in the entryway was oversized and made of crystal. It would make a glorious noise.

"*But then what? We make a noise, the rest of you drag it out, and we take it where? Did I miss that part?*"

"*Down to the basement.*"

"*Yes! That side that never gets used.*"

"*We can just rip open the bag and they can eat it as they need it.*"

"*We can drag some blankets or towels down there so they have a warm place to sleep.*"

"*And we have to figure out some water.*"

"*There are water taps down there. Cyril, can you figure out how to work those?*"

"*Probably. We'll need a dish.*"

"Henrie has dishes down there for us. We'll just have to move them close to the tap."

"Let's get started. We can bring them over tonight."

Their humans weren't paying attention, so they didn't think when they opened the door to Cyril. They just saw the big dog, the little dog and seven cats dancing around it asking to go downstairs to play.

And no one on The Avenue noticed when two large cats crossed with Tiger Lily, making their way around the house to the basement cat door.

Hank received a telephone call. He grunted his response, hung up and called Geraldine at home. Everett, her husband, answered.

"What do you two have cooking now, Hank? She's all tense again, just like she gets when the two of you have a scheme going."

"Not much, Everett. Just a little something to put some money in our pockets."

"You two always say that, and it never quite turns out that way, does it? This is why I have to keep working. Always working. And it goes out faster than I can bring it in."

"Oh, keep your sob story to yourself. Let me talk to her."

Geraldine came on the line. "Did they go for it?"

"They did. It'll happen tomorrow."

13

Breakfast was…well, breakfast was an event. The Bartrams were in fine form. Annie thought, it's Thursday. Only a few more days and they'll be gone. In the meantime, she was treated to a few choice comments.

"Wait your turn. We were here first."

"You! We would prefer to be served in a private room."

"You! You! There is not enough food out here for everyone! See to it we have enough for seconds!"

"This situation must change before tomorrow!"

Annie breathed and smiled at the other guests, who handled the situation with grace and style. Saying nothing but "good morning" to the Bartrams, they filled their plates and retired to the all-season porch.

Henrie took pots of coffee and pitchers of cranberry and orange juice to them, as well as a platter filled with a variety of breads and condiments.

Tillie, Kali and Ko stayed on the porch. The other cats left for their places of business as soon as Annie opened the door. Tiger Lily, Mo and Mr. Bean promised to be back by the time Hilly came in to do her cleaning, so they could get the food.

Henrie kept the television in the kitchen on, tuned to regional news. Throughout the morning, earnest reporters gave updates of the Chelsea Junior and Senior High School sexting case. They called it a "ring of child predators."

According to news reports, four teens had been arrested. Three teen boys would be charged as adults; one girl would possibly go to adult court as well. Those names would be released if the cases made it to adult court.

By mid-morning, the new guests were out of the house, ready to explore the town. Terrence and Jerald were dressed for a long walk up and down the beach and out to the lighthouse. Nathanial and Joline borrowed the Inn's car and said they planned to explore the lakeshore as well as the town.

Cressida and Alistair, after finishing the second and part of the third box of Henrie's special biscuits, were out again to who knows where. Hilly arrived and was upstairs, changing the sheets and dusting the furniture.

She hadn't been there long when she heard a loud crash. Running to the stair railing, she looked down to see two big cats looking up, all innocence, and sitting amidst broken glass and fresh flowers.

"Don't move!" she cried. "You'll cut your feet!"

Hilly ran downstairs while Tiger Lily and her crew ran for the front bedroom. The food was right where Tillie thought it would be. It was a big bag. Tiger Lily was glad she had called on Fat Cat and Scaredy Cat to help. Five strong cats and a dog worked together to drag it to the elevator. In their efforts to push and pull the bag, little claws tore holes into the bag. They didn't notice a trail of kibbles from bedroom to elevator.

Finally, the bag was safely in the elevator and they were on the way to the basement. Being the spoiled children of Annie Mack, the cats had specially coded foot pads to make the elevator go up and down.

When Hilly finally got back to the second floor, she looked at the trail of dry dog or cat food, she wasn't sure which, and wondered why she had not noticed it before.

Alistair and Cressida, in their rental car in a public parking lot, trembled with excitement and fear. They had just received a call from a man who said, "We're gonna do the job. Tell us what we need to know."

Now, they considered their circumstances.

"Who do you think they are?"

"Could be that new couple at the Inn."

"Oh, certainly not. At our Inn? Why would they come to the same place?"

"Well, it could be them. Actually, it could be either couple. I heard those gay boys say they're 'married' to each other."

"Not those gay boys. Surely!"

"It could be someone who already lives here."

"Your contact said they were in town 'now;' it sounded like they were arriving."

"That could mean they live here, that they are already here, here 'now.'"

"Or they could have come from somewhere else and they're at another hotel, or another bed and breakfast."

"It couldn't really be either of those couples at the Inn. They don't have cars."

"But they can use the Inn's car."

"But they can't count on having it when they need it, not with other guests around."

"It could be them."

"I'll bet it's someone else. Someone who knows the town."

"You're probably right."

"Probably."

Fat Cat and Scaredy Cat thought they had died and gone to heaven.

"How long do you think we can keep this up?" asked Fat Cat.

"As long as we have to. If Mommy finds you here, we'll protect you. When she sees we like you, she'll try to take care of you."

"Then why don't you just introduce us to her? Why go through all this?"

"Well, she's in the middle of another rescue. She's trying to make sure Tillie is taken care of. We don't want to overdo it with her."

"Sure, okay. We're cool. We can stay hidden for a while. We'll wander around town during the day, if that's alright with you."

"Sure. You know who your friends are. All of us, and Cyril, and eventually you'll meet Jock. He's okay too. He's another big dog, a big black dog."

"Okay. If we run into a big black dog, we'll call him by name, and we should be alright."

While the bigger cats and strong Mr. Bean took care of the dog food, Little Socks and Sassy Pants had a different experience altogether.

A young couple, fashionably dressed, ate a late breakfast at the Café, looking all around as they ate. The man asked Cindy, the server, "Where's the cat, Tiger Lily, the one that's supposed to be sitting on the hostess stand?"

"I'm not sure. She left a little while ago. She'll probably be back soon."

The couple paid for their meal and dropped in at Lil' Socks' Virasana.

While Diana finished a class, the couple looked around. The woman sat on the windowsill next to Little Socks. The man looked at the literature on the counter. He quickly slipped one stack of papers into his jacket.

When the class was finished, Diana approached the counter.

"Can I help you?"

"Yes. My wife wants to take some of your classes. Can we take a schedule with us?"

"Yes, there's a brochure right here on the counter." Diana turned to look for the brochures but the stack was missing. "That's odd. I thought I saw them this morning. I must be losing my mind. Give me a minute and I'll get one from the office."

Diana turned to go to the office. The man stepped over to Little Socks, pulling a canvas bag out of his jacket. He quickly dropped the bag over the cat and pillow, scooped them up and left the studio without notice. The woman approached the counter and, on Diana's return, took the schedule and thanked her.

The woman went next door and waited outside for the man as he returned from a car parked on the other side of The Avenue. They entered Mo's Tap and sat at the bar.

He ordered two beers, looked around and asked, "Where's that cat I heard about? Mo."

George looked around and said, "Not sure. He was here earlier. He must have seen a pretty woman walk by."

When George turned to get the beers, the man said, "Just a minute; some friends of ours are on the other side of the street. We'll be back."

George, leaning over to pick up a towel, looked out the window as he straightened. No one was across the street, and he though he saw the backs of the couple going toward Mr. Bean's. Oh well. No great loss.

At Mr. Bean's, the man went to the counter, kneeling in front to get a good look at the pastries. The woman took a seat at one of the few café tables in the small room, looking around the room as she did so.

Carlos approached the counter. "Can I tell you about our selections?"

"I think we just want to share one of these cream cheese Danish." The man stood up. "Hey, where's that cat I hear so much about?"

Carlos looked at the window, then took a quick look around the shop. "Can't say. He's usually right here. He must have run down the street for a minute. Do you want this on a plate?"

"No, we'll take it to go."

The woman put the bag containing the Danish in her purse and they left the shop.

At Sassy P's, the little girl dropped to the floor in front of the woman so she could scratch her tummy. The man put himself between the woman and Minnie, who was standing behind the counter. Minnie didn't notice the woman as she picked Sassy Pants up and slipped her beneath her coat. The woman left immediately. The man looked around, saw her leave, and said apologetically, "She hasn't been feeling well. Must have had to go out and, you know. I'm sorry. We'll come another time."

The woman went to the other side of the car, and, just in case anyone was looking, leaned over as if to throw up. She threw Sassy Pants into the back seat, next to the canvas bag.

They got into the car and left. Their orders were to get the cats from the smaller businesses, because the two at the Inn were big girls, too big to handle.

While the woman drove, the man picked up a cell phone and made a call to the only number he had. A soft voice answered.

"We only got two."

"Only two? We paid you for five."

"You haven't paid us anything yet. We'll get the agreed amount for two. If we can't get as much money, we'll take a larger cut."

"You won't get a larger cut. Ask for the full amount for the two. She'll pay it."

"I told you before we got them that we need a larger cut. We're taking all the risk."

"It was our idea. You made a deal. You'll stick with it."

Silence.

"Are you still there?"

"Okay. We'll meet you at the place and time we discussed to split the money."

"Which ones did you get?"

"The black one and the multi-colored one."

The couple, driving through town, made several turns, checking to see if they were followed. Satisfied they had not been noticed, they drove slowly through one of the less fashionable parts of town.

They stopped. The man looked in the back seat. Sassy Pants was terrified. She clung to the bag containing Little Socks and would not let go. As the man looked at her, she gave out a long, low hiss.

"The one in the bag won't hurt us, but that little one could scratch."

"She looks more scared than angry."

"Even so, I'm going to put my coat over her before we go in."

The capture was made. Sassy Pants, wrapped in a coat, and Little Socks, still locked in the canvas bag, didn't go quietly into that good night, so to speak. By the time the couple had them safely inside, with food and water set out, they were ready to shoot both cats without blinking an eye.

They didn't even let Little Socks completely out of the bag. The woman opened the zipper part of the way, then said to her companion, "This is a mean one. They can figure it out after we're gone."

"You know they're gonna die in here."

"But we'll have the money. All of it. Those people are idiots, thinking we'd share."

Clara stopped at the Inn to make her weekly delivery. Her black jeans were complimented by a black leather bomber jacket, black neck scarf, black leather gloves, and knee-high black boots with a modest heel. She wore a bright red calla lily behind her ear. This was a signature touch, setting off her exotic Haitian good looks. She pulled her covered wagon just inside the door, to keep it out of the weather.

Annie watched Clara cross The Avenue from her third floor apartment and went down to meet her. They chatted while Clara pulled out a medium-sized fresh flower arrangement for the dining room and a bundle of wrapped flowers without a vase.

Clara owned the flower and gift shop across The Avenue, Bloomin' Crazy. Every week, she made a delivery of fresh flowers to each of Annie's businesses. They were color coordinated to each place, and the vases matched the personality of both the cats and the places they called their own. As Clara delivered flowers for one week, she took the vases and flowers from the previous week away.

The Inn received flowers in hues of blue, and typically the vases were crystal. An oversized arrangement graced the foyer, a smaller arrangement with similar flowers the dining room. Clara always made a small bundled arrangement for Kali and Ko. The girls were pleased to be allowed to inspect each week's offering.

Annie called Kali and Ko.

No response.

Clara called out, "Girls, the flowers are ready for your inspection."

No response.

"Oh, well," she said. "I'll leave this little bundle with you. You can give it to them later."

The flowers this week were in Italian cobalt lead crystal vases, matching, but one larger than the other. The flowers included blue roses, blue cymbidium orchids and psychedelic daisy flowers. In place of the typical filler flowers, Clara had inserted red, white and pink hearts in various sizes and styles, on plastic dowel rods in a variety of lengths. Some appeared at the bottom of the arrangement, others above, and others were peppered throughout the flowers.

Clara came in from the dining room carrying the old vase and flowers, placed them in the wagon, picked up the large vase, turned, and stared at the empty table.

Annie, who had been looking at the arrangements to go to the other storefronts, noticed the change in atmosphere. She stood and looked in the same direction.

Annie asked, "Where did it go?"

"Um, maybe the flowers were looking puny?"

"They were still beautiful this morning. I'm sure I saw them this morning."

Annie went to the kitchen. "Henrie?" A note was on the counter. Henrie was across the street, purchasing light bulbs at DoubleGood, then he would shop at Babar Foods for fruits and vegetables. He might stop to have a cup of tea with Mem.

Annie went to the second floor. "Hilly?"

Hilly came out of the front bedroom. "Yes?"

"By any chance, did you notice where the flowers got to?"

"Oh, yes. I cleaned that up."

"Excuse me?"

"Kali and Ko had a little accident. I was going to say something to you or Henrie before I left, but I'm running so late. I wanted to finish these rooms first before your guests returned. I did clean it up, and I checked their paws. I don't think they got any glass in their feet."

Annie was still stuck on the first sentence. "Kali and Ko had a little accident."

"This was a first. They have never knocked over a vase before. Did you see it happen?"

"No, I just heard it. I'm surprised you didn't hear it up on the third floor. It made quite a noise."

"Do you know where they went? After you checked their feet?"

"No, I'm sorry. They typically stay out of my way."

Annie returned to Clara. "Kali and Ko, apparently, broke the vase. We'll replace it, Clara. They aren't cheap."

"You will do no such thing. You keep me in business. Between the regular orders and the ongoing advertising, people seeing what I do in your places, I have a thriving business. I can afford a vase."

"But you shouldn't have to. Let's not argue about it now."

Clara finished placing the new vase and said, "Did you see all of the others?"

"I did. I can't choose a favorite."

Clara's next stop would be Sassy P's, with reds. A square white marble box sat slightly askew atop a square marble tile. In the box, red roses floated on a field of green trick dianthus. It managed to be both romantic and whimsical. At Mr. Bean's, a rectangular, low green ceramic vase held potato vine, petunia, geranium, and Spanish dagger. One white heart poked through the middle.

Mo's Tap received yellow arrangements. In an oversized champagne glass, several ranunculus ranging from white to bright yellow swirled in beautiful abandon. The glass itself was painted with red hearts in a variety of artsy shapes and sizes. Little Socks, whose yoga studio boasted a bright orange theme, would receive a variety of pansies, each with some amount of orange coloring, curling attractively in a ceramic oversized ballet slipper. One artsy heart poked out of the top.

Tiger Lily's Café received purple hues, almost always in a crystal vase. Today, Clara had twelve tinted long-stemmed roses, ranging in shades from the lightest lilac to the deepest purple.

Annie gave Clara a hug. "I don't know how you do it, week after week."

As Clara left to deliver the remainder of her flowers, Annie got ready to go to the Café.

Tiger Lily, Mr. Bean and Mo waited until they heard Mommy go upstairs and waited for just a couple minutes more, to be sure Clara would be inside the Winery. They slipped from the basement and back to their posts, unaware of the fate of Little Socks and Sassy Pants.

Annie went to the Café to help during lunch rush, found a note addressed to her on the hostess stand, read it and fainted dead away.

14

Felicity and Trudie acted quickly and on instinct. Felicity read the note, and while Trudie called for Pete and medical help, Felicity called Henrie and told him to round up all of the other cats to keep them safe.

Henrie, rushing out of the Inn, took the time to open a drawer on the hall table and place an object in his pocket. He got Hilly's attention on the second floor, yelled at her to lock the doors and let no one in unless she knew exactly who they were. "And keep those cats safe!" He set off at a run for the Café.

He pulled open the doors of the Confectionary and Mo's for just enough time to tell Carlos and George to get the boys to the Inn. He would explain later. Both Carlos and George, hearing the frantic tone, did exactly as he asked without question.

When Henrie arrived at the Café, Pete was there with Cyril. Jennifer, a nurse practitioner and a nine-one-one responder, dealt with Annie, She was on the floor, sitting up now and sobbing. She clutched Tiger Lily to her chest.

Henrie leaned down next to Annie and took Tiger Lily from her. He took a harness from his pocket and slipped it over Tiger Lily's head and front legs; he snapped a leash into place. Tiger Lily was too scared to be angry. He kept hold of one end of the leash, and placed her behind the hostess stand where Cyril waited, ordered by Pete to "Stay." He was anxious, shifting weight from one foot to the other.

Henrie couldn't read the note because Pete had it in evidence, but Felicity told him again what it said.

"You'd better tell Diana and Minnie."

"We already sent a server to tell them, and she's going to let George and Carlos know what's going on, too."

"Why would they take those two?"

Pete joined them. "Felicity, was anyone new in the Café this morning?"

"Cindy, the server that went down to tell Minnie and Diana what happened, said something about a couple that asked about Tiger Lily. She didn't know them, but they looked like normal people, maybe tourists?"

"They just asked about Tiger Lily?"

"Yeah. Well, they ate, but before they left, they asked where Tiger Lily was. For some reason she wasn't at the hostess stand. I think she left the Café. She came back, though."

"When was this note seen on the counter? Was it there when the couple left?"

"I don't think so. I don't know when it was put there."

Pete motioned Marco over. "Go to each one of Annie's businesses, ask if they saw a couple, probably someone they didn't know. Make sure you talk to Diana and Minnie, but talk to the others as well. They may have tried to take more of them but didn't have the opportunity."

He turned back to Felicity. "Does Cindy have a cell phone?" At Felicity's nod, he said, "Call her and get her back here. I need to interview her."

Trudie made sure the business kept going. She gathered the other servers and cooks, told them to focus, and they managed to operate close to normal.

In the midst of the excitement, and during the transition from panic to 'let's keep things going,' guests at two tables had different reactions.

Terrence and Jerald were at one table. They arrived just after Tiger Lily's return and just before Annie received the note. They were seated at a table close to the Bartrams. As Annie found the note and fainted, Jerald jumped to give assistance. Terrence put his hand on Jerald's to stop him. "Stay here. Don't get involved. See? They're already helping her."

Alistair turned to look at them, nodded his head and turned back to his meal. Neither he nor Cressida had missed a bite.

Tiger Lily felt impotent. She and Cyril were able to figure out what had happened. Little Socks and Sassy Pants were taken by bad people. Mommy received a note that said someone would ask her for money later. It sounded like all of them would have been taken, but she and the boys had gone back to the Inn. It was just luck they had gone at the same time the catnappers were looking for them.

Tiger Lily was sure she had done something wrong to cause the catnapping of the other two. She should have asked them to help with the dog food. She should have stayed here. She should have been the one taken.

Cyril felt the same way. If only he had been on the sidewalk when this was happening. If only he had felt the presence of bad people. If only. If only.

They didn't know it, but they were experiencing survivor's guilt. They would not get over it soon.

Someone had called Chris. He was there now, beside Annie at one of the tables, helping her stay focused as she gave a statement to a police officer. He took a minute to turn around and give a reassuring nod to Tiger Lily.

It didn't help.

At the Inn, the cats and Hilly were confused. Hilly found Kali and Ko in the library, hiding under the television table. She locked them, and Tillie for good measure, in that room. There was no cat door for Tillie to pop open. Also no litter, no food, no water, but that was beside the point at the moment. Knowing no different, the girls thought they were being punished for breaking the crystal vase and for moving the dog food.

Soon Mo and Mr. Bean were in the room as well, just as confused. George and Carlos arrived with them at the same time, almost throwing them into the library so they could go back to check on the police and ambulance activity at the Café.

The cats pooled their information and realized it wasn't a punishment, but they still didn't know what was wrong. Where was Tiger Lily? Where were Little Socks and Sassy Pants? It seemed they had been locked up forever. Certainly they would starve to death if they had to wait in here for Mommy!

Their ears perked up when they heard scratching at the door that led from the library to the basement. The door was at the far side of the room. Because a guest had once used the door to take her husband to the basement – he didn't recover from the trip – a bookcase now stood in front of it. The scratching came from Fat Cat and Scaredy

Cat. Mr. Bean called out, *"What's happening? What have you heard?"*

The two cats told them what they knew. Little Socks and Sassy Pants were missing. Some bad people took them. There were lots of police and an ambulance at the Café. As far as they could tell, Tiger Lily was okay; she was with the big dog they met last night. Their mommy, Annie, was being taken care of by the ambulance lady. Lots of people were asking if the other cats were safe, so that's probably why they got locked up.

Tillie backed all the way up. She couldn't bear to look at her new friends. Mo noticed and gave a trill. Tillie looked at Mo in confusion.

Kali and Ko said together, *"He wants to know what's wrong." "He thinks you know something."*

All eyes were on Tillie, and she could tell the cats on the other side of the door were listening, too. *"I'm just worried, is all. I want my friends to be safe."*

15

Mo and Mr. Bean tried to make a break for it when Hilly came back to the library. She closed the door quickly, nearly catching a little paw in the process. She apologized and looked around at the scared kitty faces looking back. All of them. And a little dog.

"I feel like a fool. I hear Annie talking to you sometimes, so I'm going to do the same thing. I'm going to tell you what's happening, and if anyone looks through the window and says I'm losing my mind, then so be it. Here goes." Henrie had called, filling Hilly in on everything he knew. She shared it all, including the fact that Tiger Lily was safe with Henrie and would be home soon.

As Hilly talked, she watched as each of the cats and the little dog settled down on their rumps. Their faces stayed focused on hers, upturned and with worried expressions. As she talked, Hilly realized it was therapeutic. This isn't so bad, she thought. I should talk to them more often.

She didn't realize two additional cats listened from the door to the basement.

Hilly heard someone enter. She excused herself, then thought, I excused myself to cats and a dog?

Outside the library she encountered two people she had not seen before, most likely new guests. The only way they could have entered was with a key, as each guest had a key to the front door.

"Hello. I'm Hilly. I started to clean the rooms, but I was interrupted. I'm so sorry, but you will see my cleaning equipment in the upstairs hallway."

A man with a southern drawl answered. "Please don't apologize. We were at the Café and we know what's happening."

Another man, another southern drawl. "We just got here and our room doesn't need a thing. As a matter of fact, if you'll tell me where the closet is, I'll just put your cleaning supplies away."

"Oh, no, I'll get it. If you're sure you don't need anything?"

"We're sure."

"Then I'll just nip upstairs and put that cart away. I have to ask you to stay out of the library. In fact, I've locked the door, and I'm keeping the key. I…I don't know how to explain it to you."

The first man said, "I assume you're keeping the other cats safe. You won't have a quarrel with us."

The second man added, "Don't worry. We'll hang out here in the foyer for a while. We'll keep an eye on that door."

"Thank you," said Hilly. As she went upstairs to put away the cart, she wondered if she should be so trusting. I'll just hurry along, she thought, and get right back down there. When she returned, she nodded to them, now sitting in the comfortable chairs in the foyer.

She didn't know this couple, after all. Could they be trusted?

Back in the library, she counted noses and said, softly, "I'm going to stay in here with you until Henrie gets back. I'll keep you safe."

Just in case, she called Boone.

Boone took the call as he and the boys cleaned the sidewalks and steps behind the buildings on the other side of The Avenue. He left the boys to it and went to the Inn, letting himself in with the key Annie had given him.

Two men stood as he entered. One man, in a southern drawl, said, "State your business, sir."

Another man, another drawl, said, "Now, Jerald, you got no call to…"

"State your business."

"This man obviously has a key."

Boone didn't know which persona to put on, so he stood for a while, watching and listening while these men looked to have a lover's quarrel of some variety. When they wound down and once again looked at him, Boone made a choice. In an Appalachian sing-song voice, with the requisite head and arm movements, he said, "Wall, I wuz jes gettin' to my work an all, an a nice lady from this here Inn called, and she sez, she sez, now wot wuz it she sez… Oh! I wuz to come down an make shore ever'thin' wuz okay here."

The library door opened, and Hilly stuck her head out. She hissed, "Boone! Stop that and get in here!"

Boone nodded politely at the men as he got in there.

Pete didn't have a lot of information at his disposal. He had general descriptions of a man and woman who made the rounds of each of Annie's businesses, asking about the cats or distracting staff attention long enough to get away with them.

Unfortunately, this general description could apply to anyone not well known on The Avenue. It could be tourists, someone from the region, or someone local who did not frequent this part of town. The couple appeared "kind of" familiar to some, so it was possible others in town knew them. Or maybe they just had familiar traits, like the way they dressed or talked.

He had the description of a car. Again, unfortunately, the description fit many other cars in town, including the one his wife drove and one of the cars used by the Inn.

Diana and Minnie were more than distraught. They loved their girls and couldn't stand the thought that they had done anything to aid in their catnapping. Pete assured them there was nothing they could have foreseen. The cats had clear run of the premises and The Avenue. They were in and out as they pleased. If they were missing for a time, it wasn't unusual.

As Annie recovered from the shock, she walked back to the Inn, Chris by her side and Tiger Lily in her arms. She stopped in at both the yoga studio and the winery to essentially say the same things Pete had already said, trying to put them at ease.

It didn't help.

Pete's officers canvassed the businesses on the other side of The Avenue.

Mem, at CyberHealth, had seen the car and had seen the man approach the car at least once before leaving. That one time, the man had thrown a canvas bag of some sort into the back seat of the car. He had then gone back across The Avenue to join the woman. She wasn't watching the street to see where they had walked, and she didn't see the car leave.

The couple was young, well-dressed, professional looking. They looked like any tourist or anyone that could be visiting from the region. The car looked familiar, in fact it looked like one from the Inn. But didn't Pete's wife drive the same kind of car? And that science teacher? And Steve, from the dry cleaner?

Clara had been making flower deliveries at about the same time of the catnapping. Her first stop after the Inn was Sassy P's Wine and Cheese. She entered the door as a man left, and she glanced back as he crossed The Avenue to a car. A woman was there, on the other side of the car. She had been leaning into the car. She closed the door to look up as Clara turned to go into the shop.

They were average looking, white, maybe someone in town or from somewhere in the region, maybe tourists, but no one she had seen on the street or in any of the businesses before. Nothing stood out to her as descriptive. The car was a common type of car. Lots of people around Chelsea drove the same model.

Her assistant could be of no help. A young adult, he claimed to be busy during the time in question. Clara assumed he had been busy with his nose pressed to one or another of his electronic devices.

Pastor Teresa had been at the church, Soul's Harbor, but she was tending to the gift shop and had not looked outside during the time in question.

Twin sisters Holly and Jolly, from the hardware and electronics store DoubleGood, offered a bit more information. The couple had pulled up around 10:00 and had stayed in the car for a time, talking on a cell phone. The conversation was an animated one; they were possibly arguing with whoever was on the other end of the line. Holly, who had been at the counter in the front of the store at the time, thought the two looked angry when they exited the car and walked to the Café.

Sisters Marie and Jennifer, from The Drug Store and The Clinic, were not aware of anything until they were called to the Café to provide medical care to Annie.

Laila was no help at all. Pete called Jennifer to come tend to her, as she could not stop sobbing. As Jennifer arrived, Pete said, "If you get her calmed down, please ask if she noticed anything that I need to know." He didn't think he would get anything of value.

Pete hadn't seen Cyril since shortly after they left the Café.

When Pete and Cyril left the Café, Cyril sniffed around and realized the two stray cats had been on Annie's side of The Avenue. That was different.

He looked for Pete and saw he was still interviewing Diana. Cyril trotted down the sidewalk to the Inn, went to the basement cat door, poked his nose in and gave a *"Woof!"*

Scaredy Cat remained at the library door, but Fat Cat went to the entry.

"Did you see or hear anything?"

"We didn't know there was a problem until it was too late, but I think we saw who did it."

"Who?"

179

"Neither of us got a good smell, but it was a young couple. It could be the couple staying here, they look kind of similar. But it could be that couple that owned that restaurant."

"Which restaurant?"

"You know that restaurant that was open for a little bit? On that other street? They used to have lots of food in the trash because no one ate there."

"Oh, yeah. I was there a couple of times with Pete. It was awful."

"It was awful, but to us, it was food, so we hung out in the alley a lot until they closed. Anyway, that young couple on The Avenue today could have been them. Or those new people staying here. They went into all of the places on this side of the street, and they were back and forth to their car a couple of times."

Cyril huffed to himself. How was he going to get Pete to look into these two couples? And where did that restaurant couple live? Was it possible they had the cats at the restaurant, now closed?

Fat Cat, who might have been mind-reading, said, *"We can go with you to that restaurant. It has a second floor. We can climb up if we have to."*

Cyril was grateful for the help. *"We'll leave in a few minutes. I have to call a friend to come help."*

Cyril went to the parking lot of the Inn. Then he stood and bayed toward The Marina.

At The Marina, a big black head came up. Jock trotted through a dog door to the wharf and gave two sharp, loud barks in reply.

Cyril stood looking across to The Marina; Jock looked around to make sure the coast was clear and took off at a run to join his friend.

Cyril asked, *"Can you help me hunt for Sassy Pants and Little Socks?"*

"What?"

"Oh, you don't know." Cyril explained the problem.

"Ray's not home right now, and Cheryl probably didn't realize I left. I can come."

"We might be gone for long time."

"I know. It's okay. Ray's meeting with people about fixing his boat. He won't be paying any attention to me."

Fat Cat returned to the library door. He hissed softly to get the attention of the cats. He didn't want to raise the attention of the woman in the room.

The cats looked around at one another. Mr. Bean made his way to the Library door, snuggling into the bookcase in front of it. He whispered, *"What is it?"*

"We're going to go help Cyril find those bad people. We'll come back if we have anything to tell you. But you need to know it could be someone staying here at the Inn. You have to be careful."

When Mr. Bean reported this to the rest of the group, they heard Henrie enter, followed by Annie and Chris. Tiger Lily gave a loud meow and they sighed with relief.

They could hear Henrie talking to the guests, and Boone rose to go to the door. He unlocked it just as Terrence said, "They're all safe in the library."

Tiger Lily leapt from Henrie's arms, leash and all, and ran into the library to be with her siblings. Annie, to assure herself that everyone else was okay, entered as well, shutting the door behind her. She got to her knees, sobbing again, and they all ran to her.

"We'll get through this, kids. We'll get them back. Everything will be fine, but for now, you're staying right here."

Without realizing it, Annie talked to them as if they already knew about Little Socks and Sassy Pants.

Henrie entered softly, again closing the door, and he had food! Food! They were not going to starve, after all!

Ray arrived at the Waffle House in Marsh Haven. It was an easy-to-find meeting place, on the outskirts of town and just off the highway. He entered and walked toward the table from which a woman had just stood, waving him over. "I'm Ray."

"Hello, Ray. Cindy Stiles. Thank you for driving here. It was just easier, you know, since I'm here, and the contractor, too."

"Not a problem. I assume I need to sit with an adjuster since this will be my third claim within the year?"

Cindy Stiles seemed confused, then caught herself. "I'm not sure, Ray. You see, I am focused only on this claim. They didn't give me the whole file, obviously."

"So, the claim will go through? Even though…you mean, I can expect to get some reimbursement?"

"Certainly. Everything seems to be in order. We just have to agree upon a contractor, and then you can get started."

"Is there a cap to the amount?"

"I've been told that the contractor will set the cap. He'll give an estimate, a not-to-exceed number, and the insurance will pay up to that amount and no more."

"And I just need to get the one estimate?"

"We're introducing you to one of our preferred contractors. We trust him implicitly. Oh, here he is now."

Cindy pointed out the window. A man got out of a gray Ford Fusion and walked to the door of the Waffle House.

Chris made arrangements to stay overnight at the Inn. Henrie made fresh coffee and placed a plate of fresh fruits and vegetables in front of him.

"Thanks, Henrie. I imagine there will be several people in and out. Can I help you do anything?"

"You can help by staying with Annie. That is all this house needs at the moment."

Chris nodded. Then he said, "Henrie, I'm sorry about..."

"Do not give it a thought. I believe a slip of the tongue happens on occasion, especially under duress. I imagine a word two were, shall I say, premature."

"What do you think?"

Henrie looked at Chris steadily. "I think that is something for the two of you to discuss. You have my full support."

Chris would have responded, but instead, he rose to answer the first of many knocks at the front door.

16

Ginger drove to The Avenue. Parking spaces were at a premium. She considered going to the public lot but decided to drive up and down until a place came open on the street. For some reason, she didn't feel safe parking in the lot.

She thought about her day. At school, she received a cold shoulder by almost everyone, even James. James would not meet her eyes and seemed to avoid all of the places they used to see one another.

Shellie approached her at lunchtime and called her a witch-with-a-b in front of everyone. But she had used the real word.

One girl, a freshman and a friend to Penny, sought Ginger out to thank her. True, the girl talked to her in the relative privacy of the girls' bathroom, but it was human contact nonetheless. Ginger took the opportunity to pump her for information.

Marc and Justin, the two bullies who had not been arrested, stalked her after each of her classes. One or the other or both would be in the hallway as she exited a class and would follow her to the next class, close enough that if she stopped quickly, they would run into her.

Lia was not in school. Ginger now knew that Lia had been in the third photo, the one of "a girlfriend." Ginger had not seen the photo. Penny's friend described it to her. Nothing had been left to the imagination. Since Lia had agreed to the photo, she was as guilty as Billy. Lia regretted the photo the instant she realized it had been shared with just about everyone.

Ginger tried to be empathetic.

It didn't help.

At the end of the school day, tired, discouraged, and just a little scared, Ginger stayed in the office and called her mother to pick her up. Now she was headed to the Inn to pay her respects to Annie. A parking place came open in front of Mo's and she swung in. She got out, locked the door, and started down the sidewalk toward the Inn. Behind her, she heard footsteps, but it was a busy street. She didn't look around.

She was hit in the back of the head with a rock hard snowball. Now she did turn around. No one was there. There were recesses, doorways, in which someone could be hiding, or someone could have gotten in between the cars and ducked down.

It could be little kids, having a lark. It could be Shellie and her friends, not dangerous, just angry. It could be one of the bullies. Dangerous. She hurried on to the Inn.

It was evening. Annie couldn't bear to be upstairs by herself, so the cats had been settled into the library with food, water and litter. Dog food for little Tillie was provided as well, and Chris took her for walks on a leash a couple of times.

Someone was always near the telephone.

Hilly had gone home, but she, Boone and the boys came back later, bringing a pot roast casserole. Tender bites of beef with carrots, onions and mushrooms atop a layer of mashed potatoes, topped with gravy, steaming and redolent with the smell of thyme and rosemary.

Visitors came and went all evening, no one staying long. Some brought food, some brought flowers, some brought just themselves and a kind word. Everyone from The Avenue was in at one time or another, business owners from the other side and staff from each of Annie's places.

Ginger gave a tense glance behind as she walked into the Inn. Chris noticed the glance.

"What's wrong?"

"I just thought I saw someone. Something."

"Did you walk over?"

"No, I drove. But there are lots of cars here. I'm parked up by Mo's Tap."

"Don't leave the Inn without me. I'll walk you to your car when you go."

Ginger smiled and seemed to relax.

Annie, realizing she had the guests of the Inn to consider, asked Henrie if everyone had plans for the evening.

"Terrence and Jerald are dining at Mo's Tap. Nathanial and Joline seem to be nesters. This evening, they had pizza delivered to their room. Again. Perhaps they are making the most of their 'alone time.'"

The Bartrams stormed in as Henrie spoke. "And there," he said calmly, "you see the last of them. How lucky for us they decided to return."

Cressida was in typical form. "You would think a convention had come to this place. We could hardly fight our way down the street with all this traffic!"

Chris stood to meet them and introduced himself. "We've not had the pleasure. I'm Chris, a friend of Annie's. I would be very pleased if you could allow Annie the time and space she needs while we get through a crisis."

"She can have her crisis on her own time. We didn't arrive in time for afternoon tea. We'll have it now."

Chris didn't quite understand why he was being asked to serve food to this couple, but knowing that Henrie would be unfailingly polite, he nodded in reply. He turned to go to the kitchen but was met by Henrie, carrying a tray of packaged snacks.

Henrie placed the tray on the hall table next to the Keurig corner, turned to the Bartrams and said, "I am delighted to provide tea for you this evening. Please avail yourselves of these offerings."

Cressida's nose went up at the prepackaged chips and cookies, but before she could say anything, the telephone rang and everyone's attention went to the sound.

Annie answered, breathless. The quiet voice on the other end of the line was succinct. "They're alive. They will stay that way until we receive $250,000. Each. You'll receive instructions tomorrow." The line went dead.

Annie sank into her chair. "$250,000. Each. Instructions tomorrow. How will I come up with it?"

Pete called Chris on his cell. "They called from a burner. They weren't on long enough for us to pinpoint it"

"Okay. Thanks. Hey, I'm going to follow Ginger home. She seemed a little nervous on her way in, like someone might have been following her."

"Thanks, Chris. She may just be spooked, but it's possible some of those kids from school want to get even."

"That's what I was thinking."

As he hung up, he noticed Ginger putting her coat on. He hurried to her and said, "Give me just a minute to tell Annie where I'm going. I'm going to follow you home and you aren't going to argue, because I promised your dad I would do it."

She waited, grateful.

Marc and Justin waited in the median, crouched behind one of the concrete flowerpots. They watched as Chris pulled up to Ginger's car in his own SUV. Ginger got out and opened her car door. Chris followed as she pulled away.

"We're never gonna get close to her."

"Maybe after school tomorrow."

"So, what are we going to do when we get her? We can't just rip her clothes off and take a picture. We get caught, they'll throw the book at us."

"We'll get a little more personal. Put her in a frame of mind so she wants to do what we want her to do."

"I thought Billy was the only one insane enough to think he had magical powers."

"Shut up. Let's go by her house, see if she's the only one home. Maybe she'll invite us in."

"It's freezin' out here! She lives several blocks away, and last I looked, you don't have a car."

"Neither do you. Come on. Walkin' will warm us up."

"I don't know, man. I don't know if this is a good idea. After today, it's a good chance we'll get caught."

"Let's just get close to her, first, then we'll decide what to do about it."

Little Socks and Sassy Pants were safe, but they were cold, and their water was beginning to freeze. They didn't have the luxury of a litter box, so they made do by peeing on a blanket in a bathroom. It smelled and felt like it had been used before for the same reason. A lot.

Sassy Pants said, *"We cants be uppity ups bouts it. We gots to pee somewhere."*

Little Socks, still traumatized by having been in the bag for so long, let Sassy Pants take the lead on everything.

It had taken both of them working together for what seemed like hours to get the zipper open wide enough for her to leave the bag. They had to stop several times while Sassy Pants cautioned Little Socks to, *"Breve. Just breve. Mommy sezs you tinks better when you breve."*

They were locked in a building that had no apparent weak spots. Nothing they could break or pry loose to get out. All of the windows were covered with slick black stuff, so they couldn't see out, either. They had looked everywhere. Well, to be honest, Sassy Pants had looked everywhere. Little Socks could do little more than huddle near the cat food.

Sassy Pants thought she might have peed right there, too. But she couldn't say anything. That would be rude.

Sassy Pants, investigating the kitchen one more time, found a loose corner on the black stuff at the window over the sink. She poked her head underneath. Nothing looked familiar.

Sassy Pants thought about it. If they did get out, they didn't know where they were. They would never find home again. They would starve before anyone found them. There was only one mound of food in the bowl.

While the catnappers left enough food for a couple of days, the little girls were cats, and they were positive starvation was just around the corner.

Sassy Pants, after thinking for a very long time and trying to be brave, said, *"They has to be looking for us. Tiger Lily an everybody. They has to be."*

Little Socks couldn't think clearly, so she didn't answer.

"And Cyril. And Jock. They has to be looking, too."

Little Socks said nothing.

"We has to stay awake. We has to listen. They'll call to us."

Little Socks said nothing. She seemed to drop off to sleep suddenly.

"Is you okay?" screamed Sassy Pants. She pounded Little Socks on the haunches, then on the shoulder, then on the head.

Little Socks wouldn't wake up.

Sassy Pants did what she had seen both Jennifer and Marie do on occasion. She put her face close to Little Socks and satisfied herself that she was still breathing.

Sassy Pants had planned to sleep close to that window, so she could see when their rescuers arrived. Instead, she lay beside Little Socks, cuddling into her to keep her warm, trying as hard as she could not to fall apart herself.

Soon, she fell asleep, exhausted. She didn't hear Cyril and Jock barking down the street.

17

Pete had a full plate. Not only did he have the sexting case and the case of Annie's cats, but he was sure someone was stalking his daughter. Ginger denied having a problem, but he noticed tension in her face.

Three boys had been charged as adults. They would be able to bond out by this afternoon. Two other boys had been seen in the vicinity of his house. A neighbor, aware of the situation, noticed the boys and went to his porch, calling out to them, asking what they were doing. They ran. The neighbor called Pete with a description.

Pete thought the two matched the description of Marc and Justin, two of the school bullies. It wasn't enough to make an arrest.

Interviews with students and their parents were ongoing, as were the investigations into cell phone usage during each interview. Thankfully for Pete, county deputies and the state police managed most of the interviews and investigations.

Also, Cyril had come up missing while he questioned people on The Avenue. He had stayed out all night. Not only was Cyril missing, but Ray had called, saying Jock had run off.

Pete and Ray, knowing that nothing would keep breakfast from being served at the KaliKo Inn, arranged to meet Annie and Chris there at 8:00.

As he drove down The Avenue on this Friday morning, everything felt different. People moved down the street warily. Faces peered from buildings on both sides of the street, people taking careful note of the car and driver.

The new guests were served coffee, juices and breads again in the all-season porch. The Bartrams took up the entire dining room and enough food for four people. Maybe six.

The cats and Tillie were once again allowed free access to the house, but the exterior doors were locked and the cat doors were double barred. Except, of course, for the basement door that remained forgotten. They were wary of all the guests. Annie saw this and wondered about it, but she could hardly ask them what was going on.

Jerry had come over from Mr. Bean's to bring additional breads and to help serve. Trudie was here as well, helping Henrie in the kitchen and making sure refills were plentiful in the dining room and on the porch.

The Bartrams finished the fifth box of biscuits. One box remained.

Henrie sat at the kitchen table next to Annie and asked, "Do you believe the dogs have been taken as well?"

Pete answered quickly. "No. I think they're trying to find those cats."

Trudie and Jerry, eating breakfast at the end of the kitchen counter, gave one another a speculative glance. They said nothing but kept their ears tuned to the conversation.

Ray spoke up. "Cheryl heard a dog from this direction about the time Jock left The Marina. She looked around and didn't see him, so she went to the door and is positive she saw the tail end of him over here by the Inn."

Annie, still teary from time to time, said, "Not to speak ill of you or the police department, Pete, but if anyone can find them, it will be Cyril and Jock. I'm glad they're on the case."

Jerry and Trudie looked at one another again, then looked quickly back at their plates. Henrie turned in his seat and stared until they looked up again. He motioned, with his finger to his mouth, that they were to be silent about the matter.

Pete turned to Annie. "Jeff Bennett took a couple of days off. It appears the FBI doesn't want to be involved in catnappings, even with a ransom demand of a half million dollars. Anyway, he'll be here early this afternoon and will bring some surveillance equipment that we don't have access to. What are your thoughts about that ransom?"

Chris answered. "We've talked about it. It's a bad idea. A very bad idea. She could pay it and still never see the girls again. But she's adamant. I can come up with $250,000, but not $500,000. I left a message for my broker."

"And I left a message for Gwen. She gets to the office early, so I should hear from her soon. If I liquidate almost everything, I can come close to getting all of it. Chris shouldn't be doing this."

Ray said, "Liquidate? You mean sell the businesses?"

"Yes. What else do I have?"

"Annie, think clearly here. You can't sell everything, and even if you did, there is no way you would have that in cash by tonight."

"I don't have anything else, Ray. What else can I do?"

"Someone thinks you're rich. Who would think that?"

The five friends looked at one another. They said as one, "Geraldine."

Pete took a drink of coffee as he got up, picked up his radio and called for Marco. On his way out the door, they heard him say, "Meet me at the police station. We have a couple of interviews to do right away."

"Oh, my," said Annie. "Marco and Geraldine. That's an interview I would want to listen to."

A couple of months before, Geraldine had enrolled Marco in a scheme that left Marco nearly without a job and totally embarrassed. There was no love between the two of them. Annie assumed the other interview would be with Hank, another boil on the backside of Chelsea and a great friend and confidant of Geraldine.

The phone rang. Henrie picked it up. He handed it to Annie. "Your accountant, Gwen."

The cats and Tillie, sensing activity, ran down to the basement. Fat Cat and Scaredy Cat had arrived. Fat Cat sighed. *"We haven't found them yet."*

They were tired, cold and hungry. Tiger Lily insisted they be allowed to get warm, have something to eat and some water before asking them to talk. Scaredy Cat threw a grateful glance her way and headed to the water bowl. Fat Cat sat on the dog food bag to eat some kibbles. Kali, Ko, Mo and Mr. Bean danced around, impatient. Tillie was impatient as well, but she showed some reserve. This was unusual.

Finally, the two strays had refreshed themselves enough to speak. Fat Cat took the lead. Scaredy Cat threw in some snippets when she thought something had been left out.

"We thought we recognized a man and a woman on The Avenue, and we told Cyril we thought it might be the people at that restaurant that opened and closed real quick."

Tiger Lily looked confused. *"What restaurant?"*

"It had a big green door. It opened right about the time we got lost, and it was only open for a few weeks. No one ever came."

"The food was awful."

"Yeah. The food was awful, but there was always plenty for the trash, so we at least had food to eat for a while. Anyway, we took Cyril and that black dog, Jock, to the restaurant."

"They couldn't smell the cats, but that doesn't mean they aren't there. After all, they wouldn't have walked into the place. They would have been carried somehow."

"So we climbed up the railings and got to the second floor porch."

"Yeah. We tried to look inside, but all the windows are covered with black stuff."

"We called for them, but they didn't answer."

"But we're going to keep an eye on that place, just in case."

"What if it's the wrong place?"

"That's the thing. We talked to the dogs about this. This is a place where one of the couples could be, but maybe they had a house, too. And maybe this other couple that is staying here could be a problem, too."

"That young couple? The man and woman?"

"Yeah."

"*Not the two men?*"

"*No. A man and a woman.*"

Tillie spoke up. "*What about my humans? Those evil ones?*"

Tiger Lily looked at Tillie in surprise. "*Why would you say that?*"

"*They were trying to figure out how to get money for me, probably lots of money, but then they asked Annie how much she would sell you guys for. Maybe they decided to try to get money out of her by holding you guys for ransom.*"

Tiger Lily was now glad Kali and Ko had shared that information. She looked thoughtful. "*They put that note on the hostess stand, the one that made Mommy faint.*"

Choruses followed. "*What?*" "*Trill!*" "*Why didn't you say anything?*" "*How could you forget that?*"

Tiger Lily hung her head. "*It didn't seem important. They came to the Café and she leaned down and then put it there. She kind of looked around and said, 'Someone must have dropped this,' then they were seated. I should have thought about it.*"

Mo trilled.

Kali and Ko translated together, "*You can't think of everything.*" "*You remembered it now. That's okay.*"

Tiger Lily sighed, shook her head and sat up straighter. "*It's possible they wrote the note; it's also possible she was right, and it was on the floor. We have to keep an eye on them. Can anyone remember where they were when those calls came in?*"

"*Well,*" said Mr. Bean slowly, thinking it through, "*Mommy got that call from the catnappers last night, and those people were here in the house. It couldn't have been them.*"

They all thought about that for a while.

Kali and Ko said together, *"They could be partners."*

"There could be more people than just two."

Saddened at the amount of information to sift through, they sat, morosely, as the strays ate and drank some more.

Eventually, Fat Cat said, *"We have to get back out there."*

As they left, Mo called out, *"Trill!"*

"What?"

Kali said, *"He was being polite, something all of us forgot."*

Ko added, *"He said 'thank you.'"*

Tiger Lily, upset with her lack of manners, said, *"Yes. We all owe you a debt of gratitude."*

18

Ray returned to the The Marina. The marine carpenter he met yesterday was to give an estimate on repairs to The Escape. His name was Guy McNally, and he waited on deck.

"I saw it here, and thought I'd take a look before going into The Marina to get you."

"That's fine, Guy. I was running a little late. So, what do you think?"

"I think it's not in bad shape, but I need to go below to take a look inside. Is it okay?"

"Sure. Follow me."

Ray moved nimbly from place to place, but on occasion he had to turn to help Guy. "Not used to being on the boats yourself?"

Guy laughed. "That's why I have a crew. I'm great at crunching numbers, but swinging a hammer on a moving boat? Not on your life!"

Guy looked at everything. Even, thought Ray, things that would not have been in the least affected by the winter storm.

"Could you turn the engine on, let me listen? And then use some of these instruments?"

Ray, not loving much of anything to do with insurance companies and people trying to upsell him, grudgingly complied. Almost immediately, issues arose.

"Here," said Guy. "You took some damage to your sonar equipment. Something must have hit the boat from underneath."

The two listened to the hum of the motor some more, and Guy looked at everything. "Can you try the radio?"

"Sure." Ray picked up the handset and tried to raise Cheryl inside. She didn't respond. He tried again with the same result. He used his cellphone and got an immediate response.

"Hey, can you get to the radio? I'm trying to raise you."

"I'm in the radio room. I've been here all morning."

"You didn't hear me?"

"No. Try it again."

With Cheryl still on the phone, Ray tried again. The radio was dead in the water.

The contractor finished his review and sat at a table in The Marina to work on his quote.

Ray and Cheryl were astonished at the amount. It was over $200,000. At the bottom of the page was the damage due upon hire. Thirty-five percent, over $70,000.

"Um, I think I need to get another quote."

"You can do that, but remember, the insurance company is going to pay, so you won't be out anything. Matter of fact, once I get started, they'll pay you for everything, so you only have to front the down payment, the retainer. You'll get it back. This company has a quick turn-around time."

"Maybe I'd better call…"

"Good idea. Here. I have Ms. Stiles' business card."

Guy fished around in his wallet until he came up with a much-used insurance company card, personalized with Cindy's name, photograph, telephone number and email.

"This doesn't look like the number I called."

"It's probably not. This is Cindy's cell phone number. Call that, or call the company. She'll call you right back."

Ray called Cindy's number. The call rolled into voice mail, but she returned it immediately. "I'm so sorry, Ray. I was in a meeting. Did you get together with Guy?"

"I did. The price is pretty steep." Ray went over the quotation with Cindy, and his request for a down payment.

"That won't be a problem, Ray. Just fax a copy of that quotation over to me. Do you need that number?" She gave it to Ray. "Once he gets his down payment, he'll confirm to us that he's on the job, and you'll have that check within seven business days."

Ray hung up and looked at Guy. "I can have that for you tomorrow, if that's okay?"

"Sure, Ray. I can drop by, pick it up, and we'll get to work on it as soon as my crew is finished on the job they're doing now."

"I have to go to the bank. Want to meet me at Tiger Lily's Café when I get it? I'll treat you to breakfast."

"Well, tomorrow's pretty tight for me. Why don't I meet you here. Won't take but a minute that way."

People in Chelsea were caught up in a flurry of activity that day.

Pete spent time on the telephone with the district attorney regarding the ongoing findings. And he worried about Ginger. And Cyril. And the cats.

Ray and Cheryl met with the bank to get an unsecured loan to get started on The Escape. And they worried about Jock. And the cats.

Marco worked with county and state officers while they continued interviews in the sexting case. And he worried about the cats.

Chris went to Marsh Haven to pick up a bearer bond for $250,000. And he worried about the cats.

Annie met with Gwen to come up with as much as she could. And she cried about the cats. And cried.

Terrence and Jerald borrowed the car from the Inn to tour the lakeshore. They asked permission to have the car all day and Henrie granted it. They planned to visit some lighthouses to the south and have a late lunch at a highly-rated restaurant.

Nathanial and Joline asked for the car but were told it was already in use. They seemed unsure what to do with themselves. Henrie told them there were many places of interest, gift shops and restaurants, within walking distance, but they decided to spend the day in their room, watching movies from the Inn's library.

Henrie wondered again why they bothered to pay for the lodging. And he worried about the cats.

The Bartrams were wherever the Bartrams got off to. Sometimes Henrie thought they just left to go sit in a car for the day. They were odd people.

The cats and Tillie were under lock and key again. At least they had the run of the Inn. And no one found the unlocked cat door. Yet. Tiger Lily warned all of them to use it only in an emergency, so they would not be discovered. The door might have to stay open all winter for Fat Cat and Scaredy Cat.

Henrie and Hilly worked together to clean up the dining room, all-season porch, kitchen and bedrooms. When the telephone rang, Henrie was cleaning a toilet in the front bedroom. He let it go to voicemail.

Soon, Hilly shouted up the stairs. "Henrie, whoever called said Annie was hurt!"

Henrie rushed to a phone and hit the message button. It was Felicity. Annie had been found in an alley on Main Street. She had been knocked cold and her billfold taken. Marie was there with the ambulance and they would probably take her to the hospital.

"Hilly, can you stay?"

"Certainly. I'll lock the doors, and I'll put the safety catches on. Even the guests will have to ring the doorbell."

"Thank you. Keep those cats safe!"

Henrie got the Inn's SUV out of the garage and sped up The Avenue, honking the horn at the corner so Felicity would know he was on the way. As he rounded the corner, the ambulance hit the gas in front of him, siren blaring. Henrie kept up. No way was Annie going to go into that hospital all by herself. As they left the town limits, Henrie heard sirens behind as well. Pete. Well, Pete was just going to have to follow him. He wasn't going to pull over.

At the hospital, everyone jumped out, Marie first, running to the back to get the stretcher. Hospital attendants ran to help. Henrie was just able to look at Annie, meet her eyes and assure himself she was at least alive. She gave him a very weak smile.

Henrie stood back, backing into Pete and Marco.

Marco asked, "Did she have the ransom money on her?"

"I cannot imagine she did. She had an appointment with Gwen. Gwen is her accountant. She is not the bank."

Marco opined, "I wonder if some idiot thought she would be leaving with money?"

Pete looked at him, then down at his with a shake of his head.

Henrie asked, "Has anyone talked to Gwen?"

Pete answered, "Officers are there now. We'll hear soon what she has to say."

"Who found her?"

"You don't know?"

"No. I thought the police would know."

Pete looked at Marco. "I guess one of us needs to get back to town and start a proper investigation. Marco, take the car. I'll ride back with Henrie." Pete looked at Henrie. "Let's go in and see how our girl is doing."

"I must make two calls first. I doubt my cell phone will work inside the hospital."

Henrie made the first call, the easiest call, to Felicity, who would text the information to everyone on The Avenue. Annie had made eye contact. He assured Felicity he would call as soon as he knew anything more.

Then he made the hard call. He called Chris, who picked up his phone while still in Marsh Haven.

"Chris, this is Henrie. Do not return to Chelsea. Join me at the emergency room."

"What's wrong?"

"Please, just come. I will tell you as soon as I see you."

Henrie heard a click, and he walked slowly to join Pete in the waiting room.

Ginger was ready for another day of cold shoulders and stalking at school, but after the first period class, James finally stepped up.

"I'm sorry. I've not been a good friend. Let me hang with you. If people are going to stalk you or call you names, they'll have to go through me."

As Ginger left a class, James waited. He walked with her, arms interlocked, from class to class, followed closely by Marc, Justin, or both of them. They endured stares and some catcalling, particularly from Shellie and her friends.

Ignoring everyone else as they walked, they caught up on gossip.

After one class, James said, "I hear Billie, Porter and Dallas were charged in adult court. They'll bond out this afternoon."

"I heard that, too. I also heard they would be waiting for me and I'll never know when they'll come at me."

"Why haven't you asked your dad to protect you?"

"I can't do that. I can't play into their 'Little Miss Piggy' perceptions."

"Well, I think you need to talk to him. Maybe I'll do it for you."

"No you won't!"

After another class, James told her, "I heard Lia swallowed a bunch of bills from her mother's medicine cabinet."

"No! Is she alright?"

"I just heard she was in the hospital."

At lunch time, their conversation veered into the worst of the sexting situation.

"Do you know Pam? The junior high girl? Dallas's sister?"

"I just know who she is."

"She's a friend of Ava. Ava told me last night that Pam wasn't in school yesterday, and they don't expect her back."

"Are her folks going to home school her?"

"They're sending her to live with an aunt and uncle."

"It's like she's the one being punished."

After yet another class, Ginger shared a thought with James. "You know, the other day at the mall, Lia was laughing with everyone else at what was probably Penny's picture. She was already embarrassed about her own. Why do you think she would laugh at another girl? A girl that didn't want her picture taken?"

James didn't have an answer.

And so the day went.

As the day wore on with only brief conversations with the doctor, Henrie, Chris and Pete began to fray at the edges.

Pete knew he should be in Chelsea, taking care of the ongoing investigations. Marco called, alerting him to the presence of Jeff Bennett. Marco brought Jeff up to speed on everything, including the sexting case, to make sure all avenues were covered.

He also told Pete what they knew of the mugging. Not much. According to Gwen, there was nothing Annie could do to raise all the money – or even half, to match what Chris could give – with the possible exception of borrowing money, using her businesses as collateral.

Having made calls to every bank in the region, no one was willing to give her that kind of money today, no matter what the reason. Possibly, after a financial investigation, they would be able to give her some. Annie's cash on hand amounted to tens of thousands, not hundreds of thousands.

Annie left the office, disappointed and fearful she would never see the girls again.

Gwen didn't have anything to add to help the police department. Her assistant, Minnie, reacting to someone running in front of the window, stepped out to the sidewalk. She saw nothing, but was compelled, for some reason, to look in the alley. She found Annie and called nine-one-one using her cell phone. Minnie didn't see anything that would be descriptive of the runner.

A hole burned in Chris's pocket in the form of a $250,000 bearer bond. Since Annie had been mugged, he feared a connection with the catnapping and wondered if his money would help get the girls home.

Henrie was so worried about Annie, he almost forgot to worry about his duties at the Inn. He had just thought to call Hilly when his phone rang.

"Henrie, this is Hilly. Those catnappers called. They were supposed to tell Annie how to get the money to them."

"Oh, my word. Oh, my word. Good gracious me. How could we forget?"

Pete took the phone, as Henrie was making no sense. "What's going on?"

"Those catnappers called. I didn't know what to tell them. I said Annie was at the hospital. They said they would give me a half hour to get things together and they would call back."

Chris could hear Hilly and he said, "I'm on my way, Hilly. I'm leaving now."

"I'm going with Chris," said Pete, handing Henrie the telephone.

They rushed off. Henrie, holding the phone, could hear Hilly saying, "Henrie? Henrie?"

"Oh, yes, Hilly, I quite forgot myself. I am supposed to be taking care of the guests. There is the matter of the afternoon snack, and, um, I do not know what else."

"Now Henrie, you just stop, right there. I didn't know how to handle the ransom situation, but I certainly know how to take care of people. I called Felicity about an hour ago and she brought over some finger sandwiches and fresh fruit. And I've gone through the pantry and fridge to make sure things are on hand for breakfast. So everything is fine here. How is Annie?"

"I do not know yet."

"It's been so long."

"I know. They are not forthcoming with information. I should probably call her mother."

"Don't you dare. Don't you call her until you know something."

"You are probably right. How are the cats?"

"They're fine. They are up and down, up and down, up and down. I guess if we used the stairs more often ourselves, we'd be a lot healthier."

Henrie, in his mind's eye, saw the cats going up and down the main stairs, to the second and perhaps the third floor. Hilly had not thought to say the basement stairs were the ones in question.

Sassy Pants woke with a start. What had she just heard? Was it possible? She shook Little Socks, who didn't respond right away. She jumped onto the kitchen counter, poked her face under the plastic and yowled as loudly as she could. She yowled, and yowled again.

Then she heard it. Barks! Barks! She heard barks! And yowling! The cats were here!

Little Socks heard it, too. Finally roused from her stupor, she joined Sassy Pants on the counter and added her voice to the chorus. Her voice was more scared than Sassy Pants could have imagined.

Soon, they were looking through the window at two beautiful dog faces! Cyril and Jock pranced around, looking for a way in!

19

Henrie was there when she opened her eyes.

"Henrie. How are you?"

"How are you? You are the one in the hospital bed."

"Oh, it's just a little boo-boo. That's all. How are my kids? Oh! My kids!"

Annie tried to sit up. Henrie held her down.

"Where are they, Henrie? Are they home?"

"Not yet, Annie, not yet. Chris is taking care of it."

"I didn't get the money! How is he going to take care of it?"

Henrie wanted to alert a nurse, but one came in, responding to the monitor.

"She is worried about her cats. Can you calm her down?"

"Let's just turn up this drip a little bit. That will calm her down. Annie? Breathe deeply. We can't have you getting so excited."

Annie tried to take some deep breaths. Henrie breathed with her, talking as he did so.

"Chris was able to get half of it."

"He paid it? Chris paid for my babies?"

"He is at the Inn, tending to payment and delivery instructions."

"He didn't get them?"

"Not yet. You know how this works. They get the money, then they tell us where to pick them up."

The county sheriff came into the room. "Henrie, if Annie's up to it, let me ask her some questions."

Henrie moved to the side, keeping hold of Annie's hand, while the sheriff moved into view.

"Annie, what's the last thing you remember?"

"Leaving Gwen's office. And then falling down."

"Do you remember falling down first, or being hit on the head first?"

Annie got a puzzled look on her face. "I was hit on the head?"

"Yes."

"By the people that took my babies?"

"We don't know that yet."

"Well, who else would do that?"

"We don't know that either."

Annie could barely keep her eyes open. "Do you know anything?"

"We're pretty much in the dark about everything, Annie, but we're working on it. Your friend Jeff Bennett is here, too." The sheriff and Jeff had worked together before, on a case involving the Inn.

Annie shook her head to stay awake. "The FBI is looking for my cats?"

"Well, Jeff is looking for your cats."

Annie was losing the battle to stay awake. "That's good enough. Thank you, Sheriff."

"Is there anything you can tell me, Annie?"

"Scruffy shoes."

"Scruffy shoes?"

"Scruffy, dirty tennis shoes."

Annie closed her eyes and didn't open them again for a couple of hours.

After the last class of the day, James headed for his locker, knowing Ginger would wait for him there. He walked around the corner and ran into two large male bodies. Marc and Justin.

"Where ya goin', towelhead?"

"Just let me pass."

"No, I don't think so. You see, we number one don't like towelheads in Chelsea, and B, we don't like towelheads takin' up with our ladies, black or white."

"I didn't realize I had taken up with a girlfriend of yours," said James, as he tried to walk around.

Marc stepped in front of him. "We asked politely. Where ya goin'?"

James turned to walk the other way.

Justin moved to cut him off. Now they were in close quarters, one on either side. "He asked you a question. Politely."

"I'm not going to answer. Now excuse me."

Once again, James tried to move around them, but before he could react, Marc had an arm around his head, hand over his mouth, and an arm around his chest, holding one arm tight. Justin grabbed his legs. With just one arm to defend himself, James was at their mercy.

They took him into an empty bathroom.

Ginger waited for James at his locker. He didn't come. As the halls emptied, students heading for buses, cars and other ways home, she became worried.

She approached the nearest classroom and asked the teacher, Mrs. Hobbs, if she had seen James.

"Why, no, Ginger. Maybe he's already gone home."

"He wouldn't leave me," said Ginger. "Maybe he's hurt somewhere."

Ginger was beginning to panic. Her breath came fast; she clutched at her chest. Mrs. Hobbs took her into the classroom and called the principal.

He came at a fast walk, and Ginger told him her concerns, that the two boys, Marc and Justin, had been stalking her, that James had been escorting her from class to class and he would have waited for her. He would have waited.

The principal called the office from the telephone in the classroom. Then he called nine-one-one. Over the school's intercom, the calm voice of the office administrator asked each administrator, teacher and custodian to look around to see if a student was sick. This was code for, "Lock the building; lock your offices. No one enters; no one leaves; look for a student in trouble."

James was found in the second floor east bathroom, beaten and unconscious.

Marco's car arrived, sirens and lights going, about the same time James was found. As he pulled into the lot, he noticed two teenaged boys running. They were in the distance, and they ran in the other direction, but Marco recognized them. Justin and Marc. They got out of the building before the lockdown.

Pete said nothing on what seemed to be the longest ride to Chelsea he had ever taken. Never mind Chris was driving thirty miles over the limit. Never mind that he would have some 'splainin' to do if they blew past flashing red lights. Thank goodness, they saw no police on their way.

They tore into the kitchen door just as the phone rang. Hilly, shocked at their entrance, reached for it, but Chris held up his hand, took a deep breath, picked it up and said, "KaliKo Inn."

Pete listened to Chris's side of the conversation. "I have half what you requested." …. "That's what I have. We turned everything we could into cash, and we have a quarter of a million dollars." …. "I have it with me."

Chris's eyes closed, and he slowly put the phone in the cradle. "They hung up."

Pete's eyes closed as well, and Hilly had a sharp intake of breath.

"They'll call back." As he said it, Pete hoped with all his heart it would be true.

Pete heard Hilly say, "Excuse me," and she left the room. In the kitchen, he leaned on one counter, eyes on Chris. Chris leaned on another counter, head in his hands. He heard Hilly say, "It's good to see you back. I hope you had a great drive today." A southern drawl answered, "We surely did. This is pretty country. The snow makes it look like some kind of wonderland." "Well, we certainly think so. Please, help yourself to curried shrimp and fresh fruit. You'll find it in the refrigerator. Oh, before I forget, Henrie would probably ask for the car keys." Silence. Then a different voice, another southern drawl, "Ma'am, we were just up the street getting this wine. When we returned with the car, oh, about an hour ago, that other couple asked if they could take it. We didn't think there would be a problem?" "Oh, I'm sure it's fine. Anyway, help yourself to shrimp." "Are you okay, ma'am?" "I'm fine. Well, we're just waiting on a call…"

The telephone rang again. Chris picked it up. "KaliKo Inn." …. "Good." …. "I'll make the delivery." …. "Yes, I'll be alone." …. "When and where?" …. He replaced the cradle again. "They said they'd get back with me."

"When?"

"They didn't say."

Pete didn't have time to respond. He picked up his cell phone and listened while an excited dispatcher told him about James, and Ginger, and Marco's information about two boys running away from school. While he listened, he took off on the run. He'd have to get to the police station to get another car. He was going after those boys. Now he could arrest them.

Laila forced a calm demeanor onto herself and stepped into Annie's hospital room. She touched Henrie gently on the shoulder and pressed. He awoke, hand still on top of Annie's. She remained asleep. Or knocked out.

Laila motioned for Henrie to follow her into the hallway. "How is she?"

"She woke only one time. They are watching her for concussion. She has some scrapes and bruises. I am sorry, Laila. They are allowing only family now, and they placed me in that category. They will not allow you to stay."

"I'm here for another reason, Henrie." She took him by the arm and led him to the open door of the room next door. Henrie looked in and saw James.

"My word! What happened?"

Laila explained the details as she knew them. "He's in pain, but there were no broken bones. Probably a concussion."

"And Ginger?"

"She stayed with a teacher until her mother got to the school. I understand she is home under lock and key right now. Pete threatened to withdraw her college fund and spend it on a boat if she left the house."

"I assume that worked."

"I believe it did. Now he's out looking for those boys. He might not be able to charge them with stalking, but they'll be charged with this. James woke up long enough to tell Marco who did it."

"Forgive me for not thinking of this in the first place. Who is with Ava and Carl?"

"Jolly. And Teresa said she'd be over just as soon as she could. She's packing a bag to stay, and she expects both of us to go home and sleep in our own beds tonight."

"How can I possibly…"

"Sleep. Right. You need it, and half the town is depending on you. I need it, and my children – all of them – depend on me. Teresa said…"

"I do not care…"

"Yes, you do. Annie will be fine. If you have to, wait long enough to see her open her eyes again."

"That could be forever…"

"She's in a hospital, and she needs her sleep. Those two things are enough to guarantee a nurse will be in every ninety minutes to wake her up."

Pete made the rounds. He was becoming familiar with these boys and their families. He knew he would find the most sympathetic ear with Justin's parents.

Professionals, Justin's father worked at an accounting firm in Marsh Haven, and his mother worked as a loan officer at the local bank. An older brother would graduate from engineering school in a couple of months, and a sister was in medical school. The parents were perplexed at the continued inexplicable behavior on the part of their youngest child.

No, they had not seen Justin since he left for school that morning, but if Pete could please charge him with something, perhaps it would be a turning point. And, they wanted to know, why hadn't he been charged with that sexting situation?

"That was out of my hands, ma'am. I presented the paperwork to the prosecutor, and he declined to press charges. If it had been up to me, and pardon me for saying it, he'd be at the county jail charged as an adult right now."

"Well, I hope you find him. And Chief, we're really sorry for what he's doing to your daughter."

Pete's next stop was at Marc's house. Marc's father was long missing from the home, and Marc's mother was about as useless as it came to being a parent. Pete stood in the doorway as his mother cried elephant tears. He walked through the living room and into the kitchen as she continued to cry. He sat at the table with her as she cried and blew her nose – many times – into tissues that had been used and used again.

Pete asked if he could look around, just make sure Marc wasn't there.

Through sobs and tears, she replied, "Go ahead…just go ahead…I hope you find him…I can't do anything with him…his dad left me…."

Pete didn't find him and asked that she call if he came home. He knew what would happen. Marc would come home and would bully his mother into not calling.

His next stop was at the home of Dallas and his family. Dallas, bonded out of jail, sat in the living room with his father. His father was surrounded by beer bottles. His mother was not there. Pete pressed Dallas about Justin and Marc.

"Have you seen them?" "No."

"Have you heard from them?" "No."

"Do you plan to see them?" "No."

"Where's your mother?" "What's that got to do with anything?"

Pete turned to the nearly comatose father. "Sir, where's your wife?"

"None-a-your bizness."

"Sir, I can make it my business. I'm searching for two felons."

"She leff."

"When will she be home?"

The father had finally passed out. Pete turned to Dallas. "When will she be home?"

"She took that prissy little sister of mine to live with Aunt Phyllis. And she stayed. Sent Uncle Jack to get her stuff. She ain't comin' back."

Good for her, thought Pete, as he walked out the door.

He went next to Porter's house. His mother answered the knock on the door. She was drunk. Or stoned. Pete thought it was drunk. "Have you seen…"

"Get outa my house, pig."

"Ma'am…"

"Out!" She turned to shout at someone, probably her husband, "The pig is here, an' he won't leave!"

A man, drunker than the woman, stumbled to the door. "Outahere, pig."

"Have you seen…"

"No!"

The door slammed in his face.

One last home. The leader. Billy. Pete did not conduct the interviews with this family, and he didn't see them come and go. This could be interesting. He knocked on the door. A woman, slope-shouldered, answered. Clear-eyed, but the look of defeat was written all over.

"Ma'am, I'm looking for a couple friends of your son, their names are Justin and Marc."

In a soft voice, she said, "Knew you'd be here sooner or later. Get some help and go round the back, to the basement door. Sorry about what I'm gonna do now." She stood up taller and said in a loud voice, "We ain't seen nobody here tonight, Chief. You get on out of here, now. Go!"

Pete stayed in his car, around the corner and out of sight. When Marco arrived with another officer, they walked through back yards until they got to the basement door. Pete sent the officer to the front door to knock again, and to demand entry. When Justin and Marc ran out the basement door, they ran right into two large men and two sets of handcuffs.

Chris didn't want to do this alone. With Pete gone, he called Ray to come over. While they waited for the call, the Bartrams were a loud presence in the coffee corner and foyer. They complained about the sandwiches (too small, no flavor, the bread was stale) and the fruit (can't you find some fruit in season?).

Chris, anxious already, was cheered to hear Hilly's response. "You are the rudest, the crudest and the most boorish people to ever visit the town of Chelsea. No one can stand to be around you!"

Hilly had stormed into the kitchen, a twinkle in her eye. "Henrie would never have allowed that, but it felt good!"

Finally, the call came. Chris wrote the instructions as he listened.

"Put the suitcase inside a black trash bag. It has to be black. Go to the intersection of..." Chris gave the paper to Ray, who went into the basement stairwell to make the call to Jeff. "Put the suitcase on the northwest corner, close to the road … Leave. After we pick it up, we'll call again, tell you where you can find those cats."

"It's windy out there. The money will blow away."

"What? That suitcase isn't going anywhere."

"I don't actually have a suitcase. I can put it in a black trash bag. But I don't have a suitcase."

"You're carrying that cash around in your pocket?"

"Well, yes, actually, I am. It's a bearer bond."

"A what?"

"A bearer bond. One piece of paper."

"What kind of trick are you trying to pull?"

"You didn't specify how the money was to be delivered. My bank gave me a bearer bond."

"We want cash."

"This is cash. Kind of. Any bank has to honor it, no matter where you go. No matter what state, what country. A bearer bond is just like having a two hundred fifty thousand dollar bill."

Chris waited while the phone on the other end was muffled. Apparently, the catnappers didn't know how to deal with this wrinkle.

Finally, the voice was back on the line. "Okay. Put it in the black bag and put it at that intersection." The caller hung up.

Ray had been in the kitchen for most of the rest of the call. As Chris hung up, he gave the thumbs-up sign. Chris walked out the kitchen door, stopping at the pantry long enough to pull out a black trash bag.

He left town slowly and carefully, driving the speed limit. When he got out of town and into the country, he drove a little under the limit, keeping his eye out for deer that might cross the road in the near dark.

He approached the intersection slowly, looking around as much as possible without moving his head. He was looking for Jeff, who, hopefully, was able to set up his surveillance equipment, trained on this intersection. The intersection, unfortunately, was flat and clear for a half mile in most directions, and a quarter mile in one. He pulled as far off the road as he could. This was as busy an intersection as could be found in the country. It was busy enough to demand four-way stop signs.

The northwest corner fronted a cornfield. No fences. Chris moved his feet around, looking for a rock under the snow, or anything that could weigh the black bag down. With the wind tonight, it would blow away if he didn't find... Finally, his toe felt something hard. He got onto his hands and knees and dug around a medium sized rock. It wouldn't budge. It was frozen into the ground.

Chris cursed under his breath, then went to the trunk and pulled out the crowbar. He took the bag from the passenger seat, put it on the corner, close to the road, and put the crowbar on top. If nothing else, his attempts to find a weight would have given Jeff some additional time. If Jeff was out there.

On the way back to the Inn, Chris answered his phone. "Sorry, man. Closest I could get with cover was a quarter mile. My equipment isn't good at that distance. They chose their spot well."

Henrie returned to the Inn shortly after Chris returned from delivering the money. The only way Henrie could calm himself was to keep busy. He thanked Hilly profusely and sent her home. He went to the freezer and returned with two armfuls of frozen dinners from the Café. With Chris's help, he heated the meals to serve to themselves, Ray, and Jeff, who was now a guest, registered in the back room on the ground floor level.

Tillie came into the kitchen and hopped around for a few seconds, getting his attention. "Yes, my pretty girl. Let me find your leash."

"I've got it, Henrie," said Chris. "I took her out earlier. I'll take her again."

Henrie noticed that Chris picked up the handheld receiver on his way out of the kitchen. His crutch. He would not let go of it unless the battery started to die.

Ray said his farewells and Jeff went to the back room, exhausted.

Henrie puttered around in the kitchen, and then in the dining room, where he overheard a conversation from the foyer between Chris, on his way in with Tillie, and one of the men from the south. A low southern drawl clued him to this identity.

"My name is Jerald Timmer-Schmidt. And you are?"

"Chris. Pleased to meet you."

"Chris. I know you're a friend of Annie's, and I know, just from being around town, that she was, well, I guess 'mugged' is the right word for it. Tell me, is she doing alright?"

"Yes, thank you. But she's still in the hospital."

"I, well, Terrence and I, are very sorry to hear that. And we know about the other situation. We were at the Café when she got that note. Dreadful. Just dreadful."

"Thank you."

"Well, I don't want to bother you, but, please, if there is anything we can do...anything at all...please let us know. We've gotten to know some of the people here, at the Inn and in town, and, well, it's a lovely place. Lovely. We're just heartsick for you."

Sometime later, Henrie walked the downstairs, picking detritus from the tables, emptying trash. He looked in the library. Chris was sound asleep, surrounded by five cats and Tillie, with the receiver still in his hand. Henrie got a comforter and placed it over Chris, being careful to tuck it so that cats and dog were not disturbed.

Pete slipped out of bed. Janet was used to his comings and goings all hours of the day and night and didn't wake. He checked the rooms of their younger daughters, then looked in on Ginger. She was asleep, thank goodness.

Marc and Justin were in the county jail, but would probably only face juvenile charges. Three boys, now charged as adults, were bonded out and, according to Ginger this evening, had made threats against her.

And where was Cyril? There had been sightings of a big brown and white dog and a big black dog, together and all over town. They were on the move. On one street. On another corner. On the other side of town. For some reason, they were roaming. At least reports put the two dogs together. Cyril was not alone.

Pete, still unable to sleep, lay down to get what rest he could.

The cats slipped away in the wee hours of the morning. Fat Cat and Scaredy Cat, unable to wake them by scratching at the library door, had come upstairs. They slipped quietly around until they found them in the library, hissed softly, and led them downstairs.

"We found them."

"Where?" "Are they okay?" "What do we need to do?"

Tiger Lily shushed them all. *"Let Fat Cat and Scaredy Cat tell us what they know!"*

They shut up, but still pranced, nervously, around the two stray cats.

"They're in a little house on the north side of town. Nobody lives there."

"How did you find them?"

"It was a team effort. We roamed through town, calling out on every block. Cyril and Jock did the same thing, barking, like dogs bark. We'd been all through town, but Cyril said we had to do it again, block by block."

"Mostly we split up, to cover more ground, but a little bit ago we were in the same area, us calling and them barking, and then we heard it. They called back."

"Why didn't you bring them back?"

"We looked and looked but couldn't find a way to get them out. They've been looking, too, but they're locked in tight."

Fat Cat looked Tiger Lily straight in the eye. *"We have to get them out of there. Those people are gone."*

"Gone? But they haven't told Chris how to get them back!"

"They aren't coming back."

"But…"

"They're gone."

"Maybe they're just driving around…"

"No. Sassy Pants heard them talking. They were supposed to share the money with some other people, but they had already decided that when they got the money, they would just leave."

"Leave, and let them starve to death in that house?"

"They aren't starving yet. There's food. They don't have a litter pan, so they're peeing on a blanket. They say it stinks and they can't stand it."

"But at some point they'll starve."

"And it's cold in the house. There isn't any heat, and the water that was left for them is frozen."

"What are we going to do?"

"The dogs have a plan."

"A plan?"

"Yeah. They're real tired and hungry. They caught a squirrel to eat, and they're resting on the porch of that house. When they feel better, they're going to go to Cyril's house and wake Pete up. They're going to figure out some way to get Pete to follow them."

"We're going to go back and stay with Little Socks and Sassy Pants, so they aren't alone."

Mr. Bean said, "I'm going too!"

Tiger Lily gave him a stern rebuke. "No you aren't! You're going to stay right here! Mommy's been hurt and she *doesn't need you to be running all over the place! There's nothing you can do. Cyril and Jock will figure it out."*

Mr. Bean seemed to consider this, and then said, *"Oh, alright."*

Mo gave a *"Trill."*

The stray cats in unison said, *"What?"*

Kali and Ko said together, *"He wants to go, too, but he'll stay." "He knows we have to stay here."*

The cats nodded to one another, then the strays left.

20

It was Saturday, typically an active day at the Inn. Henrie generally prepared early breakfast for guests who had plans for the day. Early breakfast was prepared, and everyone ate, but no one moved.

Henrie put a complete breakfast on the porch using the credenza on the back wall. The sun couldn't quite get up past the clouds, and Henrie had to turn on the lights. Weather reports promised more snow today, not as much as before, but enough to prompt caution on the roads.

Eventually, Terrence and Jerald came down for breakfast. They served themselves on the porch, happy to escape even the briefest encounter with the Bartrams. Nathanial and Joline had not yet come downstairs, but Chris and Jeff joined them on the porch.

Henrie came in to make sure the group had enough of everything. Jerald asked Henrie about Annie. Henrie was, for once, unable to speak. Jeff took over. "Henrie, go do what you need to do; we'll fill them in."

Once again, Trudie and Jerry were on hand to help, making Henrie's life tolerable. They took the brunt of everything – criticisms, commands and sarcasm – from the Bartrams, leaving Henrie to sit and eat breakfast in the kitchen. He could have joined the group on the porch, but he wanted to be alone.

He watched as Trudie opened the sixth and final box of biscuits. Tomorrow the Bartrams were checking out. He would make sure they received a special gift.

Henrie and Chris both called the hospital, getting the same information from Laila. Annie had a peaceful night, and the doctor was hopeful she might be able to come home late this afternoon. Laila and James planned to leave earlier, maybe mid-afternoon. Laila, when told the cats had not been returned, said, "I'm not going to tell her that." Then she hung up.

Pete tried to sleep in, but about the time the sun would have risen, if only the clouds would roll away, he woke to a dog alarm clock. Cyril was on the front lawn with Jock, raising a ruckus. Pete stuck his head out the door to see them cavorting in the yard, lights coming on in house after house in the neighborhood.

They looked tired, hungry and filthy. They saw Pete, ran toward the porch, turned and ran toward the street, turned and ran toward the porch, turned and ran toward they street. There, they stopped and barked for him to follow.

"Get in here, right now. I'll follow you, but I have to get dressed, and you need food and water."

The dogs looked at one another and jumped to the porch to go in.

Pete yelled at Janet, to "Please feed those dogs; I have to get dressed." While he dressed, he called Ray, who also dressed and jumped into his truck. Pete called Marco, and after thinking about it, Jeff Bennett.

Jeff took the call during breakfast, rose without finishing and said to Chris, "I don't know what's happening, but those dogs are back, and they want Pete to go somewhere."

"I'm coming."

"You're staying. Someone has to be here in case they call about the cats."

"Henrie can do that."

"Well, then, come on!"

Alistair and Cressida had finished breakfast and were on their way out the door. Chris and Jeff nearly collided with the them.

"You oaf! Watch where you're going!"

"I'm sorry, Mrs. Bartram. We're just in a hurry. We might have news of the cats."

Alistair and Cressida stood still, watching them run down the walk to Jeff's vehicle.

Alistair walked back to the all-season porch. When he saw Terrence and Jerald, he asked, "What did you do with the cats?"

Surprised to have been asked a question by this man, Terrence took a second to reply. "What? The cats? Nothing. I think they're around here somewhere."

"I mean the other two cats."

"Excuse me? I think…"

Jerald cut in, "Do you think we had something to do with…"

Alistair realized his mistake. "I'm so sorry. Very confused. Tell me, where is the young couple? Did they have breakfast already?"

"They haven't come downstairs yet."

Jerald added, "They must have gotten back late. They're probably still in bed."

"Back late? But didn't you have the car?"

"Yes, but they took it when we got back."

"About what time was that?"

The men looked at one another. "I don't really know," said Jerald slowly. "We had lunch about a half hour from here, we got back maybe 3:00?"

Terrence added, "I'm not sure. It could have been later."

Alistair thought a minute, then asked, "Were you here when the ransom call came in?"

"Yes," they said together. Jerald added, "At least, they said they were waiting for a call, then the telephone rang, and, well, things got pretty busy."

Alistair walked out and went upstairs. He knocked on the door of the guest room facing the lake but received no answer. Downstairs once again, he and Cressida looked at one another, eyes wide, faces white, as they sank into two nearby chairs in the foyer.

"We should go on to the meeting as planned," said Alistair.

"Yes. You're right. Let's go on. After all, we can't be sure." replied Cressida, in the softest voice she had used at the Inn.

Pete took the dogs in his car to the police station, where he met Marco, Ray, Jeff and Chris. "Chris, Ray, I really need to make you reserve officers, but until I get around to doing that, just don't get yourselves hurt."

"No problem. What's the plan?"

"Well, I'm not sure where we're headed. I think, since we're in town, that I'll just let the dogs loose, but we don't know where we're going, so I'll drive behind them. You all can walk or ride."

Jeff said, "I'll follow in my own car. Might need two."

Ray agreed. "Might need three. Chris, come with me."

The dogs knew what to do. They took off at a run, stopping to look back every now and then to be sure the vehicles still followed. They went east on the highway until they reached Linden, then they turned north and headed to the farthest part of the business section. They turned left, and after a couple of blocks, turned left again. They stopped in front of a vacant house and scratched at an already much-scratched door. The dogs barked as if they had cornered a raccoon in a tree. Of course, neither of them were coon dogs, but they knew what coon dogs did. And fox hounds.

Pete recognized the neighborhood. Most of the bully boys lived nearby. He ordered Ray and Chris to stay in the vehicle. He, Marco and Jeff approached the house carefully, guns drawn. Marco and Jeff went wide, around the sides and toward the back. Pete went straight on. He could hear Little Socks and Sassy Pants, howling as if they were burning in hot oil. Then he saw them, standing in a window. Looked like black plastic in front of the window, but they got in between. Good for them.

He pounded on the door and identified himself as a police officer. He got no answer.

The house was small, only one story. Pete returned to his vehicle to get a battering ram from his trunk. Marco and Pete rammed the door once. It didn't move, but the cats jumped off the windowsill and vanished. Twice. Some headway. Three times. The door broke open.

Little Socks hurled herself at Pete, causing him to drop the ram. She scrambled to his shoulder and hung on for dear life, as if he might decide to leave her. Sassy Pants sauntered out the door as if she owned the house.

Chris, out of the vehicle but keeping next to it, almost as ordered, noticed two cats at the side of the house. They seemed anxious, watching as the scene played out. At one point, Cyril went up to them and touched the nose of each. Huh. The heroes were drawing more animals into their detective games.

At the moment the cats were free, he was amazed to see Little Socks vault through the air into Pete's arms. Well, into Pete's chest. Then up to his shoulder. He looked down as Sassy Pants nearly waltzed toward him. Then she was distracted. She saw those two cats.

She changed course and went to them. They stood until Sassy Pants had licked both of their faces for several seconds. Actually, it was a mutual licking session. She finally turned and headed once again for Chris, rubbing his pant leg until he reached down to pick her up.

Chris, as he waited for Sassy Pants to come to him – and near tears – first called Laila, then Henrie, then Felicity.

He almost forgot about the $250,000 bearer bond.

Almost.

21

Pete finally got Little Socks off his shoulder, but only when Ray took her. She then clung to Ray's chest, digging in her claws for dear life. Pete chuckled as Ray, Chris and Jock drove away. Little Socks wouldn't be moved. Ray drove with a new appendage on his chest. Little Socks seemed to wave good-bye, sitting on Chris's lap, pounding the window with one paw. He could swear the little girl smiled.

Pete thought he knew who the catnappers were. Early on, he had focused on the young couple, new to the community, who had opened and quickly closed a restaurant. They fit the general description, and their car fit the description as well. He had not been able to find a local address for them and didn't know where they had gone, but he got warrants for this house, the restaurant and the upstairs apartment.

Pete, Marco and Jeff waited on the warrant, and Cyril seemed content to sleep on the porch. Poor guy. He must be beat, thought Pete.

When the warrant arrived, they walked in, guns drawn, just in case. Until they had to put the guns away to cover their noses and mouths. It was disgusting. But they found nothing interesting.

Marco, who had returned to Pete's car to get a face mask, now took notes on everything they saw. Some broken down pieces of furniture. A urine and feces-filled blanket. Urine and feces in other places, some recent, some old. A nearly-empty food bowl. A bowl filled with ice, which was probably the cat's water for an hour or two.

The restaurant was dark and cold, but they found nothing interesting except mouse droppings and evidence of cockroaches. The apartment upstairs mirrored the house. Windows covered in black plastic and the smell of animal urine.

Pete was confident he was on the right track. Odd. The black plastic over the kitchen sink was loose, just like the one at the house.

Sassy Pants had her proudest moments that morning. Ray parked his vehicle at the Café. They got out. Two men, a big black dog, and two cats. Sassy Pants talked to Little Socks. *"You doesn't has to be scairt now. We's wit Chris and Ray. We's safe."*

Little Socks didn't answer. She continued to cling to Ray.

Sassy Pants snuggled a little closer into Chris's shoulder. She rarely allowed herself to be carried, but today was special. Inside the Café, everyone came up to touch them. Sassy Pants purred, mewed and tapped her paw on Chris's cheek. What she said was, *"We's safe. We's happy to be home. Tanks you for caring."*

Little Socks didn't spit, snarl or hiss when anyone touched her, but she didn't purr, either.

At the yoga studio, Diana leaned into Ray's chest, face against Little Socks' soft side, and cried. Little Socks graced her with a purr, but she didn't let go of Ray's jacket.

Sassy Pants said, *"You should be nicer to Diana. She was really worried bouts you."*

At Mo's Tap, Candice came close to touch each girl. Little Socks stayed mute, but Sassy Pants purred her thanks.

Carlos gave them treats. Well, Carlos gave Sassy Pants a treat and handed Chris one to give Little Socks later. Little Socks hid her face in Ray's jacket and would not take the proffered piece.

Minnie took Sassy Pants from Chris and held her close until the girl squirmed to get away. Minnie handed her back to Chris, then turned to have a cry.

Sassy Pants could hardly stand the suspense leading up to getting inside the Inn. As soon as they were in the door, she pushed away from Chris with such force it almost knocked him backwards. She landed in a pile of five cats and a little dog.

Ray kneeled to the floor, steadied Little Socks with one hand, and gently pried loose her claws with the other. He noticed Tiger Lily off to the side of the group, and he placed Little Socks gently on the floor beside her. Little Socks pushed her face into Tiger Lily's chest, and the big girl put her front leg around the little girl's back.

The Bartrams barreled down the stairs and through the foyer, nearly knocking that man over. He was on the floor, kneeling, for goodness sakes, in the middle of the foyer! Couldn't he get out of the way? Neither Alistair nor Cressida could be bothered to apologize.

Cressida, on her way out the door, turned to look back. That black cat and the other one – what color could she be called? – were there. With the rest of them. And their own wretched dog, Tillie.

Tillie snarled, just a bit, at her, then hid behind one of those big cats. A big black dog literally glared, daring her to approach the cats. Just so he could take of her nose. At least, that's what his expression conveyed.

Cressida turned and slammed the door shut.

Chris put his hands on Henrie's shoulders in a gesture of support. The big man had collapsed into a chair in the foyer in tears. Then he looked around. Little Socks and Tiger Lily stayed to one side, the little girl's face buried in the big girl's chest. Apparently following some direction from Tiger Lily, the two were left alone.

During the walk from the Café to the Inn, Chris had looked back every now and then. The two strays followed at a distance until the group reached the Inn. Then they ran past the Inn and around the side of the building.

After Ray and Jock left, the cats and the little dog settled into a pile in the library. Little Socks and Tiger Lily were just a little to the side of the group. Chris went outside, walking slowly and softly in the direction the strays had gone. He noticed a cat door going to the basement. It was open, just a little bit. He picked up a rock and set it so the door couldn't be opened from the inside, then went into the house and down to the basement.

Busted.

Two cats. They stood, rooted in place, staring at him from the top of an open bag of cheap dog food. Chris stood still and looked around. A water dish, messy, underneath a spigot. Blankets in a corner, dirty and mussed.

He felt something at his ankle and looked down to see Tiger Lily at his feet. She sat and looked up at him.

"So, big girl, are these your new friends?"

Tiger Lily blinked once, slow and easy.

"They helped save Little Socks and Sassy Pants?"

Tiger Lily blinked again.

"Do you think your mother needs two more cats?"

Tiger Lily looked at him but did not blink.

"So. We have to find a home for them?"

Tiger Lily blinked again.

"Alright. I put a rock at that cat door, but I'll take it away for the time being. Until you hear otherwise from me, they have to stay down here, okay?"

Tiger Lily blinked.

"We'll get them some decent food and a few more blankets. And a litter pan."

Chris shook his head and walked back upstairs. He was turning into Annie.

Tiger Lily whispered to the strays, *"It's going to be alright!"*

She followed Chris upstairs and trotted to the library. Little Socks was awake, fearful, watching for her return. Tiger Lily nodded solemnly in her direction.

Decision made, she woke the other cats and Tillie to make a pronouncement. *"This is the way it's going to be. We are not going to discuss the ordeal until Little Socks and Sassy Pants are ready to do so."*

Little heads nodded. Little Socks and Sassy Pants looked at one another, then quickly looked at the floor. It would be a while before they spoke again.

Ray returned to The Marina, once again late to meet with the contractor.

"I'm really sorry, man. There was this situation…"

"No problem. I've got all the time in the world."

"I thought…never mind. I'll get the money. It's a cashier's check. I hope that will work."

"Sure. I'll come in with you. We need to get this scheduled."

As they walked in, Guy explained, "My crew called last night. They finished that other job, so we can start Monday, if that fits into your calendar."

"The sooner the better. How long will you be working on it?"

"Count on us being here the better part of the week. Will 9:00 be good for a start time?"

"Sure. What do you need from me?"

"Just the check."

With the check in his hand, Guy called Cindy and said, "Put that claim through. Ray and I have a deal."

22

In the early afternoon, things had settled down at the Inn, just to heat up again.

Henrie realized he was missing a couple of guests. And a car. He called Pete to make a report and locked the deadbolt to the guestroom door.

He came downstairs and saw Carlos, arriving from the airport with his mother and lady friend. To himself, he said, "Good gracious. I forgot they were coming." To Daniela and Isabela, he said, "I am delighted to have you. Please, sit. I will take your bags to your room. Certainly Carlos can find refreshment."

Henrie wheeled the luggage cart into the second floor room facing the state park. Thank goodness, Hilly was on top of things. The room was clean, fresh truffles were on the bed stand, the two doilies – red, green and white, the colors of the Mexican flag – rested on the pillows.

Henrie returned to the foyer to hear Carlos telling the story of the catnapping and their return. "They came into the bakery right before I had to leave to pick you up. Hey, Henrie, is Little Socks doing better? The poor little thing seemed so frightened."

Henrie, beside himself for missing that, said, "I am certain she is doing well. But to alleviate any fears, I will find the dear and check on her myself."

Henrie excused himself and walked softly around the downstairs rooms, starting with the library. No furry bodies to be seen. Well, they were probably all scared, and they probably went into hiding as soon as Carlos and his family came in.

Henrie vowed to keep an eye out, especially for Little Socks.

In the kitchen, he prepared a meal for Annie and Chris. Annie would be home this evening, and they would most certainly stay in, although no one had said anything. What day is this? Saturday.

Saturday! Date night! The night before Valentine's Day! Where in the world is my mind?

He turned suddenly as Daniela entered the kitchen. Most assuredly to "help."

"Let me help you, Henrie. What are you doing? Making a nice dinner, I see. I'm going to be alone tonight. You can take that as a hint. Tonight's date night, you know."

Daniela's Mexican accent trilled and purred as she talked nonstop. Henrie took a deep breath and realized her chatter could be therapeutic. He casually took two more servings of everything from the refrigerator and freezer, adding them to the preparation.

"I hope tonight's the night. Isabel is upstairs resting, but I'm supposed to make sure she gets up on time to get 'ready' for her date. I've seen that dress. It's black, tight, has a plunge down to there and a slit up to here. There's no way my son sees that and doesn't pop the question. No way."

On The Avenue, life was as normal as it could be.

It was Saturday, February thirteenth. Date night. The date night before Valentine's Day.

Cheryl pulled four steaks from the refrigerator. She had aged them the past four days and intended to "grill" them in the convection oven. That, some sweet potatoes, fresh vegetables steamed with herbs, and strawberry cupcakes from Mr. Bean's would be their meal for the night. The meal they would share with Pete and Janet.

She sighed as she prepared the steaks. She and Ray were supposed to be moored a little way out in the lake, under the stars, with a group of lovers who scheduled a Valentine's Day cruise. That had to be cancelled after the storm. And the damage to the boat. Apparently, the damage was much deeper than cosmetic.

Now free, she was just as happy to spend the evening with their friends. This would give the big boys – Cyril and Jock – something to do as well.

Cheryl picked the mail up from the counter where Ray had thrown it. The monthly Chamber of Commerce mailing was on the top. Hmmm. They had done an article of the new restaurant. The Green Door. The place that opened and closed too soon for the mailer to be updated. She noticed that photographs of the restaurant and the new owners were inside. She put the mailer on top of the microwave. She'd look at it later.

Cheryl had a start. She picked up her cell phone and dialed. As she waited, she went to the freezer to extract a fifth steak. When the phone was answered, she said, "Jeff, I'm not going to accept no for an answer. I'll call Pete and Ray and make sure someone brings you over on the skiff for dinner."

Marie, at The Drug Store, sold an unusually large number of treats for intimate pleasure, but business had died down. She called Jennifer at The Clinic. Jennifer was bored. No appointments, no walk-ins, no emergency calls. "Why don't you close up? I'll be done here soon, and we can take some extra time to get ready."

The sisters planned to join a group of friends, both male and female, at a fancy club in Marsh Haven. It would be an upscale event. Two new dresses had been purchased for the occasion. Marie's was little and purple. Jennifer's was little and rose-colored.

Jennifer said, "I've got that one last trip to make, then I can get ready!"

Bloomin' Crazy did a brisk business with deliveries, pre-orders and walk-ins. Most orders were for fresh flower arrangements; Clara had stocked for the rush. She planned to meet a blind date at a restaurant in Marsh Haven. A smashing red dress awaited her in the upstairs apartment.

Ginger and Janet, her last customers of the day, picked up a small vase with three long-stemmed roses, one each, red, pink and white. Ginger explained. "James will be home soon, and I want these to be waiting for him. I haven't had time to really, you know, thank him."

Before Clara left, she received a telephone call.

"Clara, this is Mazie. How ya doin'?"

"Fine, Mazie. I'm getting ready to close. I have a new red dress, and I plan to have…"

"…about that…"

"…Yes?"

"Well, see, it's like this. He went back to his wife...."

Holly worked alone at DoubleGood. Few people had need for hardware or electronic items on Valentine's Day. She and Jolly planned a movie night: pizza ordered in and three movies that arrived from Netflix the day before.

She watched as Clara closed the shop. Funny. Clara has a blind date. Why is she closing up from the outside? Well...maybe she's taking something with her, a bottle of wine or something. Holly watched as Clara went into Sassy P's.

Next door, Jolly kept the grocery store open and sold several deli meals. She also sold a lot of fresh fruits and vegetables for homemade romantic meals. Jolly was thankful Laila was prepared ahead of time.

She called up the back stairs. "Kids, it's almost time for your mom and James to be home. Did you clean your rooms?"

"Yes, ma'am."

"For the last time, I'm not a ma'am!"

"Yes ma'am."

Ginger and Janet walked in with the vase. "Please make sure this is the first thing he sees."

"On my honor."

Laila and James walked in the back door. Jolly picked up the flowers, walked them to the back and said, "For you, James, from a grateful friend."

When James went upstairs, Laila and Jolly walked to the front. "I'm closing up. I'm going to take some of my kids' favorite foods, and we're going to celebrate. What are you doing tonight? Anything special?"

"Holly and I are watching movies and stuffing ourselves with pizza. It will be perfect."

Jolly and Laila looked at the window, distracted as they watched Clara storm across the street. She carried three bags from the winery, and her face looked like she needed every one of them.

Mem kept CyberHealth open a little later in the afternoon, allowing Saturday afternoon visitors to The Avenue a place to sit and drink tea. Her gamers were gone for the day and few people shopped for health food items.

She and Frank, whose antique shop was already closed for the weekend, planned a night in at Frank's apartment over the antique store. Mem had purchased new clothing, but nothing that would be seen in public. Ever.

Mem called Diana. "Do you have everything you need, dear?"

"Yes, Mom. I'm set."

"I'm ready to go, so I'm going to lock up from the front and walk over to Frank's."

"I saw that little package, Mom. Have a hot time."

Pastor Teresa, after her overnight stay with Laila and Annie, planned a homemade Italian dinner with Jerry. They were not dating; they had become good friends. She knew Jerry would supply dessert. She now sat at the gift shop at Soul's Harbor, but this afternoon was especially quiet. She used the time to polish her sermon, wondering, not for the first time, if anyone from The Avenue would be in attendance.

Felicity and Trudie, tired of hearing servers and cooks talk about their dates for the evening, sent everyone home to get ready. "Get out of here, and you'd better have a good time!"

The two friends finished several orders for take-out meals, each one made to romantic perfection. Best of friends, and living next door to one another in the apartments above the yoga studio, they planned a night in. Leftovers, movies and wine.

Diana closed Lil' Socks' Virasana just after her mother's telephone call. It was a little early today, as no one showed for the last class. This was typical of a holiday weekend. She knew she would have the apartment she shared with her mother, Mem, to herself tonight. She planned an evening of leftovers, wine, and skyping with her long-distance boyfriend.

She hoped her long-distance boyfriend enjoyed the surprise she planned. And she hoped his mother was nowhere near his room.

George and Candice, in an on-again stage of their relationship, prepared for date night at Mo's Tap. An upscale blues bar, it was a perfect romantic location for people who wanted something just a little less formal. And beer. People who wanted artisan beer.

Because it was date night, George and Candice planned a date for after hours. Private. Exclusive. No intrusions allowed. They had several hours to anticipate the experience.

Jerry and Carlos took care of pre-orders and walk-ins for both pastries, breads, desserts and truffles. Jerry had prepared more truffles than ever before, and he was afraid there would be a lot left over, but by the time the doors closed for the night, merely three remained. Jerry packed those up and hoped Teresa would be satisfied.

Carlos became more nervous as the afternoon wore on. He checked and rechecked his jacket pocket to assure himself the ring was there. He had reservations at Sassy P's. He planned to ask Isabel to marry him over dessert.

Jesus and Minnie, a committed couple in life as well as at the winery, prepared for a full house. They had accepted reservations to fill the winery's back room and they expected walk-ins as well. They prepared special appetizers and small plate meals and had a few wines on special. They would also feature a wine and cheese flight and a wine and chocolates flight. They would have their personal celebration on Sunday, the actual Valentine's Day.

Minnie shook her head sadly as she bagged Clara's purchases. Clara had said nothing, but she didn't have to. Those beautiful eyes were on fire tonight.

Henrie – with Daniela's help – prepared a meal fit for kings and queens. He was chagrined at the absence of the Kerschners and the car but was delighted to have all of the cats on hand. He expected Annie home late in the afternoon. More than that, he was, in fact, Henrie, and he continued to take care of everyone else.

He found Little Socks. She allowed him to pick her up, and she even let him carry her around the kitchen for a while as he puttered, getting things just right. Eventually, she tired of the attention and asked to be put down. She sat on the table and watched him for several minutes before she slipped down to hide somewhere.

Henrie presented Daniela with a formal invitation to have dinner with him. The card was exquisite, and the printing looked as if it had been engraved. She accepted his invitation. He had a few board games from which they could choose. He intended to take up a good portion of the evening to keep her mind off the lateness of the hour until Isabel was escorted home.

Terrence and Jerald had early reservations at Sassy P's. Henrie placed special truffles and a bottle of chilled champagne in their room.

The Bartrams were apparently staying in. Earlier in the day, they stockpiled the newest and best DVDs from the library, enough to provide at least twenty hours of viewing. Henrie decided he did not need to cater to them on this final night. No Valentine's Day truffles for their room. This was probably the only time Henrie could be accused of being churlish.

He finished the preparation of their bill. He would present it before they escaped in the morning.

Before beginning his evening with Daniela, Henrie tended to several details in Annie's apartment.

Chris prepared for date night as well. The apartment was clean, and so was he.

He had done something completely out of his comfort zone. He gave flea baths to two stray cats. He had reconsidered and left the rock where it was, not allowing them to leave. Not just yet.

He invited them to follow him to the apartment. Henrie looked on in surprise as they paraded up from the basement.

Chris shut them in the bathroom, and before they knew what was happening, he had them in the tub, one at a time. He scrubbed dirt and fleas away. They didn't fight him as much as he thought they would. He began to realize they were domesticated and had become lost, or perhaps they were dumped. But, through all of that, the cats did get away from him in the end, running through the apartment with wet bodies stinking of flea soap.

After the cats were caught and dried, Chris had to clean the apartment, then himself. He was ready for date night. Finally.

Tillie was in the apartment with them. She had become a part of the family, and there was no question she was here to stay, at least until a good home could be found.

Jennifer made her final trip late that afternoon. She drove the ambulance to Marsh Haven and put one passenger in the front seat for the return trip.

Annie was coming home.

The snow, promised by forecasters, finally came. Big, heavy, wet flakes fell softly on The Avenue.

23

Pete had a busy day. Some would say it was a harsh day. He knew he'd be in the doghouse if he was not ready for date night, and Marco was in the same situation. Jeff Bennett didn't really care. He didn't have a date, and he didn't need to be anywhere in particular.

They worked hard, sometimes together, sometimes separately, on a variety of cases. The sexting case was put on the back burner for the weekend, but they still had the catnapping, the theft of the car from the Inn, and Annie's assault. Pete and Marco believed the assault to be connected to the catnapping, but they didn't know how. The best news was that Jeff, with a $250,000 bearer bond at stake, was able to bring in the resources of the FBI.

Pete took responsibility for the case he considered to be the most important, the case against Tim and Susie Phillips. Pete believed them to be the catnappers and he hoped to find them before that bearer bond was cashed. Since it was Saturday, and the bond was so large, he believed he had until early Monday morning at the latest.

Shortly after the cats had been kidnapped, Pete and Marco interviewed Geraldine and then Hank. Those interviews produced no leads. Today, Pete revisited both, but he wasn't going to make it easy. He called both to come into his office, put them in separate rooms, and sat down first with Geraldine. It was as if he had uncorked a bottle of champagne. She. Would. Not. Shut. Up.

He learned that Hank met the Phillips couple when they were looking for a building to open a restaurant.

They were working with that friend of Annie's, Greg, such a bore, and Hank thought he could do something better for him. He hooked them up with his brother-in-law, for a fee, you see, and then, of course, we had to see to it that they succeeded. We did everything we could to help them.

Some people thought the location was bad, but it wasn't, really. Hank wouldn't steer them to a bad location, would he? Well, anyway, that area needs to be gentrified, and this restaurant would be the tip of the iceberg. The TIP, I tell you. Businesses would have flocked to the area following the success of the Green Door.

Well, let me tell you, this couple would not be able to manage their way out of a paper bag. First of all, Hank tried to sell them a marketing package, but they said, poor, poor them, that they had spent all their money on the building and renovations, and they couldn't afford the monstrous marketing fees. That was their word. Well, you know, you have to spend money in order to make it.

And then, they had to be the "new thing" in town. Well, I tell you. That Felicity puts some strange things on her menu, but it was nothing compared to these people. They served minute portions of – what I would dare to call the haut of haut cuisine, like snails and crickets and steak tartar. And they charged an arm and a leg for it! The Rotary group insisted on a decent breakfast, and Susie finally came up with a menu of scrambled eggs, made with fake eggs, because they didn't want to use the real thing, tofu bacon, sliced potatoes – well, those could have been alright, but they always sliced them too thick and didn't cook them long enough – and some kind of bread that could best be described as cardboard. I tell you, if they hadn't closed down, the Rotary Club would have gone there one last time and then said toodle-oo.

And then, well, everything was money, money, money. They couldn't be open long hours, because they were the only employees. They handled everything. Marketing, the menu, cooking, cleaning, serving. They said they couldn't afford to pay staff, because they paid too much, blah, blah, blah. They couldn't afford to pay their vendors because no one was buying the food. They couldn't afford to make their mortgage payment because, well...it just went on and on. There was literally nothing Hank and I could do to help them. They were so stubborn and hard to get along with!

By this time, Pete's head rested on two fists. He dropped his fists to the table to stop Geraldine's tirade and tried to steer her in another direction. Did this couple have ideas for making money? Something quick, perhaps?

Well.... Geraldine decided to wait until an attorney could be present.

From Hank, Pete gathered essentially the same information, albeit from his smarmy perspective. He was a businessman. They should have listened to him. When asked about a possible get rich quick scheme, Hank, too, asked for an attorney.

Pete brought Geraldine, Hank and their attorneys together for a final interview. Certainly, they could think of something, from prior conversations, or from the realty file, that would help the police locate this couple. Certainly, they were not aware the couple intended to bring harm to a community member. Certainly, had they known the cats would be in danger, they would have said something.

Geraldine and Hank were more reticent that normal, but after consultation, one of the attorneys said, "Chief, our clients insist, quite forcefully, they know nothing about the, er, incident involving the cats. However, they are willing to share their knowledge of the couple's possible whereabouts. They will give that information to you, with the understanding that they will be allowed to go home. They are certain you will learn they had nothing to do with anyone's, um, cats."

Pete nodded, and was given the name and address of Susie's parents, who lived in a town about one hundred twenty miles up the coast. FBI field agents were dispatched to keep the house under surveillance.

By late afternoon, the couple was observed arriving and entering the home. They were taken into custody without incident. Tim and Susie claimed ignorance of the catnapping. The bearer bond was not located in their possession, but their car reeked of animal urine. They were booked for further questioning. Pete asked the arresting officers for a description of their shoes, both on their body and in their luggage. Neither had scruffy tennis shoes.

Jeff Bennett headed north to interview the couple.

The second case involved the Kerschners and the stolen car from the Inn. Deeply involved in the Phillips case, Pete put Marco in charge of this investigation.

Marco called Pete's focus on the Phillips couple into question. The description of the couple and the car of the catnappers could very well fit the Kerschners. Against

Pete's orders, he put out the want and warrant for the couple and the stolen car, including the possibility of the bearer bond, just to cover their bases.

While Pete interviewed Hank, State troopers found the Inn's car at a hotel one hundred twenty miles up the lakeshore. The couple was taken into custody without incident. Marco made the trip to conduct the interview.

Joline and Nathanial Kerschner noted their awareness of the catnapping incident, but claimed ignorance of the specifics and said they knew nothing about a bearer bond. They just wanted to get away from it all, and, well, they made the mistake of borrowing the Inn's car to do so.

Marco conducted a search of the car, the hotel room and their luggage. He did not find the bond. Following Pete's orders to "cover everything," Marco looked at the shoes they wore and all the shoes in their possession. There were no scruffy tennis shoes, dirty or otherwise.

Marco asked that they be held for a few hours while he did some thinking. When he called Pete with an update, he learned Jeff Bennett was headed to his location. He called Jeff to ask if he could sit in.

"Sure. You're at the jail now? I'll be there in fifteen."

Late in the afternoon, Pete received a call from Social Services. Penny, staying with a foster family in another town, had been at the mall with her new foster sisters. They were approached by her brother and her father, who threatened harm to all the girls if Penny didn't return home with them. Penny left with them to keep the other girls safe.

Pete was free, having just released Geraldine and Hank. He took a couple of officers to the house, not far from the house where the cats had been held, and took father and son into custody. Not without incident.

The mother cursed them as they led the men and Penny away. Before they got to the car, she accosted Pete and another officer with a baseball bat. She earned herself a personal visit to the county jail, with a stop first at the local police station.

Pete put Porter and his father in one cell, and the mother in another. The mother took off a shoe and threw it through the rails at Pete. As he bent to retrieve it, he stopped, stood, and looked at the shoe in his hand and at the feet of his three new prisoners.

All three wore dirty, scruffy tennis shoes.

Marco made it home before his wife divorced him. Pete, Janet and Jeff arrived at Cheryl and Ray's a little late, but they came with news.

Ray was starving. Jeff and Pete – and by extension, Janet – were late. Pete had called, but knowing they were "only" an hour out didn't help his hunger pangs. The day had been long, and the food – what was prepared, the steaks wouldn't go on until he saw the whites of their eyes – looked and smelled enticing.

Ray scrounged around in the refrigerator, then the pantry. He came out of the pantry with a container of microwave soup. That wouldn't spoil his appetite.

Ray followed the instructions and popped the container in the microwave, picking up the local magazine as he pressed the start button. He leaned against the counter and flipped to the story about the restaurant, the Green Door.

When he saw the photograph of the owners, he stared, then rolled up the magazine, pounding it on the counter. The words that came out of his mouth brought Jock running. He thought the house had been invaded by three men armed with Uzis.

Annie was a firm believer in Valentine's Day. She believed that no one, ever, had a Valentine's Day date that met commercially-advertised expectations. She was happy to be home. She still did not remember anything about her attacker, with the exception of the shoes.

She didn't care. She wanted her cats and Chris.

Henrie had noticed Chris with the stray cats. He didn't ask Chris, but he asked himself, where did they come from and why were they in the basement?

But, again, being Henrie, he took care of the details that had escaped Chris.

He made a meal with Daniela that would delight them both. Long before closing time, he called Clara, who dropped off a bouquet of fresh flowers with every color in Annie's rainbow. He called Minnie, who dropped off a dry red, a dry white in a chiller, and another chiller with champagne.

Henrie put the flowers on the dining table of the apartment, arranged the wine at the table, set the table with fine china, crystal, silver and cloth napkins, put the cold portion of the meal in the refrigerator, and set the oven to warm the remainder. He made another trip with special cat and dog food for the festivities.

He added a couple of puppy pee pads, assuming, correctly, that Chris would not remember to take Tillie out. And then, as an afterthought, Henrie took Tillie out.

He added a litter pan to Annie' collection, figuring that two more cats would require at least one additional large pan.

By the time Annie arrived, her apartment was prepared for date night.

And what a night.

Annie was tired and allowed herself to be pampered, accepting the love of her cats one by one and in groups. She gave special attention to Little Socks and Sassy Pants, both of whom stayed close to her throughout the evening.

In fact, Little Socks kept one paw on her at all times. If Annie moved from a chair to the table, Little Socks followed. If she couldn't be on Annie's lap, a paw remained softly but firmly on an arm or a foot.

Annie made Tillie feel at home, assuming, correctly, that she would never have to spend time with that horrible couple ever again.

She graciously met the new cats, accepting Chris's explanation for their presence.

"Tiger Lily seems to think they helped to find Little Socks and Sassy Pants, and she wants us to find a home for them."

"So, should we name them?"

Tiger Lily looked at Annie and then at Chris. Chris looked back at Tiger Lily. She didn't blink.

"No. I think their new family should have the honor of figuring out their names."

"Who do you think?"

"Well, I was thinking of Holly and Jolly. They love your cats. I don't know why they have never chosen pets of their own."

"They would be close. If they helped save our girls, we owe them a home where we can keep an eye on them."

Fat Cat and Scaredy Cat knew they were being discussed. They stayed close, purring, knowing they would have a new home. Soon. They would be safe in this home until that time.

Annie was not supposed to have anything to drink for several days, so she was not able to enjoy the wine. Chris was under no such drinking ban. He opened and enjoyed the red, saving the champagne for later.

Annie was in bed very early, sleeping on top of the covers with a duvet to keep warm. Chris slept in a recliner, moving it close to the bed to be able to hear if she needed anything.

Nine cats and one small dog joined Annie in bed with a minimum of hissing, spitting and scratching. They allowed Little Socks the honor of sleeping at Annie's shoulder.

25

Henrie had help again on this Sunday morning. Daniela refused to allow him to do everything on his own. She floated on a cloud in an upper stratosphere, now that Isabel was engaged to Carlos, and she needed to ground herself with work.

She prepared a casserole with eggs, chorizo, poblanos, onions, red bell peppers, garlic, chili powder, hot sauce, green onions, pepper jack and cheddar cheeses, with sour cream and salsa on the side.

Henrie added unsweetened cornbread to his always-extensive bread offerings.

Daniela set up the all-season porch for breakfast. She and Isabel would dine with Carlos, Terrence and Jerald, and Jeff. Perhaps Chris and Annie, if they came down. Frankly, she did not expect them to come down, but plates were ready.

In a sing-song voice, Daniela tripped along to those bedrooms, knocked three times on each and said, "Wake up, wake up! It's Valentine's Day! Start the day right with a lovely breakfast!"

Henrie made up a special place setting for Cressida and Alistair. On a photo stand, he placed two copies of the bill for their stay. The bill included several charges from the Café, Mo's Tap, the Winery and the Confectionary. Charging items at Annie's companion businesses was not unusual for guests, but this bill also included charges from businesses across the street, charges which the Inn had covered. The Bartrams had walked out without paying for items from CyberHealth, Babar Foods, The Drug Store and Bloomin' Crazy.

Sitting flat on the table, in between the two plates at their settings, was an empty box of El Loco's Coyotas.

Cressida and Alistair made entrance as they did every morning. They were haughty, loud and obnoxious. Cressida stopped short at the bill.

"What is this?" she demanded.

Henrie stood at the kitchen door, hands behind his back. "Today is the day you planned to check out. This is an itemized bill for your stay."

"We will not pay this! Your Inn is disgusting! It's dirty, the food is atrocious, and you have a horrible reputation in the community! You should be grateful for everything we've taught you during our stay!"

Henrie said nothing. His face belied nothing.

"And what is this disgusting box?"

"That is my gift to you."

"What?"

"My gift to you. I apologize that I have no biscuits to offer this morning, but I can offer you the information to purchase them in future."

"What?"

"I called your bakery in Uppingham, and they directed me to this provider. This, Mrs. Bartram, is what they have served you for years. I ordered six boxes; they have been consumed in their entirety."

"What?"

"In future, you can purchase this product – from Mexico, by the way – on Amazon dot com, and eat them to your heart's content. By the way, you will find the charge for them on the itemized bill, noted in services upon request that are above and beyond the typical breakfast fare. In that section, you will find also the luncheon you requested upon return from your trip north."

"Well, I never!" stormed Cressida. "For this, you will not receive a single penny! Not a single penny!"

"I believe you will find otherwise. You offered a credit card when you checked in."

Alistair, for once as brittle as Cressida, sneered at Henrie. "You just try to get your money. You won't get a cent. We gave you a card, but it hit the limit. We couldn't even buy petrol for that blasted rental car. The money's gone."

"Ah. Then it is well I placed the charge on your card a few days ago."

"What?"

"You did offer a credit card upon check-in, and I did run the card to assure you could handle a bill for several days. After communication with the bakery in your home town, I ran a charge that came very close to meeting the expenses on this itemized bill."

"You had no right!"

"I assure you, I did. You gave me the right when you signed the agreement."

"We did not!"

"A copy of that signed agreement is attached to the back of your bill. I regret, as this charge was made a few days ago, that I was not correct, or, to the penny, as some may say. Here is your change."

Henrie handed over a dollar bill and a few coins. A quarter, a dime and three pennies.

He backed away to the door, hands behind his back once more. "Our establishments are closed on Sunday, but if for some reason you should remain in town tomorrow, you will find you do not have the ability to charge against the Inn. You will find the businesses across the street are also prepared to, let us just say, demand payment for goods you acquire."

Cressida could only splutter.

"Please," said Henrie, "help yourself to breakfast. Our offering is unique this morning. As we have no Mexican 'biscuits' to offer, we have a Mexican casserole, prepared by an excellent cook from the middle regions of that fine country."

With that, Henrie pivoted on his heel and left the room.

Kali, Ko and Tillie were in the detective agency. Tillie quivered underneath a blanket. Fat Cat and Scaredy Cat, believing themselves to be quite at home, sauntered into the dining room, looking for stray crumbs.

Cressida screamed at the new cats.

"They're multiplying! Alistair, the cats are multiplying! Let's get out of here!"

She sprang from the table and aimed a kick at Scaredy Cat's midsection. Scaredy Cat yowled in pain, and suddenly the room was filled with snarls, hisses, sharp yips and the screams of both Cressida and Alistair.

Henrie ran to the dining room, followed closely by the diners from the porch. The cats had stayed back, adding only noise to the mix. Tillie, however, lunged, biting her humans at the ankles and calves.

Henrie was able to grab Tillie, holding her away and calming her at the same time.

"That dreadful dog! That traitor! That turncoat! Alistair! Let's get out of here!" They fairly ran up the stairs.

Henrie looked at the other guests. "I do hate to ask this of you, but if a complaint is made, you will be asked to say what you saw. Please tell me what you saw."

Terrence answered for everyone in his low, slow southern drawl. "Those people kicked at each and every one of these cats, who politely declined to offer resistance. If bite marks are found, we would regretfully say that perhaps the dog – that belongs to the people in question – protected the cats from the kicking legs. But we certainly didn't see that."

In minutes, the Bartrams, apparently already packed to leave, came down the elevator with their luggage. Henrie prepared to help them with the door, but in came Pete instead, warrant in hand.

"Alistair and Cressida Bartram, you are under arrest for criminal conspiracy."

26

Teresa called on Annie late in the morning. She sat with Annie, Chris and Henrie in the library and shared an early lunch, an excellent Mexican casserole left over from breakfast. She was able to report that at least ten people had been in church that morning!

"And I spent so much time preparing my sermon. I used Ephesians 4. It seemed appropriate."

Annie pulled out her King James Bible. Teresa said, "Read from verse twenty-five to the end."

Annie read aloud.

25 Wherefore putting away lying, speak every man truth with his neighbor: for we are members one of another. 26 Be ye angry, and sin not: let not the sun go down upon your wrath: 27 Neither give place to the devil. 28 Let him that stole steal no more: but rather let him labor, working with his hands the thing which is good, that he may have to give to him that needeth. 29 Let no corrupt communication proceed out of your mouth, but that which is good to the use of edifying, that it may minister grace unto the hearers. 30 And grieve not the Holy Spirit of God, whereby ye are sealed unto the day of redemption. 31 Let all bitterness, and wrath, and anger, and clamor, and evil speaking, be put away from you, with all malice: 32 And be ye kind one to another, tenderhearted, forgiving one another, even as God for Christ's sake hath forgiven you.

Annie chuckled.

"What was funny?"

"The phrase 'be ye kind.' Mom used to say that to my sister and me when we argued. She said it a lot."

Chris proved that he had been listening even while eating a piece of cornbread. "But it was an appropriate text for the week. We've had a bit of stealing and corrupt communication going on here. And Annie, not that we need it, but I liked the part about not letting the sun go down if we're angry."

Annie smiled and gazed down at her left hand. The smile left her face. "My ring! Where's my ring? Did someone take the ring off my hand at the hospital?"

Henrie was already headed to the telephone. "I will call Marie. She treated you at the scene."

Marie was apologetic. She had not seen the ring, and if she was doing her job correctly, she would have taken if off and bagged it as a personal possession. Perhaps, though, since it was Annie, she had not been thinking clearly.

Henrie called the hospital. The hospital did not have it, and the record of personal possessions logged in did not include a ring.

Yet another call was placed to Pete. Perhaps the ring was taken when Annie's billfold was stolen.

Henrie got off the phone and turned with a puzzled look to the others. "I think the man has lost his senses. He laughed and said the tennis shoes would be enough to get a warrant and the ring would be icing on the cake. Then he just hung up. Did not even say good-bye."

27

A few people dropped by in the afternoon to pay their respects to Annie. Among the early arrivals were Holly and Jolly. Holly, from her wheelchair, called Little Socks and Sassy Pants to her lap. They both jumped up in an unusual display of cooperation, taking one leg each.

The two strays were not in view, having learned that not everyone coming into the Inn was friendly.

Annie looked at Tiger Lily. "Where are your new friends, big girl? We want to introduce them to someone special."

Tiger Lily trotted out of the room and down to the basement, where they had gone to sulk. "You have to come up. Mommy thinks these people would be great humans for you. They're really nice, and they live just across The Avenue."

The cats ran upstairs quickly, but made their way to the library with more stealth. Tiger Lily, in front, kept turning around, encouraging them to follow.

Annie explained the presence of the two cats to Holly and Jolly. "You see, the kids are very fond of these cats and very protective. We think they were either lost or dumped, maybe at the campground. We want to find a good home for them."

The two little girls jumped down from Holly's lap and went to stand next to the strays, as if to say, "They are special."

Holly and Jolly looked at Fat Cat and Scaredy Cat. The cats looked back. Jolly got to her knees on the floor and stayed still. Fat Cat soon went over to her, sniffing cautiously at first, then bumping his head against Jolly's knee. Emboldened by the response Fat Cat received, Scaredy Cat sniffed Holly's ankle, then stood to sniff her knee, paw on the side of the wheelchair.

"Oh, Jolly, we have to take them."

"We do. Annie, what are their names?"

"That's up to you to decide. We don't know what they were called before."

Sassy Pants said clearly, *"Dere names are Fat Cat an Scaredy Cat."*

The humans heard, "Meh, meh, hiss!" The hiss came as Tiger Lily bopped her on the nose.

Tiger Lily then said, just as clearly, *"They were called 'Here, Kitty Kitty by their humans,'"* but all the humans heard was 'Meow, ow.'

Jolly, with Fat Cat now purring and rubbing against her knee, said, "This is Simon Finnegan."

Holly added, "And this is Oscar McMurphy."

Chris laughed. "Holly, I think that's a girl."

"She's an Oscar McMurphy. I don't care if it doesn't sound like a girl's name."

While the women visited, Henrie and Chris took litter, food and dishes to their apartment. Chris added a cat bed and a few cat toys to the pile.

As the young women prepared to leave, Jolly asked, "Do we need a carrier?"

Chris looked at the strays-no-longer. They looked back at him, not blinking.

"No. I think they'll follow you home."

And they did.

Kali moped for the rest of the day, her dreams of a Valentine's Day romance burst, just like the dreams of so many humans who believed the advertised hype.

28

In the apartment that evening, Annie looked at Tillie, sleeping on Chris's lap. "Well, we got her, and we didn't have to pay a penny."

"Yep. We got her. And what are we going to do with her?"

"I love the little thing, and she was so brave, to hear Henrie talk, when those awful people kicked the stray. Which one did they kick?"

"Oscar McMurphy."

"Oh, yeah. The girl."

"We don't have to make a decision tonight. It will come to us, just like Holly and Jolly."

"You're right. And she doesn't take up any room."

"And the cats love her."

"We can wait."

Pete called. "Is it okay if Janet and I come over? I have news, and I've been leaving her alone far too much this weekend."

Chris looked at Annie and replied, "Come on over. We have food. And beer. And wine."

Annie, in a voice that could be heard on the telephone in Chris's hand, said, "Make it a party, call Cheryl and Ray."

Soon, six friends, seven cats and three dogs were sitting or lying, munching something good, or sleeping, at the dining room table or on the cushions in the corner.

Pete looked at the group. "I thought you had two extra cats, Annie."

"They were here for a little while, but they're across The Avenue now. They have new humans, Holly and Jolly."

"That was quick."

"Holly and Jolly were ready to be parents. I'm sure the cats will be in and out, especially since the cat doors are unlocked again."

"Is that wise, with the little dog?"

Tillie's head perked up and looked at Pete.

"She's fine. She won't run away."

"And why are you so sure she won't run away?"

"Turns out there was a cat door open downstairs in the basement. The cats and Tillie were down there a lot with the strays. Tillie didn't leave. Well, at least she didn't leave and stay away. Actually, this makes it easy for us. She has been taking herself out to take care of her personal business."

"Looking for a home for her?"

"Not looking, but keeping our eyes open."

Silence reigned for a while, then Chris asked, "You said you have news, Pete?"

"I do." Pete reached into a jacket pocket. He brought out Annie's beautiful ring in an evidence bag. "I can't let you have this just now, but I wanted you to see it. Perfect condition. Not a scratch, not a missing jewel."

A tear trickled down Annie's cheek.

Pete reached into another pocket and brought out a computer print-out.

"What's this?" asked Chris.

"Something you really want to see."

It was a photograph of a bearer bond for $250,000.

"Eventually they will release the real thing to you. For now, know that it's safe."

Chris sighed in obvious relief; Annie clung to him, more relieved than he would ever know.

"So, who done it?"

"Let's start with the easy one. The ring. Of course, this was taken when Annie was mugged. Turns out, robbery wasn't the motive. The ring and the billfold were just an afterthought. Penny's dad wanted to hold Annie accountable for their troubles."

"And this all started with Ginger and Penny. How is Ginger?"

"She's fine. Says she would do it again. Turns out, most of the kids at school think she's some kind of hero. They've been calling throughout the weekend. Things will be different for both her and James starting Monday."

"That's great. It will be a rough road for Penny, though."

"Rough, but hopefully she'll be able to stay in foster care until she graduates. She's a smart kid. She'll probably get scholarships to college."

"And what about the catnappers?"

"Well, that's a bit more confusing. I'm going to start at the beginning by starting with the last arrest."

"The Bartrams."

"The very ones. Do you remember a conversation, Annie, about buying the dog, and they asked what price you would put on the cats?"

"Oh, yes. Vividly."

"That got them to thinking, and that afternoon, they started talking about how to get money from you, using the cats."

"How did they get hooked up with Tim and Susie Phillips?"

"They didn't."

"Excuse me?"

"They didn't. Tim and Susie left when they couldn't make a go of it at the restaurant business and after another incident that I'll get to shortly. They presented themselves as clean, young professional people, but they lived like pigs. They dumped a cat and a dog at the shelter before they left, but while they had them at home, they didn't litter train, pee pad train or even house train. They peed everywhere. Their clothes were clean and well-kept. Everything else was a mess. But they didn't take the cats."

"It was the Kerschners?"

"Yep. They didn't really work in the finance industry. They were well-put-together professional con artists. In their travels up and down the coast, the Bartrams met some shady folks. They called a guy they met, who called this couple. They made a last-minute reservation at the Inn and pulled it off, using your very own car, Annie."

"Why would they come here to do a job like that without a car of their own?"

"It was a rush job. They had to get on a plane and figured they could rent a car when they got here. They couldn't rent a car in Chelsea, but the Inn had a car to use, so they just went with that. Sticking it to you a couple of different ways."

"They never even spoke to the Bartrams, as far as I saw."

"Nope. The Bartrams weren't even certain they were the people doing the job. They were not supposed to meet or talk. They just knew it was a couple, and they'd get the job done. At first, they suspected the other couple staying here, the doctors. They realized it was the Kerschners when they took off and no one else showed up at the pre-arranged meeting place."

Chris shook his head. "That was just stupid. They had the idea, they hire someone to help, and the people they hire to help were supposed to pick up the money, too? And they thought they would actually get something out of this? Dealing with crooks?"

"The Bartrams are awful people, but they aren't criminals. Except for not paying their bills. They didn't realize a double crosser would double cross them."

Pete continued, "By the way, Marco is the one to thank for this."

"Marco? Really?

"I was focused on the Phillips couple, but Marco thought there were too many coincidences, like when the Kerschners arrived, and they borrowed the car several times, and no one on The Avenue had really seen them. He added the bearer bond to that warrant, against my orders, frankly, but I didn't have time to argue with him."

"And where was the bearer bond?"

"Jeff Bennett and Marco discussed it. They were at the same jail, the two couples being arrested in the same town. They couldn't get anything from either couple, so they did a more thorough search of their luggage. Jeff searched the luggage for the Phillips couple, and Marco the Kerschners. They both came away with something."

Pete took a long minute to drink a beer. He called Cyril over and gave him a treat, then Jock wanted one, and...Chris finally said, "Pete!"

Pete laughed as he looked back. "Marco was right. The bearer bond was in the luggage of the Kerschners. Jeff found a cashier's check in the same general location – in the lining – when he tore up Tim Phillips' luggage."

"A cashier's check for what? From whom?"

"From me. For work on The Escape."

Chris and Annie nearly got whiplash turning to look at him, mouths open, and then they heard another story. This one involved Geraldine and Hank, again, who thought they found an easy mark. Ray ended his story with, "And unfortunately, they were right."

29

Once again, it was time for the Westminster Dog Show. For two evenings, television streamed the esteemed contest to the world.

Pete and Janet, Ray and Cheryl, Carlos and Isabel and Chris and Annie gathered at Pete's for the second night in a row. The men played penny poker. The women played Malilla, a game Isabel played every Sunday night in Mexico. The dogs, Cyril, Jock and Tillie, watched television.

Pete had the DVR going, because he always taped these events, but tonight, they watched the final night of judging live. On this night, the second night of the show, they had the sporting group, with Cyril's breed, the hunting group, with Jock's breed, and the terrier group, of course, with Tillie's breed. The evening would end with the grand champion show featuring the winners of these three groups plus the winners from the four groups of the night before.

Cyril and Jock promised one another they would not get silly and angry. They had not watched last year's show until just a couple of months ago, from Ray's DVR recording. The show, or rather, their reactions to the show, caused painful feelings. The dogs' friendship had suffered.

Jock didn't say it, but he thought to himself, Matisse won't be in the running this year, so I can control myself. Matisse was the Portuguese water dog expected to take the championship last year. He had come close, causing jealousy to flare. To be honest, the jealousy would not have flared had Jock not teased Cyril. Jock wouldn't admit that to himself.

Tonight was Tillie's first viewing of the contest. She was beside herself with excitement.

The first group, Cyril's group, was again a disappointment. Despite a good showing, the English setter didn't place. Cyril wasn't sure if it was the same dog from last year, but the coloring was the same, much like his own. And the hair flowed, unlike his own. Pete kept Cyril trimmed, because he was a dog with a real job.

The Portuguese water dog in Jock's group was much different than Matisse had been. He was subdued, didn't prance as much, and didn't show off in the arena by stretching. Cyril didn't say it, but he thought to himself, this one has a powder puff tail, just like that poser from last year. This year the water dog didn't place in his group.

The last group of the evening barely registered with the big dogs last year. They had suffered through it, waiting for the main event. This year, they paid attention for Tillie's sake.

Tillie jumped up when the Jack Russell terrier first walked into the arena. Cyril, confused, said, "That's you?"

"Yes! That's me! They call them a different name. They call them a Parson Russell Terrier, but that's me!"

Jock said, "He has curly hair."

"Some of us do," said Tillie, nose glued to the television. "He's a wire coat terrier. Not like me. I'm a smooth coat. That's okay. It's still me!"

Cyril and Jock looked at one another. After last year's show, Tiger Lily had to show them pictures in a book, pictures of how their breeds might look with different colors, coats and trims. This little terrier seemed to know all about her breed already.

Cyril suddenly said, "Look! It's that hairy, yappy dog that won the group last year!" The beautiful Skye terrier was taking his turn around the arena.

Unlike Cyril and Jock's breeds, Tillie's breed made the first cut. They all held their breaths as the dogs went around one last time. He wasn't picked as a finalist.

Let down, Tillie hid her nose under her front paws. Cyril and Jock both gave her a lick. "Don't worry. It's nothing to be ashamed of."

They watched as the yappy, hairy Skye terrier won the group again.

Instead of watching the final show of the evening, the championship contest, the dogs barked to go outside. They spent the rest of the evening cavorting in the back yard, prancing around a made-up arena of their own.

As the humans prepared to go, some people a few cents richer and some a few cents poorer, Isabel said to Annie, "I wish I had a little dog like that. She's pretty."

Annie and Chris looked at one another and at Carlos, who gave a slow smile. "I'll have to ask my landlord if dogs are allowed in the apartment."

At the Inn, the cats were on their own. Fat Cat, now Simon Finnegan, and Scaredy Cat, now Oscar McMurphy, were at home with Holly and Jolly. Tillie was out for the evening, with Annie at the home of Pete and Janet.

Until now, Little Socks and Sassy Pants had avoided one another. Tiger Lily had watched without saying anything. Tonight, she thought, amends must be made.

"Little Socks, Sassy Pants, we need to have a discussion. We can have it in front of everyone, or the three of us can go to the bedroom. What's it going to be?"

Sassy Pants allowed Little Socks to take the lead. The small black cat, normally the strong one of the bunch, hung her head. *"We may as well do it here. Everyone's going to know about it anyway."*

Five sets of eyes looked from Little Socks to Sassy Pants. Sassy Pants looked back. Little Socks looked at the floor.

Tiger Lily pressed. *"So?"*

"So, what?"

"Do you want me to start the conversation, or are you finally going to tell us what happened out there?"

Little Socks, finally looked at Sassy Pants, then back down at the floor. She said, *"They shut me in a bag, and I couldn't get out. Sassy Pants had to help me get out of the bag, but after that, I was too afraid to do anything. She was the only one with the courage to try to find a way out."*

Sassy Pants looked at Little Socks with wide eyes. *"I wuzn't brave, Little Socks. I wuz scairt. Real scairt."*

"You acted brave."

"Well, dat's just da ting. I wuz acting. I was scairt because I tought you wuz going to die in dat bag. It was so hard to getted you out of dere."

"Well, I thought you were brave." She looked at the other cats. *"Those people left us some food and water, but it was cold, and the water started to freeze. We thought we would run out of food before anyone found us, and we had to pee on a blanket. It smelled bad."*

Sassy Pants took up the story. *"Yeah, it stinkted. And we lookted and lookted but we couldn't find any place to getted out of da house. They didn't have cat doors."*

Little Socks spoke again. *"You'd think an old house like that, with no one living there, might have broken windows, but this one didn't."*

Sassy Pants cut in again. *"And den we was really scairt, an we wented to sleep. But den we hearded Cyril an Jock. An den Fat Cat an Scaredy Cat. An den dey lefted to get Pete, an we watchted in da window for him to come gets us. You guys knows da rest of da story."*

Throughout the telling, Little Socks brightened. Sassy Pants wasn't going to tell them how she had completely fallen apart, scared of suffocating, scared of starving to death, unable to even move, finally passing out, ready to die.

Tiger Lily looked closely at the two. *"We are so grateful to have you home again. I heard Mommy say that you might be scared of things for a while, of people that you don't know, or sounds, or situations. And she said she was going to watch to make sure you were eating like normal. I'm telling you this because I want you to understand it's okay for you to be not quite at your best for a while. But you can't shut us out. We're your family. We're going to help you get through this."*

For the most part, things returned to normal in Chelsea. The cats were more reticent around strangers; their friends quick to trot to their sides if strangers approached.

Annie, her friends and her staff were more vigilant. Annie breathed deeply every day as the kids left for "work," willing herself not to become over-protective.

Annie wanted to find a gift for Chris that would signify to him what his ring signified to her. She realized the best thing could be a watch. She could buy a practical watch, but she wanted one in the luxury category. The only problem was that she could not afford such a thing. She promised herself to make a selection before Leap Day. As February wore on, she asked Frank for help, because he wandered through a variety of antique and resale stores to keep Antiques On Main stocked.

A few days before the end of the month, Frank called and asked her to meet him at the shop. On her way, she stopped at the Tap to pick Mo up. She carried him on her shoulder, his favorite place for walking. At the shop, while Annie joined Frank at the counter, Mo and Claire shared their private dance. Sniff noses, sniff faces, sniff and lick ears, sniff butts.

Annie and Frank watched until they got to the butts. Frank blissfully drew her attention to the issue of the day. "Annie, I made this purchase yesterday. If you don't want it, I'll keep it, but I couldn't let the deal get away. Frankly, this is exactly what you want."

He opened the box to show her the watch. She let out a soft gasp. It was understated elegance at its finest. The eighteen karat rose gold finish was complimented by a grained white dial and hands that appeared to be luminescent. The black alligator strap showed no signs of wear.

Frank said, "This watch, at a minimum, would sell for $20,000 new."

Annie's eyes opened wide. "I can't afford that, Frank."

"I know you can't. I was at a resale shop, and, well, I feel kind of bad about it, but this guy didn't have a clue. He didn't know what he had. It's in perfect condition. Clean, not a scratch, and he had a $200 price tag on it."

"Perfect."

"Well, I got it for less."

"I thought you felt bad about it."

"I did, but I couldn't let him know what he had. I had to dicker with him just a little bit. I got it for $175."

"Sold! But tell me about it. Why is it such an expensive watch?"

"This is a Parmigiani Tonda 1950. It's a basic watch that just marks pure time: hours, minutes, seconds. It's flat, as you can see. There is a very thin automatic movement that has a solid platinum micro-rotor."

"Well, most of what you just said didn't make any sense to me, accept for the hours, minutes and seconds. $20,000? Really? It's perfect, but why is the price so high?"

"For both the elegance and the brand. This is a beauty."

30

The February block party was a family affair, but it capitalized on the favorite holiday of the month, Valentine's Day. This year was leap year, and today, the last day of the month, was leap day, the day women could propose to men. Men, if they chose not to accept the proposal, had to pay a penalty. Tradition said they had to give the woman money, buy her a dress or buy her twelve pairs of gloves.

This made for a great deal of fun on the part of the planners. The event was planned free of sex roles, so dresses and gowns were nixed. A charity station sat to one side with used gloves. If someone wanted to sweet talk his or her way out of the proposal, twelve pairs of gloves could be purchased individually or in pre-packaged sets.

There were winter gloves, driving gloves, golfers' gloves, mittens, wrist-length and elbow-length women's dress gloves, work gloves, gardening gloves, welder's gloves, hospital gloves, rubber kitchen gloves, muffs, and oven mitts.

Many of the ala carte and packaged selections contained mismatched pairs. All pre-packaged sets were guaranteed to be unsuited for any one person. The purchase of gloves guaranteed nothing. The suitor could still insist on a visit to the altar.

In the planning stages, George and Jerry tried to make it a Sadie Hawkins Day celebration, in honor of the tradition spun by the author of Lil' Abner. In the end, they were voted down, but not until Candice pulled up the Wikipedia article on Sadie Hawkins day, celebrated every year in some parts of the country in November.

"And," she said, "Wikipedia is one hundred percent accurate. All the time."

Felicity added, "And we must be authentic."

Trudie chimed in, "No decorations reminiscent of Dogpatch, USA."

This stopped the discussion. Mem, looking closely at Trudie, asked, "And since when did Jamaicans learn of Dogpatch, USA?"

"We have our ways."

The planners made one thing clear. Tradition or no, the option of asking for someone's hand was completely asexual. Any man or any woman could propose to any man or any woman.

The chosen charity was the American Cancer Society. Each business on The Avenue collected contributions all month. At the Café, a crystal bowl sat next to Tiger Lily on the hostess stand. Most businesses had a similar bowl, glass or jar in place.

Another fundraiser was sponsored at each business on The Avenue and at several places around town, one that would help anyone who chose not to become a spouse on leap day.

Men or women could pay a penalty up front to refuse an offer of marriage. One contribution of $20 would buy a get-out-of-marriage-free card. A contribution of $100 bought six.

Decorations included archways draped in tulle with ribbons and bows. There was a red set, a blue set, and green, orange, yellow and purple. All of Annie's rainbow colors. They were arranged strategically around the catering hall above Tiger Lily's Café.

At each archway stood a podium where a "preacher" could perform the wedding ceremony. Nearby was a tall spittoon, into which the preacher would drop the donation or get-out-of-marriage-free card. A telephone table stood near the spittoon, upon which the spouses would sign a marriage certificate.

The certificates read, "This here person (line for a name) and this here person (line for a name) do hereby consent to this here marriage ceremony, conducted on the twenty-ninth day of February in this here year (line for the year)."

Two final lines remained, one for the "preacher that done the ceremony," and one for the "witness to these here proceedings."

Teresa made clear during the planning sessions that she would not "pretend" to be a preacher on the off chance that someone might think the ceremony to be a legal one. Ray made the same caveat. He was the captain of a boat, you know.

Clara, always the designer, came up with the final touch to the marriage archways. "We have to have a post with a leg iron, so the person being asked can't run away or have second thoughts." Perhaps she was twice burned in that regard.

If the person who was asked did not want to get away, the proposer would pay the preacher a set "fee" for the ceremony. To make sure everyone in the community could participate, the fee was set at a low $5.00.

If the person who was asked wanted to get out of it, he or she could bribe the preacher to unlock the leg iron. The preacher of the moment could name his or her price. The preacher was on the honor system to charge a price he or she thought the spouse-who-doesn't-want-to-be could pay.

The preacher held the right of refusal. No matter how much was offered, he or she could go ahead with a "shot gun" ceremony.

The only guaranteed way out of a marriage was a bonafide get-out-of-marriage-free card. However, an option was available for the couple to visit divorce court, set up under a black arch in front of the coat rack. The fee was reasonable.

To add to the ambiance, music was piped through the sound system. It was a soft, easy-to-talk-over but raucous blend of wedding, dance and dirge music with a good helping of jazz and blues thrown in for good measure.

Hosts and hostesses were to dress in black. It could be anything black. A little black dress, a black tuxedo, black jeans with a black shirt or polo, black slacks with a black sweater or tunic, black miniskirt with black spangle top. Anything would work. Almost anything. The committee put a stopper on Felicity's plan to wear a black bikini.

The only catch was that over that black outfit, a pink tutu was to be worn as well, to signify the featured charity. No one was immune from the tutu. To make the hosts and hostesses stand out, the tutus of pink tulle were topped with a ribbon boosting bright red hearts of various sizes. Everyone else, children and adults, were given tutus without the red heart ribbons.

For a while, at the beginning of the evening, cats and dogs sported tutus as well. It didn't take long for them to work together to rid themselves of the silly things. Only Kali and Mo left theirs on, thinking them sexy additions to their already beautiful bodies. Throughout the evening, Kali flounced her sexy self in front of Simon Finnegan. He seemed to appreciate the extra attention.

The coup d'etat of the evening was a wedding cake. In the middle of the room sat a round table festooned with ribbons, bows and balloons. In the center was a fresh orange wedding cake. A layer cake, it was complimented with apricot mousse filling. Buttercream frosting tinted the palest orange covered and decorated the cake. Fresh orange cupcakes with the same frosting surrounded the cake, for those who preferred a finger food.

A long table on the west side of the room held the other food offerings. It seemed that each block party brought a higher level of, well, a higher level of everything.

The menu included fun takes off foods that were purported to be aphrodisiacs. Felicity and Cookie, the cook at Mo's Tap, used this evening as a way to showcase their creative abilities. Set up as a competition, voting encouraged, each food artist produced offerings made of the chosen aphrodisiacs. Placards sat in front of each food detailing the properties that made the food fit for lovers.

The strawberry, noted for its heart shape, was once known as a symbol of Venus, the Roman goddess of love. Many ancient cultures believed the strawberry held mystical or magical powers. Felicity's offering was a traditional favorite, strawberries covered in white, milk and dark chocolate, some rolled in nuts or crystalized ginger. Cookie made strawberry banana creams. Tasty and attractive, the middle of each strawberry had been carefully carved out and filled with a mixture of mashed banana and yogurt. Each strawberry was garnished with either sliced almonds, diced dried cherries, chopped cashews, crystallized ginger or mini chocolate chips. Jesus competed with another traditional favorite for newlyweds, a bowl of fresh strawberries and chilled bottles of a semi-dry champagne.

Voting was intense, but Cookie won based on high points for originality.

Coffee, and its ability to provide extra energy, is seen by some to be an aphrodisiac. Caffeine can boost the heart rate and increase blood flow, and some believe it can enhance sexual performance. Felicity did not compete in this food category, but of course Trudie provided a variety of coffees, including dark chocolate latte and white chocolate mocha. Cookie surprised the group with a meat offering, a rum and coffee brisket. The brisket had simmered in rum and espresso and was flavored with onions, garlic and red pepper.

Cookie won the coffee category. As Felicity took a bite, she turned to Trudie and said, "He is going to leave us to open a restaurant of his own someday."

Oysters are slippery and sensual, but their aphrodisiac property comes from their ability to change sex from male to female and back again. Oysters understand both the feminine and masculine experience of love. Felicity brought baked oysters with spices reminiscent of New Orleans in a nod to Fat Tuesday, which, this year, was close to Valentine's Day. Cookie provided oysters on the half shell with a twist. He called them Love on a Half Shell. Each oyster was garnished with icy crystals of a frozen mixture of pinot noir, red wine vinegar, shallots, salt and pepper. The crystals appeared as a bright red cap on one end of each oyster.

Cookie won again.

In the Middle Ages, women were forbidden to eat artichokes due to their aphrodisiac qualities. Those qualities date to Greek mythology. The story holds that Zeus, after being rejected by a beautiful young woman, created this thorny treat, tough on the outside and soft on the inside. Today, defying Middle Age convention, Felicity made a three-cheese artichoke dip and surrounded it with crispy breadsticks. Cookie offered steamed artichokes with lemon-pepper butter for dipping. The artichokes, served whole, invited the diner to strip each petal away, one at a time, until the heart of the artichoke was visible.

It was close, but the originality factor once again skewed the votes to Cookie.

Honey has been considered an aphrodisiac for centuries. The word 'honeymoon' stems from the hope for a sweet marriage. In some cultures, honey is a symbol of fertility and procreation. Felicity offered a selection of Greek pastries: baklava, finikia, loukoumades, and honey cake. Cookie brought bruschetta with lemon, ricotta and honey. George entered this competition with a combination of two aphrodisiacs, honey and figs. To maximize his ability to receive votes, he placed his honey fig cocktails with both the honey and fig offerings, to Cookie's protestations of, "That's not fair!"

"You could do the same. Make something with honey, asparagus and beets, and put it in three sections!"

George won this category, but it should be noted those returning for second and third helpings spiked the votes.

The Greeks spoke of asparagus in their love poetry; the Kama Sutra advised drinking it as a paste. Some say French men used to dine on three meals of asparagus the day before their weddings to increase their libidos. Felicity, thinking that this time, for sure, she had bested Cookie, made a sesame ginger soba noodle salad with ribbon asparagus. Cookie's offering was subtler, but very tasty. He mirrored Felicity's use of sesame with his roasted sesame asparagus.

Cookie won. Again.

Some say the forbidden fruit of the Bible was actually a pomegranate. Associated with the Greek goddess of love, Aphrodite, the fruit symbolizes fertility and abundance. Felicity entered a bruschetta in this category, made with pomegranate, fresh mozzarella and basil. Cookie made another meat dish, lamb meatballs with yogurt and pomegranate-mint relish. Jesus entered this competition with a pomegranate champagne cocktail.

Like George's cocktail, Jesus won this category, probably on the basis of return voters.

Many cultures believe the beet to be an aphrodisiac. Ancient Romans believed beets and their juice promoted amorous feelings. Felicity brought tartlets made with beets, feta cheese and walnuts. Cookie roasted his beets with tahini and pine nuts. Carlos entered this competition with mini lemon sour cream pound cakes with beet glaze.

Felicity just couldn't catch a break. The pound cakes were so pretty that Carlos won the category.

The Aztec name for avocado is the same as the word for testicle. They would not allow virgins to leave the home while avocados were harvested. Felicity brought a creamy bacon and tomato guacamole with chipotle peppers and served it with blue corn chips. Cookie had his eye on an asparagus, avocado and arugula salad but didn't think the food would translate well to a buffet. Instead, he made avocado and black bean wraps, which included carrots, tomatoes, lettuce and spices on whole wheat.

Felicity finally won with her dip. She looked at Trudie. "They must have been voting for the blue corn chips, because my cooking hasn't done well at all tonight."

Figs, whose leaves became clothing for Adam and Eve, present a dichotomy. Their seeds represent fertility while their leaves reflect modesty. They are rumored to have been Cleopatra's favorite fruit. Felicity entered her only meat dish in this category, rosemary flank steak with fig salsa. Cookie made bacon-wrapped figs with feta cheese, basil and pecan halves. George's cocktail was featured here as well, but Cookie's offering won the category.

By the time Felicity reached this part of the table, she walked away, pulled Annie back with her and said, "You have to open a restaurant for him. A fine dining restaurant."

Annie's mouth was full, and she could only reply, "Hmmmm."

"I mean it, Annie If you don't, he'll find another opportunity elsewhere. Promise me we can talk about this before the week is over."

Annie nodded, still chewing. She tried to convey with her eyes the sincerity of her response.

In the ancient Roman Empire, basil was a symbol of love. Felicity made a low-carb version of the popular margherita pizza with tomato sauce, cheeses and basil. Once again, Cookie defied convention and provided dark chocolate-covered basil leaves.

Cookie won again on the basis of originality.

Both the Greeks and the Romans thought carrots provided sexual stimulus. Others believed it to aid in seduction when cooked. Felicity offered Italian carrots, sliced and sautéed in butter, garlic and fennel. Cookie braised whole carrots in butter and carrot juice and added a touch of dill.

The carrot category had no clear winner. The competition was declared a draw.

Carlos and Jerry set up a private competition for dessert chocolates. Throughout history, chocolate has been named in many ways as a stimulant to love. According to scientists, however, two key components do play into love. Chocolate contains both a sedative and a stimulant. Chocolate can both relax a person and lower inhibitions while increasing the desire for physical contact. Carlos provided a decadent layer cake, extra dark chocolate with chocolate buttercream icing and chocolate mousse filling. Jerry brought petit cups containing dark chocolate mousse, each garnished with a raspberry on top.

Jerry received high marks, but Carlos won the category.

Not to forget children and youth, one table held dishes to hold their attention. Jell-O jigglers in the shapes of hearts, dogs and cats, fried cheese sticks and cheese balls, hot dogs, and finger sandwiches with peanut butter and jelly.

This table won the hearts of all persons under the age of fifteen and half the adults.

Carlos placed a tray of cat and dog treats – heart-shaped, of course – near the companions' cushions. Those remained untouched until the end of the evening, the companions choosing to prowl under and around the tables for morsels to drop.

Children were invited to get in on the festivities by joining in a What Would I Do With An Extra Day Of My Life game. They were presented with option cards and got to choose one to take home. It had to be something they would not normally do. For example, if a child was involved in baseball or softball, he or she could not pick the "play catch with mom or dad" card.

Other cards included help your little brother or sister with homework, teach mom or dad to use social media, pick up trash at the city park, help a teacher with a project, do extra chores at home, set grandparents up with skype or a smart phone, turn in extra credit homework, or research colleges.

An adult version of the game included a different set of cards. Adults could choose to rent a movie with the family, actually take a real sit-down-enjoy-a-break lunch break, go on a walk, have lunch at school with the kids when it was not their birthday, paint their toe nails, splurge on what's for dinner, make a list of everything for which they are grateful, do one good thing for someone, plan and take a mini vacation, volunteer at school, or volunteer at church.

As always, a game area was set up to keep children and youth of all ages occupied and active. Ginger and James spent their evening in this corner, happy to work together.

There couldn't be a block party without charity sales of charcoal sketches from Chris. He seemed to gather inspiration for his work in the weeks before each event. This month, his charcoals featured a black cat with white paws clutching a police officer's head for dear life; a sassy-looking cat pressed against a window pane, front legs extended and with an expression that said, 'get me out of here!'; two tabby cats, one markedly fat and one a bit timid, sneaking up The Avenue in front of the Café; and two dogs, looking remarkably like Cyril and Jock, holding escapees from some jail at bay.

As usual, the sketches sold quickly with orders placed for more. Many families asked that the cats or dogs be altered to fit the descriptions of their own companions. Party planners could always count on several hundred additional dollars for the charity by the time his orders were delivered.

Throughout the evening, various marriage vows were taken. Or not.

In the "taken" category were Candice and George, Carlos and Isabel, now here on an extended, unchaperoned visit, Mem and Frank, Diana and her long-distance boyfriend, Harrison Jones, Clara and yet another blind date, and Geraldine and Hank.

Yes. Geraldine and Hank. They hated Annie and her friends but could never resist their block parties for charity. The events were "the" place to be on the last day of every other month. Ray and Cheryl went high. They smiled at, greeted, and otherwise ignored them.

Annie was satisfied to see both Geraldine and Hank contribute heavily to the preacher. She noted dryly that three attorneys and a state representative were present to witness the ceremony. That had been the impetus, not any charitable nature.

In the "not" category were Trudie and an attorney, Felicity and a doctor, Holly and a regular customer of DoubleGood, Jolly and the high school principal, Jennifer and Marie in a double "not" ceremony with a science teacher and a history teacher. It should be noted that most of the individuals who were asked were already, in real life, married to someone else.

Other marriage vows were taken – or not – by teachers, attorneys, doctors, business owners, realtors, factory workers, librarians, retirees, truck drivers, farmers, vintners, gas station attendants, fast food workers, day care teachers, social workers, stay-at-home parents, and, well, just about everyone.

The final marriage of the evening belonged to Annie and Chris.

Felicity, knowing Chris had six get-out-of-marriage-free cards, lined up six women to propose to him throughout the night. She proposed, as did Trudie, Mem, Candice, Minnie and Diana. Chris found himself locked in a leg iron in each of the colored stations before the night was over, in front of a variety of preachers, most of whom questioned the authenticity of the proffered card.

Fresh out of cards, Chris would not have used one if he had it. Not if Annie proposed, that is. He decided early on that he would not make the proposal. That would be too easy. As the evening wore on, he thought Annie would never ask. She finally worked up the nerve following her second glass of wine.

"Hey, you, care to tie the knot with me?"

"Is that a proposal?"

"Yes. What did it sound like?"

"That's really the best you can do?"

"Yes, and now you're stuck!"

Teresa and Ray both wanted to perform the ceremony, but Annie wisely nixed the idea of either of them, "just in case." Henrie got the honors. She took Chris by the hand and drug him to the purple wedding station. Henrie tried without success to keep from smiling as he strapped the leg iron on Chris's right ankle.

Chris whispered to him, "You know, Annie's the one that needs the leg iron."

Henrie stood at the podium, formal black tuxedo accented by a pink tutu. He was flanked on either side by his typical bookends, Kali and Ko. Ko looked nervously from Henrie to Annie throughout the ceremony while Kali preened in her sexy pink tutu, now askew on her midsection.

Annie and Chris stood side by side, Annie in a little black dress. Little. Black. Dress. Short skirt and more cleavage than she was comfortable showing, even in private. Chris was more casual, in black chinos and a black turtleneck. As they clasped hands and leaned toward one another, their pink tutus merged and got caught together.

Tiger Lily stood to Annie's left, consciously or unconsciously taking the place of the maid of honor. Mo took the place to the right of Chris, slightly in front of the leg iron, pink tutu bedraggled with his constant preening of the accessory.

Holly had come close, the better to videotape the ceremony from her wheelchair. She was helped by Oscar McMurphy and Little Socks, one on each leg.

Carlos, also close in order to provide a videotape for his mother, was hampered by a muscular chunk of cat on his foot. An inquisitive Mr. Bean sat his shoe to get a better view.

Cyril stayed close but out of the way, slightly behind Henrie and in full view of the couple. Sassy Pants cuddled into his right leg, nervous about the attention being paid to her mommy.

Tillie walked among the group, looking up with expectation, first at Henrie, then Annie, then Chris. She finally settled on a seat near Sassy Pants, her little back firm against the soft belly of the big dog.

Jock and Simon Finnegan decided this would be the perfect time to look for more food. They walked through the guests not watching this particular ceremony, begged for treats and picked up morsels that had dropped on the floor.

Claire, usually afraid of crowds of people, sat slightly behind Mo, admiring how the tutu was tangled with his fluffy tail.

Henrie rolled into a long-winded wedding ceremony, the longest of the evening by far. He would have gone on forever, until Pete and Ray, from the beer station, loudly urged him to "Get on with it!" Finally, he got to the part about "with this leg iron, I thee wed," but Annie stopped him.

"Let me say this part."

Henrie reached into a pocket and pulled out a box, handing it to Annie. She opened it, showed the watch to an astonished Chris and said, "With this watch, I thee wed."

Annie hoped someone had captured the ceremony in photos. She didn't need to worry. Several videos and still photos hit Twitter and Facebook as soon as the ceremony started and continued to feed until the end.

Several onlookers were captured as well, all in black with pink tutus. Such a "wedding" had never graced Chelsea before.

Chris found a seat at a table. Unfortunately, Pete and Ray were at the table, and they would not let up about the "wedding." He suffered their jokes in silence until Henrie arrived. He carried a tray with four glasses of pomegranate champagne cocktail.

As he put them around, he waxed eloquent. "As the designated parson of the nuptials, allow me to warn you that this nectar may portent fertility and abundance in your marital relationship. I assume the fertility will be that of cats and dogs, and the abundance will be in the friendships the two of you shall maintain."

"Thanks, Henrie. I was worried there for a second, thinking that, you know, you had your eye on some baby furniture."

"We do litter pans and pee pads. Nothing else. Yet."

Chris raised his glass and invited the others to do the same. "To that kind of fertility and abundance!"

"To that kind!"

Chris raised his glass a second time to Henrie, in a silent toast to the knowledge they both had. That one day, Chris hoped the parson would be the legal variety.

The evening wound down. Humans cleaned up while companions took a well-deserved rest. Their special corner held a larger group than ever before. Kali and Simon Finnegan snuggled together, Simon Finnegan's head resting on top of the pink tutu. Claire and Mo napped side by side, elegant tails wrapped together, a pink tutu tangled in Claire's front paw. Little Socks hissed, so only Mo could hear, *"Just wait until Uncle Honey Bear comes again."*

Every now and then, someone rose to get a heart-shaped treat from the tray of pet goodies.

Mr. Bean lay next to Tiger Lily. *"So, are Mommy and Chris married now?"*

"I don't think so. I think it was a joke of some kind."

"Why would Mommy joke about that?"

"Because she's afraid of getting married."

"Why?"

"Well, it's a big step."

"*She makes big steps. Really big steps. I have to walk fast with her.*"

"*I mean big steps as in a big commitment.*"

"*What's a commitment?*"

"*It's a promise.*"

"*Mommy makes promises.*"

"*This is different.*"

"*Why?*"

"*It's a serious, grown-up promise.*"

"*Why?*"

"*Well, because when they make this promise, it's for life.*"

"*Why?*"

"*Because that's the way it's supposed to be.*"

"*Why?*"

"*When humans get married, it's supposed to be to the one they will live with forever.*"

"*Why?*"

"*Because.*"

"*Why?*

"*Just because!*"

"*Why?*"

"*For heaven's sake, Mr. Bean! Just because!*"

Mo, the resident Lothario, had a special offering for Valentine's Day and Leap Day. He realized he had to give his presentation now, before the humans – and companions – started to leave. He trilled to get everyone's attention. When heads came up to look at him, he was sitting straight, a little in front of the pillows and facing his audience.

Somehow, his tutu had gotten twisted so that it hung from the front shoulder on one side and caressed his back haunch on the other.

Sassy Pants, sensing a recitation of some sort, joined him. Mo trilled again.

Sassy Pants translated. *"Mo writed a poem an he wants to say it to you."*

Little Socks, mostly restored from her ordeal in the bag, spoke up. *"When did he learn how to write?"*

Tiger Lily shushed her and motioned for Mo to proceed.

Mo sat tall and proud and nodded for Sassy Pants again. *"Mo sez I can't say it to you."*

She stopped, short circuited. *"What? What you means, I can't say it?"*

Mo projected another thought to Sassy Pants. She hung her head. *"He sez I can't say it cuz I jus reads pitchers, an I won't get da words right."*

Mo gave a soft trill.

Kali translated. *"He says you are his favorite kitty, but this is a poem, and the words have to be just right."*

Mo trilled again.

Kali turned from Mo to Ko. *"It has to be one or the other of us, Ko. We can't work together. This poem is very important to him."*

Ko hissed.

Kali hissed back but looked again at Mo. *"I'll do it."*

Sassy Pants moved back to the pillows, heartbroken, to sit beside Tiger Lily. Tillie snuggled close in an attempt to comfort the little girl. Kali moved to the front, next to Mo.

Mo took a deep breath, rolled his head around on his shoulders a few times, then nodded to Kali. She nodded back.

Mo trilled, and Kali translated.

"A Romantic Tail, by Mo."

Mo stopped and gave Kali a hard stare. *"Trill!"*

"Okay, okay. Word for word, exactly as you tell me."

She started again.

"A Romantic Tail, by Handsome Mo."

Kali rolled her eyes, but she said the rest of it, word for word, as Mo trilled. Deciding to be the best sister she could be, before the end of the first stanza, she was reciting the poem with feeling.

How the heart desires the warmth
Of bodies pressed together.
Oh, sweet siren call of lust,
The touch, the hands that tether.

My body, lean and sensuous
Is wild and soft and free.
Both men and women yearn to touch
Every inch, every ounce of me.

The hands caress my face and then
They move from head to shoulders,
Embrace my back, and 'round to breast
And down to where it smolders.

Some soft, some firm, the fingers play
A song at that low place.
Upon the region Eros knows.

For explosions I must brace!

I must hold on, I cannot take
The ultimate delight.
I must hold on, must breathe, must wait,
Until the time is right.

No words describe my feelings as
The sweet release draws nigh.
Soon, very soon, I will give up
Myself, my soul, my cry.

Finally, yes blissfully,
The hands will gently trail
From end to tip, the fluffy length
Of my romantic tail.

Mo looked around, head held high, pleased with his offering.

Kali turned her back, embarrassed at the words she had uttered, hoping Simon Finnegan would not think badly of her.

Ko laughed out loud.

Little Socks hid a laugh with a yawn.

Sassy Pants and Mr. Bean blushed. Or, if cats could blush, that's what they would have done.

Tiger Lily smiled. *"Well done, Mo. A romantic tail, indeed."*

Kathleen Thompson

Thank You For Reading!

The family of cats and the author hope you enjoyed reading this book as much as we enjoyed writing it!

About The Author

Kathleen Thompson was raised on a small family farm in Indiana. She has an undergraduate degree in Sociology from Manchester College (now Manchester University) and an MBA from Indiana University South Bend.

In a variety of towns and circumstances, she served as a probation officer, parole agent and juvenile residential counselor before moving into administrative, marketing and fund raising positions in human service organizations. Ms. Thompson took a break from human services for seven years to own and operate a bar and restaurant. Let's be honest; that's another type of human service.

While making plans to return to her rural roots, Kathi and her mother discovered an injured kitten at the family farm. The kitten, whose face was a mass of injuries, decided to make Kathi her guardian. She wrapped herself around an ankle, purred like a V8 engine, and wouldn't let go.

Against the advice of her mother, Kathi took the kitten home and to a veterinarian. The vet diagnosed road burn serious enough to take all the fur from the left side of her face, and the kitten – Tiger Lily – eventually healed and took a huge piece of Kathi's heart.

Tiger Lily was joined by the rest, rescue kitties, all: Little Socks (thank you, Aunt Mary); Kali, Ko and Mo (thank you, Connie); Sassy Pants (thank you, Ant Sherwy); and Mr. Bean (thank you, Pulaski Animal Center). Recent arrivals Speckles (thank you, Tennille) and Moriah (thank you again, Pulaski Animal Center) have joined the cast but will not live at the Inn.

Tiger Lily's Café rattled around in Kathi's brain – there isn't much else up there – for all of the years since, sometimes as an actual café and sometimes as a book. It was less expensive to write the book.

Connect with Kathi and her family of cats at their website: www.tigerlilyscafe.com, or find them on Facebook: www.facebook.com/tigerlilyscafemysteries.

Find us on the web: www.tigerlilyscafe.com

Find us on Facebook: Tiger Lily's Café, A Mystery Series by Kathleen Thompson

Text to join: Emails are sent every two weeks. You can opt out at any time. LILYSCAFE to 22828 (You may also sign up for the emails from the website.)

www.ingramcontent.com/pod-product-compliance
Lightning Source LLC
Chambersburg PA
CBHW062119170626
46813CB00002B/510